ELVIS
IS
COOL
NOW

ELLIE IS COOL NOW

VICTORIA FULTON & FAITH McCLAREN

FOREVER

New York Boston

Forever
Hachette Book Group
1290 Avenue of the Americas, New York, NY 10104
read-forever.com
twitter.com/readforeverpub

First Edition: March 2023

Forever is an imprint of Grand Central Publishing. The Forever name and logo are trademarks of Hachette Book Group, Inc.

The publisher is not responsible for websites (or their content) that are not owned by the publisher.

The Hachette Speakers Bureau provides a wide range of authors for speaking events. To find out more, go to www.hachettespeakersbureau.com or call (866) 376-6591.

Print book interior design by Abby Reilly.

Library of Congress Cataloging-in-Publication Data

Names: Fulton, Victoria, author. | McClaren, Faith, author.
Title: Ellie is cool now / Victoria Fulton & Faith McClaren.
Description: First edition. | New York : Forever, 2023. | Summary: "Ellie Jenkins definitely didn't peak in high school. She was an outsider, an invisible girl with a desperate crush on Mark Wright, a guy who hardly knew her name. Ten years later, she's living in Los Angeles, trying to write a hit show about cool high school kids, when an invitation for her high school reunion arrives. She doesn't want to go, but her writing has been suffering and her boss makes her an ultimatum: go to this reunion or lose her big break forever. He even gives her a list of challenges to complete! Ellie takes the bait and returns to the school determined to find friends, fun and to prove to Mark Wright, once and for all, that Ellie is cool now"—Provided by publisher.
Identifiers: LCCN 2022047946 | ISBN 9781538739235 (trade paperback) | ISBN 9781538739242 (ebook)
Subjects: LCGFT: Romance fiction. | Novels.
Classification: LCC PS3606.U586 E45 2023 | DDC 813/.6—dc23/eng/20221014
LC record available at https://lccn.loc.gov/2022047946

ISBNs: 978-1-5387-3923-5 (trade paperback), 978-1-5387-3924-2 (ebook)

Printed in the United States of America

LSC-C

Printing 1, 2023

To our real-life crushes, Nick and Nathan

ELLIE IS COOL NOW

CHAPTER 1

I hated high school.

I hated the annoying pep rallies and the rowdy football games, the dumb jocks and the ditzy cheerleaders, the goth misfits and the dorky band geeks. I hated the overhyped importance of the honor society and the pretend power of the student council. I hated that high school was everything Hollywood said it would be but worse, because there were no flash mobs at prom or twist happy endings where the bullied nerd gets to be homecoming queen. I hated that it felt so important at the time, but the resale value on a class ring is basically zilch.

Yep, high school sucked. And so does this fictional one I write about for TV.

Cooler Than You is about a group of teens at a ritzy private high school. Rich seventeen-year-olds played by hot twenty-somethings who look almost thirty-five and drink, smoke, and fuck like stockbrokers on Wall Street.

It's a random Thursday in October, and we're sitting around

the writers' room, twiddling our thumbs, waiting for the Boss Man to finish reading the latest draft of the script.

My episode.

He chews little bite marks into the pen cap between red marks on the script, and we're all supposed to sit there and watch him do it. The whole process so far has taken an excruciating two hours and twenty-five minutes.

I should be grateful for this job. Some people take ten or more years just to break into their first TV job. It's a long, hard road for many, but it happened fairly quickly for me. I'm one of the lucky ones. I wrote a pilot right out of college that caught the eye of a swanky Hollywood producer. I drove out to LA with an agent and job interviews. The struggle didn't come until later, when I had to turn the job I got into the career I dreamed about.

The TV pilot I wrote was a dystopian drama with political power plays, war commentary, and a strong feminist leading lady. So, naturally, my new agent got me staffed on a teen drama set at a high school in Los Angeles, with scantily clad girls and the testosterone-fueled boys who objectify them.

Did I mention I fucking hated high school?

As for that TV pilot with producer interest that started it all...

It went exactly nowhere.

But you go with it. Because it's your big break!

You're disappointed, but you shouldn't be. This is the dream! You should be grateful. But every day you watch a graying middle-aged man in a Dodgers baseball cap approve a script written for sixteen-year-old girls. Because he *gets it*. It's a lot of fun, and I'm super grateful for the opportunity and not jaded at all by the years I've spent in this writers' room, working out plots that do nothing but remind me how very *not* cool I was in high school.

I've always dreamed of writing for TV shows that shift paradigms and change the world. I believe that the stories we consume on TV and in film and in books can truly change the way we think. Stories bring people together and shape the culture. I started telling stories a long time ago because I wanted to be a part of that, to contribute something that people could point to and say *That TV show changed my life.* Just like all my favorite stories have done for me.

But from where I'm sitting, the only thing *Cooler Than You* is doing for the world is causing an uptick in teen drug use.

This gig was always meant to be a stepping stone. Unfortunately, five years in, I think my shoe is stuck.

Finally, Andy looks up. He pulls his glasses off his face and leans back in his leather swivel chair just like you would expect a bearded middle-aged showrunner named Andy Biermann to do (did I mention it's basically a requirement for showrunners to have unkempt Spielberg beards?). I click my pen absentmindedly, waiting for his response. He does the same thing whether he likes it or hates it.

"It's just..." He touches steepled hands to his mouth. We all wait. I wish I could say I'm on pins and needles, but it's always a pig roast in his writers' room.

"It's a tad cynical," he says. He rubs his beard with his thumb and forefinger and locks eyes with me. I raise my eyebrows, trying to look stunned. It's the first time he's ever given me a midseason finale. It's a huge honor. I am trying so hard to feel honored.

This is supposed to be *the Dream*. Writing this episode puts me closer to a snazzy new producer title, which makes pitching my pilot or jumping to a show more aligned with my interests feel almost within reach.

But no matter how good I make the plotlines, no matter how polished the dialogue is, I can't do anything about my contempt for the subject matter.

And it shows—and puts the Dream, with a capital *D*, in jeopardy.

"Cynical?" I ask. I cock my head to one side for an innocent golden retriever effect.

He puts his glasses back on and reads a highlighted line. "Getting 'Most Likely to Brighten Your Day' in the yearbook is like getting 'Most Likely to Drop Out of College and Strip for Hair-Plugged Pervs at Cheekies.'"

The other writers in the room chuckle, and my friends Vic Musa and Tina Fitz—the only two writers in this cutthroat room I would call *friends*—give me I-told-you-so looks from across the table. They both gave me shit for that line over the weekend when I had them read the script over a ramen takeout bribe.

I told them I would take it out.

I did not take it out.

Egg on my face.

"Or what about this one?" Andy holds up the script and balances his reading glasses on the edge of his nose. "Once I'm outta here, I'm never gonna look back. The rest of these fuckers can drop dead of ass cancer, and I wouldn't even send flowers."

Shocked gasps followed by a few sadistic snickers. I funnel

my frustration into tiny inked tornadoes that wreak havoc on my already-wrecked script. I know it's not a bad script. It's impossible for me to write a bad script for *Cooler Than You*. I'm a good writer, and I've been here long enough and written enough episodes to know the rules of this tiny, stuffy room. The beats are solid, the dialogue on point, but my underlying disdain for being a teenager in high school? That, I can't hide. At least, not anymore.

Not since a certain dreaded red and gold invitation landed on my desk last week.

Andy sets his glasses down on the table and waits for my response. I look around the room at the other writers. They're all nodding like mass-produced bobbleheads, and I want to pop them right off.

"I meant to take that f-bomb out." I clear my throat. "Before I turned it in."

"You know, Ellie, it seems to me like you didn't enjoy high school very much."

"Oh!" I say, relieved to say it out loud—finally. "That's because I didn't."

Everyone's heads turn *Exorcist*-style to look at me.

"I mean, no one does, right?" I ask. "Not really. Nobody wants to peak in high school."

The writers exchange worried looks. It's like I've just told the king that I will no longer bow to him.

"Everyone wants that," he says. "Everyone wants to fit in during high school. The kids at the bottom of the food chain want to be at the top, the kids at the top fight to stay there. It's the vicious circle of adolescence, and no one wants to get eaten alive."

I cross my arms and pretend to think about this, knowing full well that he is wrong.

I didn't.

Well, maybe I did at first. But then reality set in, and for the rest of high school, it was head down, nose to the grindstone, get to graduation so my real life can finally begin.

"Something tells me I'm not going to convince you," he says before he reaches into his writerly leather satchel and pulls out something familiar. "I think *this* might help."

Oh no.

Slowly, I take the all-too-familiar red and gold card from him.

No, no, no.

Reunited and It Feels So Good!

Oh, for fuck's sake.

Stonybrook High School
Class of '10
10-Year Reunion

I look up at him, eyes wide with horror.

"I threw this away. In the trash. Where it belongs."

There's a tiny smear of lunchtime ketchup in one corner. I grimace and hold the invitation away from myself like it's *garbage*, because it is.

"It's this weekend," he says with a grin. "And you're going."

My jaw drops.

"Class dismissed," he says with a curt wave. He never lingers. He's out the door before my brain can process what the hell just happened. I throw an amused Vic a horrified look of confusion before shouldering my way through a group of buddy-buddy staff writers to dash across the room to catch up with Andy.

"Did you go through my freaking *trash*?" I ask him. All professionalism goes out the window.

"Of course not," he says. He motions to his left, where his mousy-haired assistant shuffles to keep up with him, her cheeks turning beet red. "Susie did. We got a tip that we might find something interesting in there. Lo and behold, it's just what you needed."

"What *I* needed?" My voice is incredulous. "A high school reunion is the last thing anyone *needs*."

He stops at the coffee station to refill his paper cup. His early-twentysomething assistant appears flustered, her fingers twitching at her sides, itching with obligation to pour it for him. I want to pat her on the back and tell her, *It's okay—he's pouring his own coffee right now as a power play against me.*

"The main character never knows that what she needs is exactly what she fears most." He shakes creamer into his coffee.

I hate him. Hate, hate, hate him.

"The cave you fear to enter holds the treasure that you seek." I quote Joseph Campbell's famous Jung-inspired line about the hero's journey in mythology. "Don't use patriarchal plot devices against me."

"You need perspective."

"I'm a woman and I went to high school," I say. "How much more perspective do I need?"

He sighs and stirs his coffee with one hand. "You're talented, Ellie. The best writer we have on staff—this disaster notwithstanding." He shakes my rolled-up, red-inked script at me with his other hand to make his point. "But you hate people, and that will never work for a co-EP."

"Co-EP?" I ask, stunned (and ignoring the part about me hating people). My heart drops into my butt. Even poor Susie looks stunned. "Who said anything about co-EP?"

"Me, just now," Andy says, his smile spreading slowly. He loves a surprising, satisfying reveal. I would know; he brings up the one in my pilot all the time.

God, co-EP. Co-executive producer is one of the highest-ranking jobs in television. I get co-EP, and I am one hop, skip, and jump away from being a showrunner on my own show. I would be an idiot not to do whatever I have to do (short of sexual favors) to get that job. There's only one thing in the world I can think of that could be a possible dealbreaker.

"Let me get this straight," I say, my head tilting to one side. "You're going to make me co-executive producer if I go to my high school reunion because somehow reuniting with people from high school is going to make me like people more?"

Not likely.

"I've had you in mind for co-EP for months; however, I do have some concerns..."

"That I hate people." I grunt. "Which is...mostly not true."

His thick caterpillar brows shoot up.

"Ellie..." He lets a long pause linger after my name for dramatic effect. "You can't be in a leadership position if you're constantly judging every single person around you."

"I don't care what people do," I scoff, crossing my arms in indignation.

His sigh is deep; his patience, endless. It's the reason he has this job.

He's not getting through to me. Neither of us is surprised.

He lifts his mug at me. "Just go to the high school reunion, Ellie. Have a few drinks, mingle, see some old familiar faces... gain a fresh perspective."

"*A fresh perspective.*" Clearly, he's being purposely obscure, so I have to decipher his meaning on my own, and I don't have time for that crap. I pout like a petulant child. "What does that mean?"

"Workshop it." Andy finally sips his coffee and makes a face. "This is trash." He tosses the filled cup into the tiny garbage can.

"So was my reunion invitation, but that didn't stop you, did it?"

"Go Wildcats!" He punches the air with a mock spirited salute before he disappears into his office. Susie furiously gets to work making a fresh pot of Andy's nightmare fuel.

I don't want to go. Every cell of my body is screaming *no!* But co-EP is my one-way ticket out of here. It's everything I've been working on for the last five years. To blow this opportunity just because of one (miserable) weekend in Ohio? Am I really that big of a wimp?

Yes.

No. I can do this. I can get in, get Andy's stupid *fresh perspective*, get out, and get that promotion. I can suck it up. I've sucked it up for five years—what's four more days?

I pivot-turn away from Susie, who I just realized I'm staring down as I engage in this civil war with myself. I beeline for my desk to grab my computer and my purse so I can blow this Popsicle stand early. Apparently, I have packing to do.

Because damn it all, I am going to my high school reunion.

CHAPTER 2

I shove a handful of underwear into a suitcase and then call an emergency happy hour with the LA fam, which consists of my best friends (and coworkers) Vic and Tina. We meet at our favorite post-work bar, the Salty Dog. It's dog-friendly, hence the name, so Tina usually brings her tiny shivery Chihuahua named Greta that she dresses in pink doll-sized clothes and keeps in her purse.

Tina is running late again, and Vic and I don't wait for her before ordering. Beer for him, rum and Coke for me. I don't like the taste of beer—never have. While everyone assures me I could acquire a taste for it, I've never felt the desire to dedicate any time to that process. My lack of enthusiasm for beer made college almost as fun as high school until I could legally purchase hard liquor.

Vic sets our drinks on a high table that looks clean just as Tina runs up, waving.

"I'm late, sorry." She cringes apologetically. Tina is always late and always super sorry about it. She hands Vic her purse, performing her signature pee dance. "Get me a chardonnay!" she calls over her shoulder as she skitters in the direction of the toilets.

"You still owe me a drink, bitch," he yells after her. "She never pays me back."

Greta pops her tiny tan and white head out of Tina's Louis Vuitton, her big watery brown eyes wide with angst. *You and me both, girl.*

"Get her to cover this round," I reply to his frown, which turns it partially upside down, and he promptly flags down the waiter to order her wine despite his protests. His focus drops to Greta, his god-dog, and I watch as he sings "You Are My Sunshine" to her in a baby voice until Tina returns.

Tina plops down on her seat, gesturing for Vic to return the pooch, just as her wine arrives in a chilled glass.

"Okay, I'm here—spill the tea." She strokes Greta's head, taking a generous sip.

"Andy's making me go to my ten-year high school reunion," I say, slumping forward. They gasp. "He's dangling co-EP as bait."

"Whoa, whoa, wait a minute. Co-EP? What the actual fuck? Ellie, that's amazing!" Vic starts to clap his hands together and then stops. "Wait, why are we not celebrating?"

"I have to pass through nine circles of hell to get there," I say, burying my head in my arms.

"Okay, Dante's *Inferno* aside—it's just one boring party and then voilà! Six-figure salary. Pop champagne!"

Vic adds, "Dom Perignon, Ellie's buying!" They clink glasses, and Vic forgets all about his intention to hook Tina with this bar bill.

Vic and Tina are a few years older, and have both lived and worked in LA longer than I have, starting out as writers' assistants and working their way up.

At our first family brunch—after the three of us decided to band together as besties in order to survive Andy's writers' room—Tina leaned over a pitcher of bottomless mimosas and told me she'd rather have the life she wants and the job she settles for than the other way around. A good philosophy, but I was convinced she could have both the life she wants and the job she wants. Especially because she's one of the funniest writers in the room and has a knack for nailing her third act in one draft.

Vic, too, except he loves his job on *Cooler Than You* and wouldn't trade it for anything.

"I was not *me* in high school," I tell them, looking up from the cradle of my own arms.

"Oh my God, we get it. You hated high school." Vic makes a *blah, blah, blah* gesture with his hand.

"No, you *don't* get it. You both were hot and popular."

"Hello!" Vic waves at me ironically and points at himself. "Gay."

"Gay at an art school in hipster Portland. Please." None of us is originally from LA, but we all got here as fast as we could.

Vic shrugs because he knows I'm right. Tina says nothing because she was homecoming royalty four years in a row and basically came out of the womb model perfect and loved by everyone.

"You don't understand," I start. "When you're growing up and learning how to be a human in the world, and the people around you are constantly reminding you that you're not good enough—to hang out with them, to go to their parties, to talk to them, to even say *hi* to them in the hallways? When you feel like you have something big inside of you, someone you want to *be*, and every day you have to go to this place where you're reminded that not only are you not special, you're a nobody—"

I choke back a knot of feelings in my throat. It's embarrassing as hell, so I try to cover it up with a cough and a deep swig of my drink. I blink back tears that are on the brink, because big girls and all that. I will not wander into introspective, self-pity territory. High school is behind me. Even though I'm going back, it remains behind me. This reunion is just a stupid party, just like all the stupid parties in high school, and I have much cuter clothes now.

"Oh, Ellie," Tina says with a soft sweetness that makes me just one percent want to punch her in her perfect little button nose. "You've never been a nobody."

"You write for one of the most popular shows on television," Vic says, pressing his hand on top of mine. "You're fucking cool now."

"Right," I say. "I'll steal one of the Kids' Choice Awards from the office and bring it. Everyone will be *so impressed* by my tiny orange blimp."

"You're from, like, Ohio, right?" Tina asks. She could teach a class at a community college called Valley Girl 101. It's endearing. "You're a head writer on a show that people actually watch. People say the words you write. *Out loud.* They're gonna think it's, like, the most impressive thing ever."

"I don't know, you guys," I say. "My school was mostly concerned with sports. A guy in my class has a Super Bowl ring. You really think they're going to be impressed that I write for *Cooler Than You*?"

"Damn, a Super Bowl ring?" Vic's eyebrows shoot up.

I groan. "See?"

"Whatever. The point is, you live in and write for a hit show in Hollywood. Your popularity quotient has gone way up," Tina says.

I drop my head into my hands. "I don't want to care about that shit anymore."

I never really did want to care. That was kind of my major problem.

"Newsflash," Vic says. "You work in Hollywood. Hollywood is just a gilded high school. With more cocaine and fake boobs."

"Yeah, but at least what I have now is more based on the merit of my work than on whether or not I can wave pompoms and shout *rah-rah sis boom bah*."

"Still have to be hot," Tina points out. Easy for her to say: she's tall and tan with long flowing dark hair highlighted by the sun. She goes horseback riding every weekend, which is her only workout—although she *is* vegan, and being vegan is a workout all on its own. She's perfect, and if I didn't love her as much as I do, I'd secretly hate her.

As for me, I'm not not-hot, but I've never considered myself hot either. When I was in middle school, my cheeks looked permanently stuffed with marshmallows. In high school, I unearthed an ancient aerobics workout video in my parents' basement and lost enough weight to land a spot on the Top Three Hottest in the Room list by second-string football players who sat behind me in art class. That weight promptly returned, thanks to a four-year love affair with chicken parmigiana in college. Now, at the ripe old age of twenty-eight, too many late nights at the computer have rendered me with permanent under-eye bags, though the baby face saves me from looking a decade older than I am.

"I'm not hot, but I love you for implying that I am," I say.

"I would totally date you if I was into women." Tina grins.

"Me too," Vic adds.

"My hot-or-not-ness is not the real issue. High school was a tiny blip on the radar of my life, mostly focused on straight A's and unrequited love." I shrug my shoulders as my friends' eyeballs nearly pop out of their heads. Damn it all, I just dropped the L-bomb on two die-hard romantics.

"Unrequited love!" Vic fans himself, as though he's about to faint. "Ellie, you need to tell us everything. *Right now.*"

Tina leans forward in agreement, like she's about to read a scandalous story on TMZ.

"There's nothing to tell. I talked to him a handful of times in four years, so *unrequited* is the key word here. Perpetual loser in love, remember?" I hit the bottom of my drink, and my straw makes a horrible slurping sound that somehow matches how I feel.

"That's because you're mean to every guy you like," Vic points out. Tina nods in agreement.

"Apparently, I'm mean to everyone and need to '*gain a fresh perspective.*' Which is why Andy is making me go on this stupid quest that will probably set me back another decade in the self-confidence department, promotion or not. I need another drink." I attempt to make eye contact with the server and fail.

"A fresh perspective?" Tina raises an eyebrow.

"That's literally what he said." I shrug. "God, why does he have to be so...him?"

Vic takes a long drink from his beer, lost in thought. Suddenly, he slams it down, grinning ear to ear. "Let's make it a game."

Tina nods in agreement. "We need a reframe."

"You guys aren't going to sign me up for online therapy, are you?" I shudder.

"Tempting, but no," Vic says. "We're going to make this fun. A fresh perspective scavenger hunt."

Fun? I must have heard him wrong. There's no way going to my high school reunion could ever be *fun*.

I fake a barfing sound. Tina squeals her approval, and Greta's startled bark sounds more like a squeak.

In TV writing, we use games as a plot device to elevate the stakes. They add tension, usually in act two, where the stakes always need a little extra *oomph*. It's good storytelling, but maybe not so good for real life though. My life doesn't need stakes; it needs a Xanax to get me through the weekend.

"This is my life, not a Hallmark movie." I grunt, sucking down more melted ice, but they are no longer paying any attention to me.

"We'll call it *Ellie Is Cool Now*," Vic says. He grabs a fresh napkin, takes a pen out of his pocket, and clicks it like I imagine the devil would before he asks someone to sign over a soul. He unfolds the napkin and writes ELLIE IS COOL NOW across the top of it, underlining it like an official title. "A bucket list to face the ghosts of high school past."

"And become co-EP of a major network show," Tina adds.

Vic touches the pen to his lips, thinking hard. "We'll use the senior superlatives." He pulls out his iPad and starts poking it, all while mumbling to himself.

"Best Dressed. Most Likely to Succeed." Tina counts out the ones she can remember on her fingers.

"Aha, knew it. My high school put all the old yearbooks online—I genuinely think as a small form of torture," Vic says. "Here it is, Stonybrook High School, class of 2010."

"Nuh-uh." I grab his iPad. Sure enough, my entire high school yearbook is online.

Gross.

Vic yanks it back, smirking. He scrolls through with purpose. "There she is, the cutest future TV exec ever." He turns it out to face Tina and me.

"Oh, look at you in your hot-pink polo!" Tina giggles.

"Ick. Moving on," I say.

Vic continues to flip through the virtual book until he comes to a page with a select few of the kids in my class paired off. They look like babies...and now probably close to half of them *have* babies. My sigh is tinged with melancholy.

"Number one...definitely hook up with the prom king." He writes it down. I look at the picture of the prom king and remember when all the girls used to talk about him like he was the hottest thing since *Titanic*-era Leo DiCaprio. His name is Kyle Temple, and he is not my type.

"I don't do the hook-up thing," I point out. "Diseases."

"Hooking up can mean making out," Vic says, with a shrug.

"Uh, *diseases*," I emphasize.

"Like what?"

"Oral herpes, mononucleosis, meningitis, polio..." I count on my fingers.

"Really, Ellie? Polio?" Vic deadpans. If his eyes could roll back to touch his brain, they would.

"If there's a kissing disease to be had, trust me, Kyle Temple has it."

"Fine, fine, number two," Vic says, moving on. "Hook up with Most Athletic." Clearly, he's learned nothing. He starts to write, but Tina swipes the napkin from him before he can.

"She's not living *your* reunion dream," Tina says, "to hook up with every guy she had a wet dream about in high school."

"Also, I'm pretty sure Most Athletic is married to a BLW," I add.

Boring Life Wife is a term I made up for the gorgeous cookie-cutter girl all the hot guys marry for arm candy. Most likely a cheerleader in high school, and now doomed to a life of perpetual cheerleading—cooking dinner and raising spawn in the white-picket-fence, *Leave It to Beaver* ideal of an American family. She is a victim of patriarchal ideals and is usually rock-hard-Pilates-abs-deep in a pyramid scheme.

Tina ignores my BLW comment completely. She's not into my harsh acronym, mostly because her parents once closely resembled the BLW arrangement. Her dad eventually made a ton of money in real estate and left her mom for a shinier, newer BLW who is half his age. Free from the BLW ties that bind, Tina's mom now has her own line of luxury candles (I have one in every scent), a weekend Malibu surfing habit, and a hot boyfriend a decade her junior with a six-pack.

"You need to have better hair than Best Hair," Tina returns to the subject at hand, glancing over at the iPad. "And you def need to grab a beer with Most Likely to Brighten Your Day."

I squint my eyes at the yearbook. Best Hair was a girl named

Emma Lovett. I think she cheers for the NBA now or some-thing. As far as I know, she still has great hair, but I live in LA and have the same hair stylist as Demi Moore, so maybe I could compete. As for Most Likely to Brighten Your Day...

I scowl.

"Nope, not that one."

"Really? *Most Likely to Brighten Your Day* is the one tripping you up?" Vic asks with a raised eyebrow.

"That's Roxy." I take a labored pause. "My ex–best friend. Emphasis on the *ex*. I haven't seen her since graduation. Very on purpose."

"Oooh, sounds like a juicy story!" Vic says.

"They pegged her with Most Likely to Brighten Your Day because she slept with half the class," I say, my voice darker than I mean it to be.

Tina sucks in a breath. "Jesus. Teenagers are brutal."

"Yikes." Vic shakes his head and gestures with his hands. "Two thumbs way down for the Stonybrook slut shamers of one-oh."

"I doubt she'll be at the reunion anyway," I say. "I'll grab a beer slash rum and Coke with Best All-Around."

"Look at you! All aboard?" Vic grins at me.

"Do I have a choice?" I ask. Not going to lie, Vic and Tina have made this whole ordeal more palatable. The likelihood of me actually doing the things on this list is slim, but at least they are excited. Their enthusiasm helps me feel like this might not be the dumpster fire of a weekend that I initially feared it would be.

I set down a twenty-dollar bill on the table for happy hour. "You have the yearbook, so you two have fun plotting my fate.

I have to pack. Apparently my flight leaves LAX at ten a.m. tomorrow."

Vic and Tina give me determined nods.

"I'll email you the list," Vic says, with a smile and a wink.

"Oh," Tina says, grabbing my arm. "Who did you say your high school crush was?"

"No," I say.

"Come on, please?" Vic begs. "I need to live vicariously through you."

"Me too, me too," Tina adds. They both make ridiculous puppy dog eyes. Greta is the only one with any dignity, since she's ignoring me for a plate of chicken wings the server just sat down on another table.

"I'm already on his shit list. Trust me. I doubt he'll be at the reunion anyway. He went to med school, so he's probably in the middle of a residency or something."

"You're a hotshot Hollywood TV writer, and you'll be there."

"I am being forced to go for *research*."

"What's his name?" Vic asks, brushing past my protest.

"Noooo," I protest.

"Name," Vic insists.

"No." It's a fight to the death.

"Name!" they demand in unison. People around us are staring. My cheeks turn as pink as the polo shirt in my old yearbook photo.

"Mark Wright," I concede through my teeth. They win and I am deceased. Dead, dead, dead.

Vic scrolls through to find Mark's yearbook photo. I let out an exasperated sigh.

His wicked smile turns into a lopsided grimace as he

examines the photo of my long-ago high school crush. I peek over his shoulder to see Mark Wright's big brown eyes and crooked smile. I can't help but wonder what he looks like now, after growing into himself.

He was a baby back then. I was a baby. It's amazing to me how little we all looked, compared to how old we felt. Eighteen and entering college—ready for the world, but with no life skills to speak of. Could conjugate verbs in French like a beast though.

"He's…cute," Vic says finally. He slides the iPad over to Tina. She cocks her head to one side, the same way you would when examining a weird mole to decide whether it's cancerous or not.

"I can see it," she says finally.

"Do *not* put him on the list," I say, pointing a finger at both of them. Not that I'm doing the list, anyway.

I leave with a final warning glare.

They smile and wave me off innocently.

CHAPTER 3

I can't sleep.

I stare at the ceiling as my anxiety-ridden brain takes it upon itself to flash back to every painful high school memory.

It's no secret that I wasn't popular in high school.

I didn't get invited to parties. No one asked me to a school dance until senior year. I found out later the guy only asked because his friend was going with my bestie and he didn't want to go stag. We danced once and his breath smelled like fish from the sushi restaurant we went to before the dance.

I dated a boy named Greg for three months, the only boy I ever kissed in high school. He wore those baggy carpenter jeans and enough Axe body spray to suffocate a canary in a coal mine. Kissing him was like sucking on a slug. He ruined me on saliva swapping until well into college, and even now, I remain skeptical of its merits.

The only boy I genuinely lusted after in high school was the one, the only Mark Wright.

I get up and walk to the bathroom to splash my face with cool water.

Come on, Ellie. Sleep. We must brave the airport security lines at LAX tomorrow.

LAX is the pit stain of American airports, kissing every traveler hello and goodbye with an hour-long traffic jam. It's a hellish affair, made worse by rush hour on the 405. At exactly the time I'm en route. Thank you, Andy Biermann.

I find a zit that I swear I'm not going to touch. I swear I'm just going to get a closer look, but then I attack it until it resembles a traffic light on my cheek and...Great. Now I'm going to go to my reunion with a big honking zit *and* a withering sense of self-worth.

I grab my laptop on my way back to bed. Sleeping doesn't seem to be in the cards tonight, so Facebook stalking it is.

I search for Mark's profile. We're not friends, so all I can see is a picture of him in front of a random city skyline. Is that New York? Chicago?

He hasn't changed at all, except he dresses better now and has a haircut that suits his face. I know through some friends of friends that Mark studied biology as part of a pre-med track. He probably graduated with honors and aced his MCAT and is currently doing his residency at some fancy East Coast hospital. The chances of him being at the reunion are slim to none.

Thank God.

I click on his picture to make it bigger. My stomach flips. I still think he's attractive, even after everything that happened. *Way to not give a shit anymore, Ms. Hollywood.*

In high school, Mark was not the kind of guy girls usually lusted after. He was not a football player or a basketball star. He wasn't an angry emo kid with a band or a sexually ambiguous drama club nerd.

Mark played soccer, and he was just kinda okay at it.

He was one of the pseudo-popular kids. The B-listers. The ones who were okay to talk to me in AP history but would rather have eaten a live cockroach than hang out with me at a football game. On the surface he wasn't special, but it was the little things about him—the devilish smile, the snarky sense of humor, the small gestures of kindness of a dork just barely hiding—that I liked.

I had an opportunity, and I blew it big-time.

Senior year, we were partners for an AP English project. We'd just studied *Hamlet* and had to write and perform a dramatic scene starring a hero with a tragic flaw. We decided on a fatal attraction scenario set in high school. We met every day after school for two weeks. At first it was business as usual, but after a few days there was smiling and casual touching. A knee brush here, a hand touch there. A flirtatious comment, some lingering eye contact.

We started staying longer than we needed to, talking outside until sundown. He told me that he dreamed of going to NYU for film school, but that his dad was pressuring him to follow in his footsteps and become a doctor. I told him I secretly wanted to be an actor but was going to school for business. He talked to me about his parents' divorce, and I confessed to him that I was worried about my best friend, Roxy (who was getting wilder and wilder and talking to me less and less).

He even walked me to my car, carrying my perpetually heavy backpack for me.

It was finally happening. Mark Wright was on the hook.

There was a possibility, some hope—a spark.

And then I poured gasoline on that spark and lit it on fire.

It was a small moment, but explosive in my memory. The last day before our project was due, he asked me if I was going to the basketball game that night. I was not, but I told him I was, and then I dragged Roxy to the game with me. Roxy hated games and was in a foul mood before we even got there. She'd had a bad fight with her mom, but what else was new?

When Mark saw us walking into the gymnasium, he waved at me with a big smile.

And then something horrible happened.

I chickened out.

I didn't wave back. I ignored him. I ignored the hell out of him.

"Ellie!" I heard him say my name, but I couldn't do it. I'd been fantasizing about this guy for four years, since junior high even. And now this could really happen? Mark Wright and I...could be a *thing*?

Nope, nuh-uh, no way.

We sat on the other side of the gym, far away from where Mark had clearly saved me a seat. I noticed out of the corner of my eye that he looked back at me once or twice, but I stared straight ahead, too in my head—mentally beating myself to a bloody pulp—to watch the game.

Roxy was too upset to notice or care that I was missing my big shot, and I was too angry with myself for fucking it all up to care about what was going on with her. We were two angsty teenage friend-ships passing in the night.

Afterward, I went home and cried myself to sleep. I knew it was over, that I'd blown it all to smithereens.

I was right. The next day, Mark was cold as ice with me in class. We performed our scene, got a vigorous round of applause and an A, and never really spoke again.

Way to go, Ellie.

Mark went back to his existence at the edge of the cool crowd, and I went back to not fitting in anywhere.

My small circle of mediocre friends were about as cool as I was. We weren't in drama, and we weren't in band. We couldn't have cared less about sports, and we'd rather be murdered and have our skins turned into footballs than cheer for an actual game.

We were the Miscellaneous kids, the kids with no label—the et ceteras, the nobodies, the "insert-name-here who?"s. And no matter how much we acted like it didn't matter, we all secretly wanted to be popular (while pretending like we didn't care). Sure, we'd heard all the shit about how you should be true to yourself and *not try to fit in, stand out from the crowd, don't peak in high school, blah blah blah*. But if we'd gotten invited to one of Brock Crawley's legendary parties, we'd have nearly vomited from excitement.

Which is why I should have been sus as hell when I finally got the informal invite I'd been dreaming of for four years— to attend Brock Crawley's grad party. The Stonybrook mayor's bad-boy son lived in a big house that backed up to a golf course. His place was the clubhouse of the in crowd.

Every Miscellaneous kid wanted a spot in the in crowd.

Now was my chance. Better late than never.

I close my eyes, determined to banish the creeping memories of that one horrible night and failing miserably because there she is, Roxy Draper, my best friend, leaning up against my locker, popping her gum. Her black hair spills over her shoulders in natural waves, and she wears a T-shirt two sizes too small over low-rise jeans. The school faculty has given up trying to make Roxy adhere to the dress code. She is untamable, and also terrifying, with verbal claws that cut deep before you even know what hit you.

Roxy had no problems fitting in in high school, probably because she didn't care what anyone thought about her. She was technically Miscellaneous, but she'd begun a strange transformation the summer before senior year. On the outside it appeared to have everything to do with her particular talent for holding her liquor, combined with her budding reputation as a girl who'd have sex with *no strings attached*, a combo that had earned her a precarious place at the edge of the popular crowd.

What none of them knew, though, was that her home life was in wreckage. Her mom was having serious health issues, and her dad had bailed on them both over the winter.

Roxy's family drama was always an issue, even before her mom's health took a nosedive. They fought about everything from the color of her lipstick to her plan to take a gap year and work at the DQ to save up for a trip to Barcelona (which never happened).

Her mom was extremely hard on her, berating her for scoring anything less than an A on a test, a paper, a worksheet. If there was a grade, and it wasn't an A, Roxy was grounded.

During freshman year, I went over to her house for a sleepover, and her mom grilled me about my grades and then said to Roxy in front of me, "Why can't you be more like Ellie?" Roxy turned ten shades of red, marched up to her room, and slammed and locked the door. My mom had to come pick me up.

It got progressively worse as high school went on, a spiral that no one could stop. No matter how much I wanted to help, I had begun to think I was the last person Roxy wanted to hold her hand while she stumbled.

"You're my plus-one," she'd said, handing me the folded-up flyer that served as an invitation to Brock Crawley's blow-out graduation party. A last hurrah! The dying breath of an era!

It was Roxy's first invite to a Brock Crawley party and therefore mine by association. I was one part apathetic and two parts terrified, with a splash of curiosity. I had a sneaking suspicion she just wanted me to be her DD, but when she said the words "Mark Wright is probably gonna be there," it was game over.

That was it. My second chance.

One final opportunity to fix the basketball game debacle and finally achieve the dreamy, steamy high school romance of my heart's desire, even if it could only be a summer fling.

A night to remember that I wish I could forget.

I slam the laptop closed and rub my eyes until they hurt. This is the opposite of *not thinking about that night*.

Cut to—

The night of the party. Me sitting on the landing of Brock's childhood treehouse, watching all the Abercrombie-clad prepsters in the backyard get smashed and make out in tents, zipping them tight when it was time to *close the deal*, and I wasn't drinking because *hello, underage*.

I'd climbed up there hoping to spot Roxy in the crowd—I'd lost track of her not long after we arrived—and to be honest, I was already bored. The sucky part about being a chronic rule follower is that parties aren't that much fun when you're unwilling to partake in any of the debauchery. Also, *X-Files* was on.

From up there, Roxy was hard to miss. She writhed through the crowd like a snake, carrying a whole bottle of rum, trailed by Ben Forrester, a hockey player with no neck who practically had his tongue hanging out. *Gross.* I climbed down the rope ladder and hopped to the ground, spinning around to make a beeline in the direction I'd seen her walking.

And spun right into Mark Wright.

I push my laptop aside and curl my knees to my chest. I hug them tight, like they can protect me from these feelings. I am giving in to sleep, giving into my thoughts sliding toward Mark, what happened next, and all the shit I really should have left behind, but obviously haven't.

I close my eyes, and I'm back in the nightmare.

My hands are on Mark's chest, light and swift.

"Oh, hey, Ellie," Mark said. "Shouldn't you be at home packing for Harvard?"

Mark thought I was way smarter than I was. (Note: I did not apply to Harvard.) He was just as smart, but he got a kick out of teasing me about my brain. It was a topic of conversation on constant rotation during our AP project, and even if he was mostly exaggerating my alleged genius, that cute, clumsy flirting made my stomach flutter with stupid butterflies.

I took a generous step back, removing my hands from his chest and fixing my face in a frown. Most people, when they have a crush, flirt with the other person and, you know, want them to know they like them.

Not me.

When I like someone, I end up treating them like scum or ignoring them completely. It's so much easier to live in the fantasy than take a risk on something real. Fantasy Mark was perfect and safe because he would love me forever inside my head. Real Mark was flawed and unpredictable. Dangerous, because he could break my heart.

It was so much easier to pretend I hated his guts than to finish what we started in AP English.

A God-awful habit I desperately wanted to break at that moment.

"Actually, I should be at home watching *X-Files* reruns." Me, always brutally oversharing the wrong information.

He raised his eyebrows. "*X-Files?* Really?"

My cheeks blazed. "It's a good show."

"Oh, it's a good show. I just wouldn't expect you—of all people—to be into it," he says, his eyes searching my face.

That kind of sounded like he had thought about what I'd be into, which made it seem as if he might have thought about me, and now it was more than my ears and cheeks blushing. My insides completely ignited.

"What do you *think* I'd be into?" I asked him. The words come out more hostile than was my intention. I couldn't control it. When I looked at Mark, I realized he had noticed. And he seemed to like it.

He seemed to like me.

"Hmmm," he said, considering. "*The Notebook.*"

"*The Notebook?*" I gag. He laughs. I shake my head, disgusted. "I *hate The Notebook.*"

"Not a big fan of romance, Ellie?"

Then he leaned—or staggered, I wasn't sure. I reached out

to prop him in place. His lip curled. The dimple right above his mouth popped.

"Melodrama and emotional pandering," I said, so low it was almost a whisper. I was breathless. "No, thank you."

He laughed again, and his hand wrapped around my wrist—for balance or because he liked me, I couldn't tell. My skin got hot, my head light. He leaned closer, sending me all the signals that he was into me. I could have leaned in, touched my lips to his. Done something wild and risky and vulnerable—for *once*.

But instead I stepped back.

He stumbled forward. I crossed my arms, wrecked with new, horrible self-consciousness. And that was when I saw it for real, written all over his face.

Unshakable disappointment.

I spun away from him, unable to process this Shakespearean tragedy of a moment all on my own. How could I like him this much and still not let him see it? How could I keep rejecting him when all I wanted to do was the complete opposite? What was wrong with me?

When I turned around again, Mark was gone.

Fuck it all. I needed to find Roxy.

The only problem was, I couldn't find her. For the next forty-five minutes, I searched. I sideswiped offers of beer. I avoided conversations that began with "Aren't you in my pre-calc class?" *Definitely not.* And when I was about to give up, I saw Ben the hockey player pouring shots by the pool house. No Roxy in sight.

"Ben—hey," I said, moving into his sight line.

His eyes tried to focus on me. They couldn't.

"Where's Roxy?" I pushed past his drunkenness.

"Roxy?" he asked, like he'd lost all memory of the events prior to that moment and actually wasn't sure what was currently even happening.

"Tall, skinny, wearing leather pants and a tube top?"

"Oh, Rox-Off..." he said, and then he scowled. I scowled too, but I figured it was for different reasons. "Haven't seen her since she headed upstairs with Connor."

That was enough to go on. I made my way through the backyard and into Brock's house without another word to anyone.

The upstairs was a minefield. If the tents outside were full of people fucking, the hallways were full of people living in the aftermath. Girls sobbing, boys passed out against walls. With every bedroom door I opened, I uncovered the sound of awkward sex acts and even more awkward fights about sex acts. It was almost enough to make a girl turn celibate.

At the end of the hall, I opened the door to what looked like Brock Crawley's twelve-year-old sister's bedroom and there, in the shadows, lit by a dim nightlight and moonlight sneaking through the curtains, I found Roxy.

And Mark.

His lips on hers. Her fingers twisted in his hair.

I stood frozen, watching as her tongue entered his mouth and his hand fumbled at the edge of her tube top.

This cannot be happening.

She was my best friend and she knew—she *knew* I liked Mark. Had *loved* Mark for fully one-third of my life.

She didn't care about him. She didn't actually care about anybody.

Not even me.

I had to get out of there. I turned to leave, panic overtaking me, and slammed right into Brock's sister's pink and white dresser drawers.

"Ellie?" I heard Roxy's voice. It was sharp, breaking on the end of my name.

I ran. I heard her calling out to me, slurred words on her drunken lips, but I didn't respond. I just kept running as the white walls faded to black and closed in around me.

My body jolts me awake. I'm panting and sweating. My computer is cold, and there's drool on my face.

Except it's not drool. It's tears.

I wipe them away in disgust, blinking until they dry up completely.

As much as I want to pretend I'm beyond Stonybrook, Mark, Roxy, and every crappy, insecure feeling I left behind, I'm not.

And now I have to catch a plane to the past.

CHAPTER 4

In the Uber on the way to the airport, my phone dings with a new email from Vic.

Oh shit.

I'm going to chicken out on this list. I'm not hooking up with anyone, and I'm seriously not going to stick around longer than I have to. My return ticket is for Monday night, and no doubt there are reunion activities on Saturday and Sunday, but I am going to the main event only. That's it. Get in, get out. Andy did *not* explicitly say I had to do anything more than that.

I take a deep breath and pretend to listen to the Uber driver talk about his latest screenplay about an Uber driver—a script at least one out of every five Uber drivers in LA is currently writing—and open the email.

Subject: ELLIE IS COOL NOW

ELLIE! We stayed up way too late making this list so you are 1000% not allowed to chicken out—we KNOW you are thinking about it. STOP.

Without further ado . . .

1. Hook up with the prom king.
2. Have better hair than Best Hair.
3. Grab a beer with Best All-Around.
4. Compare lives with Most Likely to Succeed.
5. Create a piece of art with Most Artistic.
6. Finally get invited to a party with all the "popular kids."
7. Go to a basketball game and out-spirit Most Spirited.
8. Pull a prank on the Class Clown.
9. Win a game against Most Athletic.
10. Get your high school crush to help you with at least one of the items on this list.

Best of luck, babe. We know you'll CRUSH it *wink*

xo
V + T

It's a good list. The last one does make my heart drop a little bit. But Mark isn't going to be there. There's no way. And even if he is, he's not going to want to talk to me, let alone help me with some random list. I hit reply on my email and start to type "You need a new number ten—he's not gonna be—"

Mid-type, my phone lights up.

It's Andy. F-U-C-K. What now?

I answer, "I can't talk now, I'm in the middle of a pitch meeting."

"Let me guess, an Uber driver gets caught up in the middle of a bank robbery." I can hear him scratching his beard.

I talk to him through a yawn. "Jewel heist, actually. Starring Paris Hilton and the Kardashians."

My driver gives me an overzealous thumbs-up from the front seat. I just stare at it.

"I just heard about the list," Andy says, not missing a beat.

I sit up a little straighter in my seat and say nothing.

"Susie is getting your emails while you're out of town." Damn it, Vic. Of course Andy is snooping in my studio inbox.

"Wonderful," I say, sarcastically. "It's a joke, really. I'm not—"

"It's brilliant!" he interrupts with more enthusiasm than I've ever heard coming from him. It's disconcerting, especially considering the context. "Way to raise the stakes!"

When he said to workshop it, I didn't expect him to give me notes on what I came up with. But he's an evil writerly mastermind. A real-life version of a list like this is a screenwriter's wet dream. He's visualizing all the ways this list will create drama, while not even giving a second thought to the real-life person it's about to tear apart. I'm the puppet; he's holding the strings.

"Sure, but I don't need to raise the stakes. This is my real life," I reply.

"This is Hollywood." Actually, it's Ohio.

"With all due respect, I don't think you can force me to do anything on that list."

"You're absolutely right. I can't force you to do anything. But going to this reunion is about more than taking a trip down memory lane. *Ellie Is Cool Now* is the perfect mechanism to drive your arc from judgmental ingenue to well-rounded leader and co-EP."

"I'm not 'hooking up' with someone for a job—"

"Do what feels right to you," he says, taking another labored pause. As if anyone in Hollywood has ever said that and meant it. "You want to be a showrunner someday on your own show. You want to be in charge."

My mouth goes dry.

"That won't happen without hefty revisions to Ellie Jenkins's character development," he says with a flourish. I roll my eyes. He could make writing analogies for days. "Do the list, and you just might make all your dreams come true."

I swallow hard. Andy is right. More than anything I want to move on from *Cooler Than You*, to be able to run my own show, preferably not about shallow teen angst. Proving myself as co-EP is just the beginning. While I've never been put in a position to compromise my morals for a job—and I wouldn't—I can damn well complete this dumb list if it means *Ellie Is a Boss Now* is at the end of it.

How hard could it be? I can bullshit some of it, if I need to.

"Fine, I'll do it," I say. But my ears are ringing, and my head is swimming. If this is the catalyst, then I guess I'm taking the call to action.

"Good, glad to hear it," he says. "Oh, and Ellie?" His voice sounds distant as the world expands around me.

"Yep?" I say, feeling dizzy.

"You're an expert storyteller, but a terrible liar. Don't make shit up."

Click.

I slowly drop the phone away from my ear.

The Uber driver pulls up to the terminal and asks for my email address so he can send me his script. For a split second I'm worried I'll end up on *KTLA 5 Morning News*, where some beautiful woman with breast implants will regale the SoCal region with the story of a crazed lunatic at LAX who murdered her Uber driver in cold blood.

Luckily, I'm without weapons, and soon I'm standing in the security line at LAX, skimming the Uber driver's terrible fucking screenplay, because I'm a chump. In front of me, a three-year-old girl drops her container of Cheerios and starts to cry—big crocodile tears of doom—and her mother begins frantically picking up the mess. I'm trapped there as the misery unfolds when my phone buzzes with a text from Tina about the list and all of a sudden...*BAM!*

I live in LA, I'm a TV writer who hated high school, and I'm going home to this godforsaken reunion to face the demons of my past.

Mark.

Roxy.

All the people who pretended I didn't exist for four years.

Oh yeah, and that stupid thing I did when I was drunk in college.

Turns out Brock Crawley's grad party was *not* the last time I talked to Mark.

It was college, and it was my first time getting drunk. I

did not expect the bravado that came with it. Thanks to a moral chip on my shoulder about underage drinking (gee, I wonder why), I'd delayed drunken shenanigans for as long as was socially acceptable and finally unleashed my inner party animal for one night and one night only. The next day's hangover was not nearly as bad as the crushing humiliation when I discovered that in my fugue state of drunkenness, I sent Mark Wright a message on Facebook.

I yank out my phone and open my Messenger app. Seven years is a long time. It's probably not even there anymore. He probably never even read it. I search for his name.

One message, consisting of the longest run-on sentence of all time. Jesus Christ.

> Hi Mark it's me ellie from ap english i used to have a crush on you but then you hooked up with my best friend and well that's not really your fault but you did go to school for something that would make your dad happy (biology??? PRE MED???) instead of film school like you wanted and idk i just think it's disappointing that you gave up on your dreams for something you hate because it feels safe...I thought you were one of the brave ones

Apparently, I had a serious vendetta against him being pre-med. Mostly, I struggled with how creative Mark was in school juxtaposed with a picture in my head of him studying cell division and photosynthesis. He always placed in art shows and turned in Sundance-worthy homemade short films for school projects. He even starred in the school play our junior year, as

Algernon in *The Importance of Being Earnest.* I secretly saw it three times. (No shame.)

Pre-med just felt like a safe choice for Mark. Not to mention, I'd just switched my major from business to creative writing, so I was riding on my high horse, *doing the damn thing* and *making my dreams come true.* And apparently, that included reaching out to old flames (well, flickers) to tell them they were not good enough.

God, Ellie.

Right below the excruciating message, a tiny check mark to prove he read it.

He saw it and never replied. Then I blocked him and never looked back. Until now.

Oh God, I can never see him ever, *ever* again.

"Can you shove forward? We're next," the guy behind me says, pointing toward the TSA officer.

The security line at LAX is a horrible place to panic. My palms are sweaty as I slide my phone back into my purse and wipe my hands on the back of my jeans. A bored TSA officer calls me up, motioning for me to hand him my ticket and ID.

My hand shakes as I fumble for what he needs.

"Nervous flier?" he asks, eyeing me with some amusement.

"You have no idea," I choke out.

"Don't worry." He checks off something on the ticket, glancing again at my ID. "Flying really is the safest way to travel."

I suppress an eye roll as he hands back my ID and boarding pass and ushers me forward.

Little does he know that today I'm praying for a crash landing.

My mother is happy as a clam when she meets me at baggage claim. Her smile is a beacon of shiny teeth in her slim, angular face. She's got incredible bone structure. I got my dad's everything except for the eyes. Mine are blue like Mom's, and I have resigned myself to the fact that I will never see my actual cheekbones. Mom wraps her arms around me, swaying from side to side like I'm an infant she's rocking.

I haven't made it home in ages, but unlike so many of my friends in LA with *complicated family relationships*, I actually miss my parents. I want to be spoiled and waited on. I want to eat Mom's homemade cinnamon rolls and snuggle under a cushy blanket watching old sitcoms while she folds my laundry and hums the theme songs, and Dad tinkers with his ancient computer in his office, switching off between playing solitaire and dodging emails from Nigerian princes.

My parents haven't been able to visit much, either. My apartment is actually a shoebox suited for mice and not people, and I hate to put them in a hotel when they came for quality time. The co-EP position could give me enough money to finally upgrade to a human-sized apartment.

Mom pushes back to get a better look at me.

"Have you been using that cream I bought you?" she asks. She scrutinizes my face for signs of damage.

I wince. "I ran out."

"You could have asked. I would have sent you more."

"Okay, okay, stop staring at me." I groan and shield my face from her harsh dermatological exam. She's endlessly concerned about my skin in the dry desert air and brutal SoCal sun.

We turn around to wait for the luggage, but she keeps her arm around my waist, tugging me close like I'm a balloon in danger of floating away.

Dad inches the car forward little by little in the passenger pick-up lane, avoiding the sharp whistle of airport security telling him to move along. He refuses to wait in the cell phone lot because no doubt he left his phone charging at home on the counter, which Mom swears is on purpose. Mom and I walk out into the cool autumn air, and as soon as Dad spots us, he hurries out to open the trunk. I can hear sports radio yammering in the background. He gives me a solid hug around the neck.

"Hi, Daddy," I say, genuinely happy to see both of my parents, in spite of the hellish circumstances.

We drive the familiar roads away from the airport. It's fall in Ohio. It's technically fall in LA too, but LA doesn't do fall quite like Stonybrook: leaves of red and gold for miles, fields of late fall hay, the lush green of summer fading to brown in preparation for winter. In town, shop windows are decorated with hokey Halloween spooks and orange and purple lights strung overhead. Pumpkins dot nearly every doorway, some carved, some not.

I once carved a Jack Skellington pumpkin in LA in an attempt to be festive. Something about the dry air meant that within three days he'd developed a massive rotted overbite. There's just nothing like Halloween in the Midwest.

You don't miss the little things about home when you're off being a Hollywood big shot, but then you come back and it's like taking a big, satisfying inhale.

Until it starts to suffocate you again.

Dad pulls into the driveway and cuts the engine. Our house isn't fancy. Brick and wood with a red front door. Small and modest, but cute. *Damn.* Sounds like me in high school.

Dad gets out and pops the trunk. He hauls my too-huge-for-one-weekend bag inside, and I breathe a sigh of relief that he can still lift sixty-pound bags. He's pushing seventy, and every time I come home he's a little grayer. The hardest part about leaving home is watching your parents age in stop-motion.

"Do you ever hear from Roxy?" Mom asks as we make our way into the house.

My responding sigh is deep and annoyed. "No, Mom." She knows I don't, and I haven't since before college.

"I saw Maureen at the grocery store a few months ago," Mom says.

"Cool" is all I say as I hold the door open for her to come inside.

"She didn't speak to me," she says with a shrug. She sets her purse on the counter and makes her way over to the couch.

Maureen stopped talking to my mom when Roxy went off the rails. Maureen always had a weirdo competitive thing with my parents: *who was better at raising their only child?* I didn't eat my vegetables as a kid, so Maureen had the edge for a little while. But last I checked, Roxy had an alcohol and drug problem (and who could blame her, with a mother like that?). Guess my parents won, though.

I collapse onto the couch in a pit of despair. My mom launches into a whole spiel about how weird it is that Maureen doesn't talk to her anymore after Roxy and I were friends for so long, and she wonders if Roxy is sober now, and Maureen just looked *so* bad, and does *she* look that bad?

I want to say something about how Maureen has been struggling with her health for years—pretty much since my senior year of high school—and Mom should check her sensitivity meter because it might be broken. But Mom doesn't take criticism well, and I'm too close to hangry to field crocodile tears so soon after arrival.

She digresses to how she's been using her cream every day and Deb from bridge club had a facelift and looks ten years younger...

I do a lot of *mm-hmm*s and *uh-huh*s, but to be honest, my mind is elsewhere.

Mom bringing up Maureen and Roxy right before my forced attendance at my high school reunion has left me feeling nostalgic—and trepidatious. Will Roxy be there tomorrow? And if so, what the fuck am I going to say to her?

It's the one high school love story that should have spanned the ages. We'd been friends since elementary school. We first met at ballet class. Our mothers became fast friends as the only non–Boring Life Wives behind the scenes of tiny tutus gone wild. Our friendship bloomed in second grade and continued through junior high, when we were both still embarrassed we hadn't gotten boobs, and into high school. We didn't actually have that much in common on the surface—besides not needing a training bra—but it hadn't really mattered. When we were together, the differences fell away into boy talk and giggle fits.

But then senior year happened, and the differences became beyond glaring.

Roxy went from the girl they all secretly watched to the girl they all wanted to bang. And the night of Brock Crawley's grad party from hell, she went from my friend to a complete stranger. Forever.

Screw this.

"Mom, where are your keys?" I ask as I walk out into the living room.

Moments like these call for baked goods.

"Give me my purse," she says, one eye on the TV, where Judge Judy is berating a divorced couple loudly. Mom pauses her. I grab her purse, which no one else is ever allowed to go through because of possible military secrets hidden inside. She fishes out her keys and hands them to me.

"Where are you going?" she asks.

"I need Stonybrook Market therapy," I say.

Stonybrook Market is the cutest grocery store in the entire world, and it's just about always the first thing I do when I come home. I go and I walk around and listen to piano music and drool over fresh-baked brownies and sparkly cakes.

"Bring your father back a cream horn," she says as I head out the door.

I drive with the window cracked because I love feeling the cool wind whip at my face. I can never drive this fast in LA. It's all gridlock and intersections. There are never any winding roads, except for the Pacific Coast Highway, and well, let's just say—you don't move to LA from Ohio to spend your days cruising the PCH.

When I pull into the parking lot of Stonybrook Market, I marvel at how *the same* everything looks, but how different I feel. I step out of my parents' Kia Soul. I swear I can already smell the bakery. There's a slight chill in the air that feels like home. I wrap my arms tightly around myself, burrowing my hands inside the sleeves of my sweater, which is not warm enough for this weather, and head into the store.

Inside the grocery store, it's clean, gentle light, the fresh-baked smell of something delicious wafting through the air. My mouth waters instantly. I grab one of the mid-sized shopping carts and push it right to the bakery window.

I stare at the colorful cookies, the gooey brownies and petit fours and cream horns and donuts and *Oh my God, what do I choose?*

"Can I help you, miss?" a male voice asks from behind the counter.

My eyes peel themselves away from all the pastry goodness to look at the bakery worker, and I feel the air get sucked out of my lungs as all instinct to breathe leaves my body in a flash.

"Ellie?" the bakery worker cocks his head to the side in surprise.

Breathe in, I tell myself. I suck in a breath. *Breathe out. Breathe in. Breathe out.*

"Mark."

CHAPTER 5

"What are you doing here?" The question is out of my mouth before I have time to remind myself that I don't care what he's doing here and haven't cared since the night he and Roxy did God-knows-what at Brock's party. But the smell of bear claws and cheese Danish has momentarily gone to my head.

Or at least that's what I tell myself.

It has nothing to do with the tiny dimple at the corner of his lips, or how his muddy brown eyes have slightly darkened and sharpened with age.

"I...work here," he replies, quirking his stupid lips again. He hooks his thumbs through the straps of his apron to show me. I don't know why I think the gesture is so hot, but I do. Probably because he doesn't show an ounce of embarrassment that he's working at a grocery store (not that he should; just that he doesn't). He's all confidence and snark, and all the reasons I ever crushed on him in the first place come flooding back to me at once, pooling deep in my lower stomach. I need to sit down.

"You okay?" he asks, lifting one dark brow.

Damn it, I am going to swoon. What is happening to me? Get it together, Ellie. "I, um—I thought you were still in New York?"

"You thought I was a sell-out," he confronts me, no doubt remembering my drunken direct message of yore. My cheeks hurt with how hot they are. I touch one side of my face to make sure it's not actually on fire. "Because I told you that I wanted to go to film school, and I ended up pre-med instead."

"Oh, well…" He waits for me to finish my thought, but I have no words. Are there any words that exist for this situation? I can't think of any. I rack my brain. All I can come up with is "I'm a TV writer now—in Hollywood. I mean, LA. Los Angeles. California."

Smooth.

I turn to leave, desperate and pastry-less.

"Wait," he says. I turn back around, willing myself to stay put and not sprint for the door. "Are you home for reunion weekend?"

I nod. I clear my throat, trying to work out a lump that has lodged itself there.

"Are you going?" I ask, hopeful. Mostly for my job, but for other reasons as well.

"I'm not sure yet," he says. His eyes scan my face. "Didn't you come here for a snack?" I'm taken aback by his wording, but then he motions to the assortment of baked goods, and I realize he means food.

You are *a snack*. No, no, no, shut up, brain.

"Just a cream horn," I say, casual. "For my dad."

"You really did it," he says, and he's not talking about baked goods. The stunning thing is, he looks impressed. Mystified. He reaches into the display and pulls out two cream horns. He wraps them in paper, and then gently slides them inside a waxy bag. "These are on me."

He holds out the bag and I reach for it, my heart doing annoying little somersaults. At the last second he pulls it away.

"Hey!" I say, annoyed by the fake-out.

"Truce?" he asks expectantly.

"What?" My voice edges up in annoyance. "Truce implies ceasefire, and we haven't talked since high school."

A brief flicker of something flashes across his face. He narrows his eyes momentarily.

Don't say it. Don't say it.

"So that Facebook message doesn't count?"

I silently curse my twenty-one-year-old self.

"I was bored. And drunk." I try to shrug it off. "I didn't mean it."

"Yes, you did," he says. He sets the bag on the counter. I don't take it right away.

The lump is back, and no amount of swallowing or throat-clearing is going to get rid of it now.

"I didn't" is all I can say.

His eyes narrow. "You did mean it. Of course you did. You mean everything you say. And everything you don't." His voice has a new, sharper edge to it.

And it surprises me.

And suddenly, I'm pissed off. Mark Wright does not get to

pretend like he *knows* me. And he certainly doesn't get to catch me off guard, dredging up ancient history when I'm here for some sugar therapy. Not here, not today, not when I'm already on edge dreading this reunion.

I want to grab the cream horns and throw them on the ground at his feet, *truce* denied, but I won't make a scene inside of Stonybrook Market. Instead, I grab the bag and whirl, walking briskly away from the bakery, leaving behind my tiny cart and a pound of my dignity mixed with regret.

I'm in such a guilt-induced fury that I nearly run headlong into the tall, blond, knit-adorned body of Brie Baldwin.

"Ellie Jenkins?" She says my name like a question.

Brie: Best All-Around.

"Hi." I smile.

Brie was always nice. That's how she earned her title, and how everyone described her throughout her high school career. Sweet. Nice. Thoughtful. She'd remember your birthday. She always knew if you were going through a tough time and would find a way to make you feel less alone.

She pulls me into an unapproved but not unwelcome hug, and some of her wavy hair gets in my mouth. When she pushes back, her hazel eyes meet mine. They crease a little at the edges as she gives me another generous grin.

"You came! No one expected you to come."

People were talking about me?

I bite my lips because they are edging up into a weird, maniacal smile. It makes me hate myself a little for caring what they think.

Still.

"I was due for a trip home," I say, shrugging.

"This is so unexpected. I really wish I had time to catch up, but my daughter has a recital in twenty minutes. Ballet." She makes a cringey face, but then quickly corrects. "It's mostly bouncing around in tiny pink tutus. So. Cute."

An image of baby Roxy and me in matching pink tutus doing out-of-sync pliés flashes into my brain, and I mentally shoo it away.

I used to assume Brie secretly sheltered a monster deep down inside. Like the Balrog in the mines of Moria in *The Lord of the Rings*. I see a flicker of that in her eyes, but it quickly passes, and it makes me actually excited to get a drink with her at the reunion.

"I'll see you at the reunion!" I say, trying to put an end to this awkward run-in that I was not mentally prepared for.

She flashes a smile. "Or tonight! A few of us are going to meet at the Local for pre-reunion drinks. You absolutely *must* join us."

Ugh, I can't think of anything I want to do less. But! It's a good opportunity to get the lay of reunion land, and maybe go ahead and start knocking items off my list.

"Count me in," I say, forcing a smile.

She makes a *squee* sound and claps her hands together before waving goodbye as I head for the Kia.

I am officially back in high school.

The Local sits on the corner of our town square, a small, dark building with leaded glass windows and a red door. I'd been there a couple times with my mom for dinner when I visited during college, but I'd never gone on my own.

I adjust my boobs inside my little black dress. Gotta look hot but not too desperate to impress. I *do* love the subtle sultriness of an LBD.

I swing the door open and step a Chloé-bootied foot inside (a gift to myself when I got the payout for writing my first episode of *Cooler Than You*). It takes two point two seconds to find the old Stonybrook High crowd when Kyle Temple guffaws from a corner of the bar they've taken hostage. Still bigger than the average man, though with less hard muscle and more soft dough, with stubble on his now not-so-chiseled jaw and a buzz cut to hide the male pattern baldness already in effect, he's impossible to miss. I am not hooking up with him; I don't care what the list says.

Brie waves as I approach. It's amazing how easy it is to pick everyone out. The bar is full of the most popular people, the fringe popular kids, and the ones who snuck into the party after everyone else was already wasted. There's *Best Dancer*, Julie Simmons, laughing it up with *Best Personality*, who both stayed in Stonybrook and married rich. By the bar, *Biggest Drama King* cries on the shoulder of *Best Dressed*, who is sucking back a mojito—and it looks like it's not her first of the evening.

And in the corner by the jukebox is Mark.

Fuuuuuuck.

He's got a pint in his hand and the whisper of his signature snarky grin on his face as he talks to *Best Smile*, who wears the same peppy high pony she sported all through high school. In this light, he looks younger and so much like he did when I was into him that I can feel my palms begin to sweat. Fortunately, I'm an adult now, one who can purchase alcohol to help alleviate the threat of panic.

I beeline for the bar.

"Rum and Coke, please," I say to the bartender. I stare at Sailor Jerry on the bottom shelf and add "Captain, please."

"Ellie-fucking-Jenkins," a voice says from behind me.

"Make it a double," I say before I pivot to face Kyle Temple.

He looks me up and down. "You look hot," he says, licking his lips. He's already *very* drunk and staring at my boobs. I try to adjust them deeper into my dress. The LBD has backfired.

"Hi, Kyle," I say. A lazy grin spreads across his face when he realizes that I remember his name. His teeth are yellower than I remember, probably from chewing tobacco. I search for words, but I have no clue what to say to him. I settle on "Are you back for the reunion?" Duh.

The bartender sets my drink on the counter, and I hand him my credit card to start a much-needed tab. I take a huge gulp. Thank God for generous suburban bartenders.

"Never left," he answers, following it up with another up-and-down assessment. "But I see California has done you *good*."

"Well, this has been fun." *Or the opposite.* I bare my teeth in the impersonation of a smile right as Brock Crawley walks up and smacks Kyle on the back.

Brock was always good-looking. Tan and blond, with a crisp polo and a pair of khakis. He looks exactly the same, only slightly broader, with overly whitened teeth that I'm not one hundred percent sure are real. I remember seeing that he was running for city council, and that he'd married Best-Looking. As if on cue, a stunning woman with bouncy boobs and blond hair comes into view.

"Welcome home," Brock says, but his eyes have already left me to roam the room for someone he deems more interesting. Christine, his wife, half-waves. I only knew Christine from a distance in high school. We didn't have any of the same classes, and I didn't even orbit her stratosphere.

So I am shocked when she says, "Good to see you, Ellie," and she actually looks like she remembers me.

I take another swig of my drink.

"You live in LA now?" Brock asks, only half-interested. Kyle Temple rips him away from our conversation, so I direct my answer to Christine.

"I do," I tell her. "I write for TV."

"Oh my God!" Christine says. "That's so awesome. I love TV."

I suppress a snort mid-sip and pretend to choke.

"What show do you write for?" she asks, completely oblivious to how naïve she sounds.

"Just this dumb kids' show. It's called *Cooler Than You*."

Her eyes light up. "Oh my God, I love that show!" Her squeal is infantile; her smile genuine and ecstatic. I feel like I'm back at Stonybrook High, expected to beam and blush for the pretty popular girl who has decided to show my measly existence an ounce of interest.

The sickening part? There's this sliver of my soul that does absolutely glow when her bright eyes shine on me. Because however gossamer-thin her adulation actually is, I never got any of that in high school.

"Brock!" she calls out for him. He looks over at us from

a conversation he's having with Kyle Temple and a girl whose name I don't remember. "Ellie writes for *Cooler Than You!*"

"Is that the show with all the dicks and the drugs?" he asks, barely interested.

"That's us," I say, thrilled that that's our show's reputation.

Brock turns away, and Christine turns back to me. "Well, it's a great show. You must be an amazing writer."

"Thanks, I'm all right, I guess," I mutter, embarrassed. My cheeks feel warm. A few others I vaguely recognize—but couldn't care less about—approach, and just like that, everyone is chatting and reminiscing, and since I don't have anything to add to the plethora of stories about every time Kyle was "so fucking wasted," I peace out, downing the last dregs of my drink as I scan the room for Brie.

Damn it. She's talking to Mark. Of course she's talking to Mark—I don't want to talk to Mark. Not at all. Not yet. Not ever.

But I can't deny that the dark-green button-down, sleeves rolled up, looks good against his light tan skin and brown eyes. His jeans fit just snug enough that I can tell he's maintained his soccer player's butt, and since I'm staring hard at the lines of his strong, lean thighs, I must be sending intense vibes in their direction because Mark's eyes trail across the room, straight to me.

Our eyes meet, and I look away fast.

Damn it, Ellie. Not this again.

I decide to detour to the bathroom to get my shit together. I'm twenty-eight years old, not seventeen again.

I walk down a short, dim hallway to another red door with the word *Gals* painted on it in chipped gold. I shove through the door and am greeted by the sound of someone vomiting in the nearest stall.

My eyes go wide. She's left the stall door open. I can see the strap of her purse from here, splayed out on the ground and coiling around the heel of her shoe. I slink forward, curiosity getting the better of me. There, wearing a pair of black skin-tight jeans, a loose-fitting sweater with leather cuffs, and about twelve bangle bracelets on her left wrist, is none other than Roxy Draper: former best friend.

"Fuck this," she says to the inside of the toilet bowl.

The edges of my vision blur. My skin feels weird and slick. I want to run away, but I'm trapped between a rock and a hard place—a slighted former crush out there and a wasted ex-bestie in here. I clear my throat and cross my arms instead. It's more armor than judgment.

"Drunk already?" My voice is cold, with an edge of hostility I kind of despise because it makes me sound nefarious and not in a sexy way. I swallow, my jaw tightening.

Roxy doesn't sit up right away. Or turn. Her shoulders slump inward and she presses her palms to the toilet seat, heaving again. It's a horrible sound. After a few seconds she spits—I can hear it splash. And then, inexplicably, I'm leaning forward with a stack of paper towels from the counter behind me. I press them into her hand. She still doesn't look at me, but she does take the towels and wipe her lips, flushing the toilet as she does.

Her sigh is heavy. Still crouched on the ground, she turns sloppily and leans back against the toilet. She lifts her eyes to mine. Smudgy black liner around big green eyes. Three earrings in her left ear. Two in her right. One side of her mouth kicks up into a half-grin. After all these years, I have never forgotten that sly Roxy smile.

"Ellie Bellie," she says, but her voice is hard. Not like ice; more like metal forged from the fires of Mount Doom.

"Do you need some water or something?" I ask.

"Awww, aren't you sweet?" she says, her tone clear. She does not think I'm sweet. "This is just great. Let's see, how long have I gone without a drink?" Her glossy eyes travel skyward, calculating inside her head.

"Thirty seconds?"

"Six months," she corrects with another sly grin. "Back to day one." She reaches into her pocket and pulls out an AA medallion. Dark blue with a triangle and a six in the center.

"Maybe coming here wasn't such a great idea." I can feel myself pitying her, but I can't let her see it. I fold my arms tighter around me, protecting my vulnerable center. I can't expose my underbelly to her, or she might gut me, leave me for dead.

If there is one thing I don't do, it's pity people—any people. Some (Andy) would say I judge others a little too harshly. But I have high standards, that's all.

Roxy never responded well to pity anyway.

"Yeah, well, I needed a drink," she says. She pushes up from the ground, wobbly, like she's got new doe legs. I extend one hand to stabilize her. I pull it away just as fast.

Our eyes meet for a split second.

"Hi," she says, swaying a little.

"Hi," I say back. I search her face.

It's amazing how you can go from the best of friends to strangers so easily. Ten years after graduation and we haven't spoken once before now. We stopped speaking after Brock's party. We stopped listening to each other a long time before that.

She pushes past me to the counter, tossing her sobriety medallion in the trash on the way to the sink. I hear it plunk. She turns on the faucet and washes her hands and the corners of her mouth. I keep looking forward, at the toilet where she was just heaving chunks.

"Back from the City of Angels." Her voice echoes in the tiny bathroom.

I turn to face her, suddenly feeling bold. "How's your mom?"

She flicks her eyes up to the mirror, looking straight into mine.

"Disappointed." She shrugs. "But what else is new."

I wait for something that looks like pain to pass over her face, to flicker in her eyes, but it doesn't happen. She's numb.

Roxy cups a handful of water to her mouth, rinses, and spits before turning off the faucet. She spins around to face me, but she's unsteady, so she uses the counter for leverage.

To say Roxy's mom is difficult to please is the understatement of the century. Nothing Roxy ever did growing up was good enough for Maureen. When Roxy's rebellion peaked in high school, Maureen did everything short of chaining Roxy up in the basement, but Roxy is untamable and cannot be contained. The wildest sort of animal.

But even the wildest animals wish they could make their mothers proud.

Roxy snatches my handbag from around my wrist and unzips it, pulling out my tube of lipstick. My face pinches in surprise. She works fast. Without looking in the mirror, she applies a coat of Chanel Rouge to her lips, caps the lid. Her lips rub together, and she wipes around the corners like a pro.

"You gonna hide out here the rest of the night?" she asks. My mind is stuck on how she flippantly violated the sanctity of my favorite lipstick. I don't respond.

She discards my purse on the counter and is out the door, leaving me behind to clean up her mess.

Like. Always.

CHAPTER 6

I quietly slink out of the bathroom and up to the bar to pay my tab. I manage to flag down the bartender and gesture the signing of a check with a thumbs-up when I see that he's got it.

"Cutting out early?" It's freaking Mark again. I quietly pray to the California god—the Universe—to *please* give me a fucking break.

"Like a bat out of hell" is my response to him.

"That's a double." He points at my tall empty glass.

"What's your point?" I snap at him.

He looks me up and down, a mischievous grin tugging at his lips. "There's no way you're not a lightweight."

"I feel fine," I snap.

I blink, as his lips drift closed, unsure of the next move. I absolutely will not think about the fact that my knee-jerk reaction to Mark may be an indication that the sludgy remains of my crush have risen to the surface. I may be a grown woman with a blossoming writing career, but my go-to with guys I like hasn't changed since elementary school. I get meaner than a stepped-on rattlesnake, and I almost never explain it's because I secretly want to kiss them.

The bartender sets down the check with a pen in front of me.

"Eight bucks?" I say out loud, astounded. "That's like, free." I wish I could order one to go.

Mark laughs, defusing the tension between us, and I let a tiny puff of nervous air out through my nose. It's almost a laugh, and he notices. The bartender is puzzled by my reverse sticker shock. I quickly add a tip and sign the check. I shove my wallet back into my purse and dig for my keys, bumping into dudes that smell like beer and farts while I speed-walk to the door as fast as my studded leather boots will carry me.

I push through the door and into a wall of water.

The rain. Oh, how I miss the rain.

Within seconds I am soaked to the bone. Ohio weather is my absolute favorite. I miss the seasons with the summer storms and winter snow, the fall chill and the spring flowers. Transitions that punctuate the passing of time.

There are so many things I love about LA, but our "seventy-five and sunny" rep is highly overrated. Our seasons are smog, fire, wind and fire, and winter months where locals wear parkas and tourists wear tank tops. The ocean is too cold to swim in, and there's too much irony to being located next to the largest body of water in the world and also in a perpetual water crisis.

I shiver and wrap my arms around myself. It's October, and the rain is freezing. I feel a hand snatch keys out of mine and I look up to see Mark jingling them at me.

I frown. "What are you doing?"

"I don't think you should drive home yet," he says. I roll my eyes.

"I had one drink!" Even as I say it I can feel the slight buzzing behind my eyes. Double the rum on an empty stomach is catching up to me fast. He arches a single eyebrow.

"Fine," I say, shrugging my defeat. "But I'm not going back in there."

He grins and motions for me to follow him to the parking lot. He pulls a key fob out of his pocket and nearby car lights blink. He drives a Honda Accord because of course he does.

"Number one car in America," I snark as I get into the car.

"Gets me from point A to point B," he responds. It's a dad answer, and all I can think is that he needs to get the fuck out of Ohio. Ohio pushes out dorky dads faster than the Kardashians push out babies.

"What qualifies you as DD?" I ask him, suddenly aware that he was just in a bar with high school classmates too.

"Half a beer," he says. He starts the car and pulls out of the parking space. Raindrops hit the windshield in a perfect rhythm that makes my eyes lull. Best sound ever.

"Are you a serial killer?" I ask him suddenly. My brain is starting to heat up. Fucking rum. "Is a jogger going to find my body in the woods behind Keller Park two weeks from now?"

He shoots me a side-eye. "That's vivid."

"As a kid, did you ever melt roadkill flesh in vats of acid in your basement so you could keep the bones?"

"No. Jesus." He runs a hand through his wet hair. "Are *you* a serial killer?"

"Does fictional murder count?" I ask.

"I think maybe it does." He grins.

"Then, yup."

"Lots of people die on *Cooler Than You*?" he asks.

I sink deeper into my seat and cross my arms over my chest with a frustrated sigh.

"Not really," I tell him. "We did almost have a serial killer story-line, but the network scrapped it. Wait, where are we going?"

Just as I ask the question, he turns into the parking lot of a Waffle House.

Oh shit.

My eyes light up like Christmas trees at the sight of black block letters against a glowing yellow backdrop. "Stonybrook has a Waffle House?! Since when?!"

"Since over a year ago," he says. I'm graced with another sideways glance. "When was the last time you were home?"

I bite my lip. Not since last Christmas. And even then I was only home a few days for the holiday before I had to head back to LA to finish up a deadline.

He's barely parked the car before I'm out of it and nearly skipping to the front door.

A few weary-eyed truck drivers sit alone at tables sipping coffee and eating melty sandwiches. I cop a squat at a table right in front of a waitress with deeply etched under-eye circles who looks like she's been working for minimum wage for twenty-four hours straight. She smiles weakly, and I make a mental note to leave her a big tip. I might be a judgmental asshole, but a miserly undertipper I am not.

She sets a menu in front of us, but I don't need it.

"All-Star Special, please. Eggs over medium, bacon, white toast, coffee—extra cream."

"I'll have the same, eggs scrambled." Mark slides into the seat across from me.

The waitress disappears into the back.

I turn back to Mark. "Okay, spill it."

"What?" Genuine confusion flashes across his face.

"Dude, I live in Hollywood. Coffee is never just coffee. Coffee is a meeting."

"But this is Waffle House."

"The point is, you want something. What is it?" I'm on my usual mean streak. Even with the double rum, my heart is pounding inside my chest—and none of it is tempered by the fact that I'm used to having my brain picked by Hollywood hopefuls, and it was not so long ago that Mark had Tinseltown ambitions of his own. For all intents and purposes, I'm his ticket in—little does he know that my own ticket only gets us seats in the nosebleed section.

But let's just face it, I owe him. Eight years ago I sent him a hurtful message during what I can only assume was a very painful dark night of the soul.

Mark doesn't answer me right away. Instead his gaze wanders off to where the waitress is pouring ancient coffee into classic diner mugs. There's a war happening behind his eyes. I sink down in my seat and groan.

"Fuck!" I shout over the sizzle of hashbrowns on the griddle. Everyone in the restaurant turns to stare, including the waitress, who nearly pours coffee down the front of her apron. Oops.

Mark's expectant eyebrows shoot way up.

I sigh audibly. "You have a script."

The look on Mark's face like I'm a fucking mind reader

annoys me to no end. The mental war wages on until finally, we all lose.

"Yeah, okay," he says, leaning forward. "I wrote a screenplay."

"I knew it! I fucking knew it."

"I don't want you to read it or anything. I know you're busy. I was just wondering if you could give me a few tips—maybe name someone, anyone I could send it to for notes?"

"Is it any good?" I ask him. "Do you have it on you?" Aspiring screenwriters always have that shit printed out and ready to go in case serendipity strikes.

Mark doesn't disappoint. "In my car," he says, and I bite back a chuckle, imagining him driving around with his script stuck inside his glove compartment. "And I don't know if it's any good. Probably not."

I roll my eyes. "Well, there's your first problem. You're gonna have to get some swagger if you want to make it in the land of egomania and grandiose delusions."

"Is it really that bad?" he asks me. The hope in his eyes is sweet with just a hint of pathetic.

"It's a mix," I tell him. "Fortunately for us, LA transplants tend to do well because we're willing to do actual sweat labor to back up our unrealistic expectations."

The waitress sets down trashy, carbolicious goodness in front of me, and I'm transported to hog heaven. I immediately get to work wrestling open a tiny individual tub of fake butter.

"You've inspired me," Mark says, catching me mid-syrup pour. I nearly drop the syrup dispenser.

"I did?" I shouldn't sound so incredulous, but I can't help it. My career has felt the exact opposite of inspiring thus far. I want to write about serial killers and mob bosses and AI technology, and instead I'm writing about underage drinking and teenagers getting it on in the back of their dad's Lexus. I want to ask the big questions, like *What does it mean to be human?* instead of *What does it take to be popular in high school?*

"You're doing it, Ellie," Mark tells me. I like the way he says my name. That soft tenor. *Swoon.* It matches him perfectly. I extinguish my swoon with a giant bite of hashbrowns. "You're in LA, writing for a living. I know it doesn't look *exactly* like you want it to, but it's impressive."

He's working overtime with the flattery here, and the way it's making me feel warm fuzzy things inside my stomach can only partially be contributed to the hot plate of food I'm ingesting. But if I'm going to succeed at the *Ellie Is Cool Now* list, then I need his help, too.

I set my fork and knife down. "Okay, fine. You've twisted my arm. I'll read your stupid script."

Mark sits up just a little straighter, and I can tell he's excited. My heart flutters. "Wow, really? That would be amazing."

"Yeah, yeah, but I don't work for free," I tell him, shoving bacon into my face. My conscience tries to remind me again that I owe him for being a dick in a DM, but I don't have time for redemption right now. I have a plane to catch on Monday, and a list that needs checking off before I board.

"Of course not," he says earnestly. "Name your price."

Why, why, *why* is he being so sweet? Come on, man! Be a jerk! Don't do this to me! Don't make me start to like you again. I do not have time for romantic, nostalgic feelings.

But it's already too late. There's that familiar tugging on my heartstrings.

"I don't want your money," I say to him.

His head cocks to one side, and he eyes me suspiciously. "What is it then?" A half-grin highlights the dimple in his cheek.

Why. Is. He. So. Cute?

Damn it.

"I need help with a list."

His grin spreads wide.

My heart explodes.

And just like that, the crush is *back*.

CHAPTER 7

This is why I didn't want to be reunited with my past. Mark's smile. Roxy's dismissal. Everything that shouldn't matter but somehow still does. For a split second I consider shooting up from the table, telling the waitress to pack mine up to go, and Ubering my ass all the way home. To LA. It should only be like, what, two thousand dollars? Who needs a savings account anyway?

"Can I see the terms and conditions before I agree?" he asks. His roguish grin is killing me—it's literally killing me. Someone read me my last rites, because I'm a goner.

"I'll do you one better." I fish around in my purse for my phone and quickly unlock it.

"Let's see." He leans forward.

I take a deep breath. I turn it so he can see the screenshot of the list I took earlier on the plane. I don't want him to see the email from Vic, and I feel oddly self-conscious about handing over my phone. His thumb brushes mine as he slides the phone toward himself, zooming in to read the text.

"*Ellie Is Cool Now*?" His smile is sardonic. I shrink down in my seat, mortified.

He keeps reading.

The waitress comes by with the coffee pot and refills our mugs. I take two more single serve half-and-half cups from the overflowing bowl and doctor my coffee until it's the optimal color of sand. The spoon comes to a standstill, and I lift the cup to my lips, blowing. I notice Mark's eyes flick from the phone to my face, and I get the funny feeling his interest in what I'm doing is not exactly appropriate. The thought makes my skin tingle and my lips automatically press together into a smirk.

"This is ambitious," he says finally, leaning back. He takes a long sip of his coffee. "Hook up with the prom king?" There's a flash of some emotion I can't place in his eyes. Is that...jealousy? No way, I'm imagining it. I need to get a grip.

"I just have to kiss him, and I will one hundred percent settle for on the cheek."

"What's it for?" he asks, still skeptical.

I sigh. "My job. Believe it or not."

"Your job?" He squints at me. He's still not buying it.

"My boss thinks I need *a fresh perspective*," I explain. "Because I hated high school and I write for a high school show."

"Is this even legal? For your boss to make you do this list?"

"You think Hollywood cares about what's legal?" I fire back, tilting my head to one side. "That's cute."

"And so hooking up with the prom king is going to...do *what*, exactly?" Mark grips my phone until his knuckles turn white. Okay, it's not my imagination. He's mad.

I take a hefty drink of my coffee before answering. "I'm not going to hook up with the prom king."

"It's on the list." He points to it on the phone screen.

"I know! I know it's on the list," I growl, frustrated. "The list is symbolic. I think."

"You think?" he asks. One eyebrow raises in question.

I take a deep breath. "My showrunner wants to promote me to co-executive producer."

"So this list is like a test," he says, eyes flying back to the phone.

"It's bait. And I'm the fish. But I want this," I say, and for the first time I feel like my two worlds are actually colliding.

I lift my Waffle House coffee—weirdly delicious, but maybe that's all the cream and sugar—in the air and raise my brows.

"*Cooler Than You* was supposed to be a pit stop for me. But it's been five years, and I'm done paying my dues." I point to the phone. The list. "That list is my ticket out of there."

His eyes are back on the phone, his brows cinched together. He clicks it off but doesn't give it back.

I put a hand on top of his, and the warmth of his fingers spreads across my palm, sending tingles all the way up my arm and all the way down to my toes. I half expect him to pull away, but he doesn't. "I know I said some pretty awful things to you. To be honest, I'm going to read your script no matter what, because I'm really sorry about what I said. If it's any consolation, working in film isn't all it's cracked up to be?" Mark's eyes widen. "I know that makes me sound really ungrateful, but it turns out pursuing your passion can be just as complicated as not pursuing it at all."

I pull my hand away, and his fingers flex subtly at the loss of my heat. When he looks up at me again, there's a spark of gold in his chocolate brown eyes. Determination. Excitement. Ambition.

"Okay," he says as the waitress delivers our check facedown on the table. "I'm in."

For a second there's absolute silence. Carb-induced silence.

"Your list…" He hesitates. "It says, *Get high school crush to help*—"

"Pssh, don't flatter yourself." I laugh him off.

But we both know why number ten is on the list.

He scoops up the check as I reach for it, fishing his wallet out of his back pocket.

"Now that I'm helping, does that automatically knock number ten off the list?"

He's trying to be sneaky. Can he assist in a single task and thereby do his duty? I feel like he wants to know how interested I am in his help. How interested I am in *him*.

"It says, *at least one*," I point out.

He throws his credit card down with the check and raises his cup. "To Ellie, for she is apparently cool now."

"Oh my God, stop." I blush and sheepishly raise my nearly empty mug.

We *cheers* ceramic coffee cups in the middle of an Ohio Waffle House. Classy AF.

The waitress comes by and picks up his card. I throw a generous cash tip down on the table, fulfilling my secret commitment to myself to make this overworked woman's day. Mark double-takes the amount I've set down. His eyes meet mine and linger, and there's something behind them. Something heated.

"You're not *that* mean," he says, grinning at me like he knows something I don't.

I shrug and squirm, unable to hold his gaze.

"How many days—" His phone on the table buzzes and lights up with a text message. He quickly turns it off and pockets it. "How many days do we have to complete the list again?" He finishes, taking another bite of what's left of his food.

"Three," I say. I nod my head to where his phone was. "Do you need to check that?"

"It's just my mom," he says. "Only three?" He sounds almost disappointed.

"I fly back Monday night." I very deliberately raise a single brow. "Also, you live with your mom?"

"No!" he says, almost in a panic. "She just…She checks in. I'm the only kid left in Stonybrook." He clears his throat. "Monday, huh? We better get a move on, then."

"So it's a deal?"

"I'll help you with the list," he says, extending his hand in an overly dramatic but totally adorably cinematic way.

"And I'll read your script when we're done." Our hands fit together in a shake that lingers a little too long, but neither one of us seems to mind.

We slide out of the booth and laugh as we walk and talk out the door toward his car, and it all feels so easy despite my lifetime of trying to combat how I feel about him. It's as if Mark and I should have always been having impromptu breakfast for dinner at the Stonybrook Waffle House. Like we should have always been flirty friends, or more.

Maybe he is exactly who I hoped he'd be, and maybe I wasted years thinking he wasn't, playing mean girl when really

I was just scared out of my mind to let him see how much I actually liked him. Scared of being rejected or having my heart broken. Or worse.

Scared that if I got what I wanted, I wouldn't want it anymore.

There's no question that I'm sober now. Even though before I didn't think I needed a DD and a massive meal to keep from disaster, now I'm certain I can get myself home.

As we approach his car, one of those uncomfortably charged romantic comedy silences hangs between us. You know the ones I mean, the girl tossing her hair back, over her shoulder, tucking it behind her ear as she walks. The boy fidgeting with his keys, hands in pockets, eyes surreptitiously surveying the parking lot while really trying to look at the girl.

It's stopped raining and the leaves that cover the pavement are slick with rainwater and mud. I nearly slide off the curb, and Mark reaches out to help me. His fingers clutch my wrist, his palm splays out against my lower back. I lean in, shoulder tucking under, and I can't help it, I smell him. Aftershave, light and woodsy, not too much, the smell of soap and sweet syrup, like the Waffle House permeated through his skin.

He even opens my car door. How chivalrous.

We drive to the soundtrack of our youth. The local radio station plays early two thousands jams for returning grads who might be feeling nostalgic. And I *am*. Buckled into Mark's Honda Accord, purse at my feet, wind blowing my hair through the cracked window.

Back then, if I were better with people, better with men, would I have ended up in Mark's car—maybe a hand-me-down then—sweater set unbuttoned, listening to No Doubt on the radio, wondering the whole time if he would reach over and touch my hand, if would he kiss me on my parents' front porch?

It feels like something I missed out on. Something that has a second chance to play out now, for the first time. Even if it's just for a little while. A few days, a weekend. Maybe just this evening.

"What?" he asks, and he clicks his blinker to turn left, back to the Local.

I didn't realize I was smiling. I make up a reason.

"Fall is the best in Ohio." It's not what I'm really thinking, but close enough.

We park, and I fumble with the handle but only because he's already out, on the other side of the car. Geez, chivalry really isn't dead.

I tug. He tugs. We stop. I tug. The door opens to him having one of those full body laughs. I feel it from my head to my toes, even as my own nervous giggle is filled with uncertainty.

I let the car door slam behind me and rest against it with a view of the bar. This late, only the diehards remain. Two cars. Mine and an unknown, sort of rusty ancient Mazda. The sticker on the fender says Go Bucks!

I clutch his script to my chest. He had it in a messenger bag in his back seat. Just a little more professional than his glove compartment.

It's time to say our friendly goodbyes. In LA we do the cute little French *la bise*, a kiss on the cheek, usually to the side of the cheek, lips meeting air, cheek touching cheek. Very posh. In Ohio, it's all about the hug. An awkward side hug if you're parting ways with someone you're lukewarm about, full body hug if you're very fond of the other person.

This is the test.

We stand facing each other awkwardly. I'm sure as hell not going to make the first move.

"Okay, I guess I'll—see you?" I say, still hugging his script. I'm pretty sure I'm looking up at him with big doe eyes, which makes me want to die.

He laughs at my obvious discomfort, but I can tell he doesn't know what to do either. He holds out a hand.

You've got to be kidding me. A handshake? What is this, Bank of America? Have I just opened a new account?

I sigh and extend my hand, sliding it into his.

He grips my hand and holds it there, our warmth mingling. Ohhhhh, this is a *handshake.*

Every place my skin connects to his, energy shoots up through my arm. We don't let go. He's looking at me like I'm someone special, like he wants to push the lock of hair from in front of my eyes and tuck it behind my ear, letting his fingertips trail down my neck.

He closes his lips. His eyes are on my mouth, so I let my teeth slide over the edge of my bottom lip, and he clenches my hand. He leans forward . . .

And then the door to the Local slams open and bangs against the outer wall.

"I'm fine—" Kyle yells at the bar employee. "I cun druv."

Mark leans back, eyes traveling to this unwelcome interruption.

Fucking. Kyle. Temple.

"Can we call you a taxi?" A frantic bartender chases a drunk and stumbling Kyle out of the restaurant.

Our hands slide apart.

"I got him," Mark says, waving and walking away.

Was he going to kiss me? Was Mark Wright just about to kiss me?!

The employee looks surprised. Mark crosses back to the passenger side and opens the door. Kyle sways and stares at him with hooded, bloodshot eyes.

"Get in," Mark says, waving Kyle into the car.

I watch it all helplessly, wondering if what I thought just happened really just happened. "He's definitely going to throw up in your car."

As if on cue, Kyle pitches forward in his seat and our ears are accosted by muffled retching noises. I feel my own stomach do flip-flops and I'm not sure if the culprit is love or the sound of vomiting.

Kyle sits up again, a new man with vomit-encrusted lips. I imagine kissing those lips, and I nearly throw up my All-Star Special right in the parking lot.

Mark pinches the bridge of his nose. "I regret everything."

"Always a hero," I say. My own voice sounds foreign to my ears, so swoony and annoying.

"See ya tomorrow," Mark says, sliding into the driver's side. "Dude, you are paying to get my car detailed—"

The door shuts, cutting off the rest of a sentence meant for his drunk passenger.

I watch him drive away, my mind following him home.

When I finally come to, I realize I'm touching my lips.

I shake off the feeling and drive my fool ass home.

CHAPTER 8

When I get home, it's nearly midnight and Mom is asleep on the couch with the TV on. It reminds me of when I spent long nights out with friends and she used to wait up for me. Our wild shenanigans always ended at a local twenty-four-hour Starbucks where we'd goof off and do some late-night people watching. It was all fun and games until a few of my friends paired off with the baristas. Then it was just me at home alone with my cat, Rosie, may she rest in peace.

I turn the TV off and cover my mom with a blanket before switching off the light. She snores lightly, and I head up the stairs to my childhood bedroom.

Nobody tells you how lonely having a chronic crush can be sometimes. You're half in love with this person who doesn't know you exist, and all other guys seem to pale in comparison. You're stuck with a person your brain has invented, a fantasy where you have the perfect relationship with the perfect guy who you can never actually talk to, lest he pop the bubble of his own perfection.

The worst part is, you never asked for any of it.

Your brain did this shit on its own.

I'm sure there's a clinical diagnosis for whatever the fuck my brain does when it likes someone, but I don't want to know what it is.

I've been sad and boyfriendless my whole life. Why stop now?

The beauty of being three time zones ahead of LA is that my night out is over before my friends' night has even begun. I brush my teeth and hop into an old pair of pink cupcake pajamas, grabbing my phone from the bathroom counter before shutting off the light.

As I reenter my room, my eyes catch on my dresser. The pink oval wood-trimmed mirror sitting on top is an antique from the local flea market. Beanie Babies peer down at me with their beady black eyes and plastic-protected heart-shaped tags, a long-abandoned, long-ago-prized collection from my preteen days. On the corner stands my rose gold necklace tree stand. Dangling from the branches are tarnished lockets and fake pearls, gold-plated chains adorned with various shapes and colors of butterfly and unicorn charms.

Right at the top, antagonizing me with its tarnished metal and chipped pink paint, is one-half of a heart with letters etched into the center:

BE
FRI

I'm drawn to it, like it's a magnet dragging me across the floor. My fingers clutch the tiny pink and gold half of a heart.

The other half—if I had it, which I don't—completes the other:

ST
   ENDS

Each half is a broken heart, and when held up to the other, spells out BEST FRIENDS.

Or as Roxy and I called it, BEFRI STENDS.

I think about how fitting it is that it's a heart broken in two.

I can't help but wonder if Roxy still has the other half, but I doubt it. We haven't worn them since middle school, and Roxy's not one to hang on to items for their sentimental value.

I snatch the gold chain from the stand, yank open my former underwear drawer, and peer inside. In this drawer are some extra socks, underwear, and a set of pajamas. Items my perpetually overprepared mother keeps around in case the airport loses my suitcase on a flight home.

I look at the necklace, and it's like looking directly into the sun. I know I should just trash it, but I can't bring myself to do so. Not yet.

I drop it into the drawer, and it plunks against the wood before I slam the drawer shut.

There. Out of sight, out of mind.

I exhale a sharp breath and ignore the melancholy on my

face when my eyes find themselves in the dresser mirror. I turn away from my reflection and head toward the bed as I hit Vic's name on FaceTime. I lie back and get comfy on a stack of pink and white pillows.

Tina answers Vic's phone in two seconds flat. She's clearly riding in the back seat of an Uber.

"Vic's your favorite," she says, pretending to be hurt. "I knew it."

"You never answer your phone. Plus, you're always with Vic." I don't think they notice the wobble in my voice, and I'm glad.

"Whatever." I watch Tina scrutinize her face in the phone. She digs in her bag and pulls out her lip gloss, then proceeds to use the phone as a mirror while she reapplies.

"Give us the dirt!" I hear Vic's voice, but I can't see him.

"Where are you guys going?" They go out all the time without me, and I'm a few thousand miles away, so I don't know why I prickle at them being together without me there. I guess sometimes, even with my friends, I still feel like I'm not sitting at the cool table. Or like I'm only there because they want to use me to ace the final exam and boost their GPA.

"The Bungalow," Tina says. "Vic's idea. He's single and ready to mingle."

"You're going all the way to Santa Monica?"

"You're changing the subject!" Vic grabs the phone from Tina. He raises an eyebrow at the camera for dramatic effect. "Give us *le scoop*."

"Those two weeks of Duolingo French lessons have really paid off."

"*Ellie.*"

I let my smile curl like the coy ingenue that I am (today, at least). "I spent pretty much the whole evening with Mark."

"Shut the front door." Vic squeals. Tina grabs the phone and checks her lip gloss job one more time.

"Wait, who's Mark?" she asks, smacking her lips together. Vic elbows her.

"Mark, dummy. Unrequited lover boy!" Vic informs her.

"Ohhh." Tina shrugs. "I can't be expected to keep all these people straight."

"It's a love story fifteen years in the making, Teen. Keep up!" Vic scolds her. Vic is a great lover of romantic drama. He rolls his eyes and snatches the phone back from her. "Did you kiss him?"

"Um, we shook hands," I say.

"Ewww." Vic and Tina both recoil.

"But like, a lingering handshake," I add.

"Ooooh," they say together, sounding more optimistic, but not one hundred percent sold.

"And then he leaned in," I continue, "but I'm not sure if it was for a kiss, or—"

"Why else would a man lean in?" Vic asks, looking at me as though I'm the densest motherfucker to ever walk Planet Earth.

"I don't know," I admit.

"Is he taking you to the reunion?" he asks.

"I don't know," I say, clueless. "This isn't prom. Do people go on dates to reunions?"

"They hire escorts," Tina says nonchalantly in the background.

I snort and Vic levels Tina with a side-eye of disapproval.

"What? They do." I can almost hear her shrug.

"What is wrong with you?" he asks, shaking his head at her.

"He hasn't asked me," I interrupt them. "So I'm gonna go with no?"

Vic's eyes roll into the back of his head. "Girl, this is *not* the nineteen fifties. You can ask him."

"I'm sorry, do you know who you're talking to?" I ask him, incredulous. "I had a crush on this guy for six years and said nothing. Less than nothing. Now you want me to ask him out on a date?"

"Give me that." Tina grabs the phone from Vic. "Ellie, listen to me. You need to *finish that list*. Like, if romance is a by-product, great, but there's too much at stake here. Eyes on that prize, sister."

I nod. She's right. I'm not going to let my big promotion get derailed by some guy I haven't seen in a decade. That wouldn't be all that feminist of me, now would it?

She squints at the phone. "Are those cupcake pajamas?"

I panic and pull the covers up to my neck. "Thanks for your help, friends!"

I finger-punch my phone to end the call before they can razz on my favorite Ohio jammies. My head hits the pillow, and I find myself staring wide-eyed at the ceiling, wired as hell.

I reach for my phone again and scroll through my newsfeed. Reunion-y photos are starting to pop up, and not just pictures from the bar. Various dinners and coffees and drinks are being had tonight all over Stonybrook.

I'm still not Facebook friends with Mark, but I go creep on

his profile anyway. It's the same old New York skyline profile picture as always. I click on it and read the comments.

Dude, get yo' ass back to NYC.

Markyyyy Mark, when's the big day? I didn't get my save the date.

The top half of my body flies upright. Save the date? Why is someone asking him about a save the date?

My fingers are quick on the draw.

Do people use "save the dates" for graduations?

I send the message to Vic.
His response is immediate.

I don't think so. Those are only for weddings.

I say:

Someone asked Mark about a save the date on his FB profile picture.

Vic responds:

Oh, hmm. He didn't mention a sigoth, did he?

Nope.

Didn't he try to kiss you?

Maybe. There was some definite lean-in action.

Ok, then there's nothing to worry about. Quit over-thinking it.

Twitter flashes a DM notification. My heart nearly drops into my butt. It's Mark.

Hey forgot to give you my number.

And his number popped onto the screen.
Oh my God. Don't freak out. Do. Not. Freak. Out.

I'm freaking out! Mark just messaged me his number.

Vic doesn't text me back right away this time, so I keep messaging him with my internal maelstrom.

What should I do? Should I text him?
Or is that too desperate?
I should play it cool. Just be cool, Ellie.
I am so. Not. Cool.
Help!!!!!!!!!
I'm just gonna ignore it forever.

I set my phone down and focus on my breathing the way I learned in that one yoga class I attended three years ago on Melrose. A white yoga teacher with BO banged a little gong and chanted some yoga phrases that everyone knew except me, so I was done forever (also because, cultural appropriation—gross).

They did teach us a breathing technique where you alternate breathing through your nostrils by plugging the other nostril. I find that if I do it long enough I start to get lightheaded, which is basically the same thing as calming down, in my book.

I can't believe Mark may or may not have almost kissed me. I kick my feet under the covers and squeal like a schoolgirl. I feel like a kid again, but I'm not. I'm a full grown-ass adult with a dream and a job, and Mark is a full decade older than when I last saw him. We're so different, but yet also somehow the same in all the ways that matter.

It makes me wonder. Does growing up turn you into a different person, or do you just become more *you*?

When I think about it now, all the best parts of me were there in high school. My ambition, my confidence, my courage. I just wasn't fully cooked yet. I went to school every day feeling naked in front of my peers, in front of my crush—half-baked and underdeveloped. But I was there. The essence of *me* was there. I just needed more time. Maybe I still do.

My phone buzzes. I release my nostrils, ignoring all the little stars that streak across my vision so I can read Vic's text.

U r romantically illiterate.

It's Vic's signature drunk textese. If *you* becomes *u*, Vic is dead to the sober world—and is totally useless to me now.

I sigh, lie back, and do the one thing I am so profoundly good at.

Ignore Mark forever.

Sleep comes more easily when you've made the decision to die alone.

CHAPTER 9

I have a ritual for days like this, days with something dreaded looming on the evening horizon like a dangerous weather warning. It begins with a full-fat, extra sweet, triple-shot latte with whipped cream and chocolate shavings on top, served up beside a vanilla cake donut.

The first layer of fortification is dessert for breakfast.

I crunch the cup in my hand and shove it in the donut bag wrapper, dropping it in the trash can beside the kitchen cabinet. I can feel my mom actively trying not to watch me from the table as she does her crossword puzzle—in the newspaper, with a pencil. Some things never change, and suddenly I feel so relieved by that thought that I could burst.

My feet move fast without warning, and my arms close around her shoulders. I feel her cheek lift against mine, just as her hand closes and opens light around my arm.

"You'll be fine," she says, her other hand tapping the pencil on the paper. I lean back.

"Have you been to any of your high school reunions?" I ask, pulling out the dining chair. Her sharp blue eyes meet mine.

"A few," she says.

"Was it . . . fun? Or at least, not totally awful?" I ask. "I mean, you went back for more."

She lays her pencil down, considers. "People don't change as much as you think they will outside the high school bubble. They still huddle up in the same cliques. But the thing that has changed is your perspective. You've changed. Even if they haven't."

My nose wrinkles. "Sounds awful."

She looks up at me, meets my eyes. They've hardened momentarily, cutting into me with a sharpness that says *suck it up*. The same person who used to comfort me when I fell down and skinned my knee is also the voice of my inner critic. "It's just one night, Ellie. You'll survive."

Maybe.

She sighs and softens, sensing my anxiety. I'm a bundle of nerves. She reaches out to take my hand. "You're okay," she says softly.

They're simple words, but they provide relief. My mom is complicated, like all mothers are, but she's the only person who knows how to make me feel better.

I sit there a little longer, just because I can.

The second layer of fortification is an obvious one.

"Turn the camera around so I can see the options in the mirror," Tina says through the phone. She's at her apartment in

LA. It's drenched in sunlight and decorated in shades of white and pink. Her hair is a fluffy brown bun on top of her head, and she's gorgeous without a stitch of makeup. She lifts her own (black) coffee to her lips and takes a sip.

I flip the camera phone to show her my three options. Clothes are everything at a reunion. You may still live in your mom's basement, but a designer dress has the power to create a diversion. My job on *Cooler Than You* hasn't made me rich (not even close), but it does give me a budget for cute clothes and a few designer bags. Sure, sometimes I eat ramen out of a Styrofoam bowl between seasons, but that's a price I'm willing to pay for Jimmy Choos.

She's silent as she scrutinizes my choices. High School Ellie would not have selected any of the ensembles that hang before me. She didn't show cleavage (because she didn't have any), and she didn't wear stilettos (because she couldn't walk in them). About the only thing hanging here that would have been on High School Ellie's radar is the tiny pink sparkly purse, and only because I've always had a thing for pink.

"Turn me around," Tina says. When we're face-to-face through the camera, her dark brown eyes lock on mine. "The pink dress with the sweetheart neckline. Put your hair up so you can show off your amazing décolletage—" I gag, interrupting her nineties rom-com style makeover pep talk.

"Stop doing that. You're gorgeous. Get over it." Tina rolls her eyes as I pretend to stick my index finger down my throat and make more fake barf noises.

She ignores me and talks over my disruptive show of self-loathing. "Now, let's talk *accessories*."

The third layer of fortification against impending doom is a game.

I made up this game freshman year of college, during my first experience with finals. For every cram session, I received a gold star. Ten gold stars meant one half-hour doing something luxurious—which at that time usually meant lunch off-campus or a new bottle of nail polish, but as I've gotten older, I've adapted the system to my changing circumstances.

A gold star per screenplay page. Ten gold stars gets me: A fancy dessert. A massage. A pedicure with all the fixings.

Currently, my stars are logged in a journal featuring a rainbow-maned unicorn and the phrase *Stay magical* in script across the front. I always have it on me in case I need a bribe. It may be childish, but it works for me.

For every step in the getting-ready process, I give myself a gold star.

Shave my legs—gold star.

Moisturize—gold star.

Flat iron my hair—gold star.

Apply that first coat of mascara—you guessed it! Gold star.

By the end of the process, I've earned a fancy steakhouse dinner out with friends when I get back to LA. And with all the cash I'll be raking in with my new promotion, I'm getting the most expensive steak on the menu (and picking up the tab for Vic and Tina).

I adjust my thong one more time and dab Miss Dior perfume behind my ears and on the inside of my wrists, taking a step back from the mirror to take myself in.

I look pretty good.

There's a knock on my bedroom door to the tune of "Shave and a Haircut." My dad's signature.

"Come in," I say.

My dad swings the door open, already talking, not really looking at me because he's fiddling with a loose screw on the doorknob. "Mom said you might want a ride to the reunion—" This is the moment he finally looks at me. His face says it all.

My dad hasn't seen me dolled up like this since high school prom.

"Wow," he says, his jaw hanging open. "You look beautiful, sweetie."

He doesn't dish out compliments often or lightly, so I know I've succeeded in making myself look at least presentable for the big R.

"Do I look cool now?" I ask him, waggling my eyebrows.

"What's cooler than cool?" he asks me, raising an index finger. He's being goofy.

"Ice cold," I say, rolling my eyes, finishing his dad joke for him.

I grab my purse and follow him out to the hearse, I mean, car.

Dad pulls the Kia to a stop in front of my old high school.

"It looks exactly the same," I whisper. A huge banner reads WELCOME BACK, CLASS OF 2010 in looming red and gold letters.

"They renovated the gym and reseeded the football field," Dad says. I don't reply. "Ellie?" I turn to look at him. I expect him to look worried, but he doesn't. He's got this determined set to his jaw and his eyes narrow, scrutinizing me for a brief moment before he says, "Knock 'em dead, baby girl."

He hasn't called me that since high school.

I swallow a nostalgic lump that forms in my throat. This all feels so weird.

I'm out of the car, and for the first time in this whole horrible process I feel ready to slay...maybe not my emotional dragons, but definitely the list that stands between staff writer and co-EP. My stilettos click across the sidewalk, marching to the beat of my triumph. I swing the door wide, step into horrible fluorescent lighting, and am greeted by none other than Brie "Best All-Around" Baldwin. Number three on my list.

Her reunion smile is megawatt and an inch too wide. She looks ready to scream, but she contains it behind a pitchy "Hi again, Ellie!"

"Hey." I wave.

"Wow, that dress is the perfect shade of pink for your skin!" she says. Her eyes are so big I'm afraid they're going to pop out of her head. I secretly wonder if she sleeps at night. I'm guessing four hours, tops.

"Thanks!" I say, trying to match her enthusiasm by even a third. I'm failing.

"We've put everyone's senior yearbook photo on their name badges, so it's easy to recognize each other." She motions to the table full of black-and-white photo badges.

"Wow, ten years! How did you recognize me?" I snark, picking up my photo badge. Her smile dims, and I can tell she's not sure what to make of me. Join the club, sister.

What I know about Brie I've learned from the digital public scrapbook that is Facebook. Brie didn't leave to go to college. She got married right out of high school to the captain of the debate team. She had a small army of children. She lives and breathes Stonybrook. Planning this reunion has probably been a major highlight of her recent life.

"God, that haircut. Who the hell let me cut my own bangs?" I hear a familiar voice save me from my foot going directly in my mouth.

I wish I could be happy about it.

Black metallic nails slide through the badges and lift one from the many. Roxy's plum-colored lips kick up into a smirk. Her eyes meet mine. Sharp, sad, saying so much more than her lips ever could.

She leans against me so she can see my badge.

"At least you gave up those Banana Republic sweater sets. Jesus, I thought you'd grow up to be a librarian, the way you dressed in high school," Roxy says.

I can't think of anything clever to say before she presses her badge against mine. Our black-and-white seventeen-year-old faces meet. She smacks her lips in a kissing sound. "Let's get this party started."

She turns, gone in a blur of red and black.

Brie and I stand in awkward silence for a beat before she finally takes pity on me. "Those sweater sets are making a comeback."

They aren't, but Brie is kind for pretending. I smile weakly at Best All-Around and start to head for the gym before remembering the list.

The list!

"Can I buy you a drink later?" I ask.

"S-sure!" she answers, surprised.

Check. Well, almost.

I drape the lanyard of my photo badge around my neck like a noose I can use later if things get ugly. Each click of my heels toward the high school gym is an alarm bell ringing inside my head.

Back to hell we go.

CHAPTER 10

I'm surrounded by red and gold balloons and streamers that say WELCOME BACK, CLASS OF 2010. I'm holding a plastic champagne glass filled with sparkling grape juice (because no drinking on school property) and stuck in a conversation with Abigail Wedgwood (now Abigail Smart), a woman I barely remember from ninth grade health class. My eyes scan the sparse crowd for Mark. I'm not happy about it, but they do it anyway. I don't see him anywhere, and I desperately want him to show up so this party can finally get interesting.

Sometime during my visual search, Abigail pulled out her phone. She's scrolling through Facebook photos one after the other, and my eyes struggle to stay focused. She's diving deep on the Disney vacation pictures of her, her husband, and their two kids (and one on the way!) in matching BE SMART, GO TO DISNEYLAND T-shirts with Mickey Mouse for the boys and Minnie for the girls. It's a play on words with her married name, and it takes everything in me not to toss my cookies (well, vanilla donut) right there on the gym floor.

"Traveling on a plane with a baby is *not* easy, let me tell you what," she says. "I brought a small bag of candy for the rows around us. I read about it on a mommy blog. I thought it was so *smart*."

She giggles at the use of her married name in a sentence. I imagine matching jerseys at her kids' sports games that say PLAY SMARTER, NOT HARDER! or the whole family pretending to read books on a holiday card: A SMART CHRISTMAS. I smile at my own interior monologue, and she thinks I'm smiling at her.

"Next time you should bring them tiny bottles of alcohol," I suggest. It's a semi-innocent suggestion, I swear, but she does not take it well. Her answering frown says it all.

"Do you have a boyfriend?" she asks, quickly gaining the upper hand in whatever war I've just accidentally waged against her. I watch her adjust the sparkly diamond band on her ring finger along with her honking Zales diamond.

I take a deep breath. "Not at the moment, no."

My eyes flick away—*someone save me*. They land on Roxy. Standing ten former classmates away, rolling her eyes at Sharon Digby, former all-state track champion who has maintained her runner's physique. My attention lingers a moment too long, because Roxy turns, makes eye contact, and smirks.

"You're so pretty," I hear Abigail say, as I snap my eyes away from Roxy. "I'm surprised no one's snatched you up yet. Don't worry, you have plenty of time." Her voice is syrupy sweet.

I almost snort fake champagne through my nose. I'd forgotten that Midwest time passes in dog years. I'm basically middle-aged. The clock is ticking, and one thing that *does not* improve with age is a female's reproductive organs.

She adds insult to injury: "You should get one of those apps. Kindling? Bumblebee? Or whatever they're called..." She rotates her ring again.

It's a not-so-subtle hint that she's happily married and has been since before those dating apps were a thing. My lips pinch closed. It will be a cold day in hell when I download a dating app. Vic is obsessed with all of them, and Tina has dabbled. As far as I can tell, they only result in the occasional hookup or disastrous date with men obsessed with feet or psychedelics.

"Oh, what a great idea." I lay it on thick. I down the rest of my nonalcoholic bubbly and pretend it's real. The DJ kicks up the music like it's time to dance. Is it time to dance?

I look out at a group of people who are shadows of their former teenage selves. Still here, still hanging out with the same people, still going to the same places and doing the same things. Still in a high school mentality, just with jobs, a mortgage if they're lucky (rent if they're not), kids who will eventually go to this high school, and the first signs of aging.

"Time to turn back the clock, y'all!" The DJ puts on "I Kissed a Girl" by Katy Perry and my soul leaves my body. A few high-pitched shrieks come from happy customers who have taken one too many trips to the virgin punch bowl and think they're virgins again. The women all gather at the center of the dance floor to grind on each other while the men watch.

Oh boy.

"I love this song!" Abigail says beside me. "Remember this song? Ben! Benny!"

She tears her hubby away from his fellow former band geeks

and drags him to the dance floor. I forgive the DJ's song choice now that it's saved me from that hellscape.

I close my eyes for a second. It's been a minute since I've been to a party with a DJ and swirling light effects, and I'm already fighting vertigo. Turns out this reunion is not as bad as I thought it would be: it's worse.

When I reopen my eyes, I see Mark in the doorway directly across from me, wearing a simple gray sweater and dark jeans. He looks good and probably smells even better. Like baked goods and sandalwood cologne.

Finally.

Adrenaline hits my bloodstream like a hammer, making my skin blaze and my heart pound. I'm ridiculously excited to see him. What the hell is wrong with me? His eyes search the room and lock with mine. It takes every muscle in my body to fight it, but I don't look away. I hold his gaze.

My smile is slow and deliberate.

His answering smile is quick and trepidatious.

He slides his eyes from me to the woman standing beside him. She's tiny, fair, and freckled, like a woodland sprite. Her strawberry blond hair is pulled up into a high ponytail. She smiles, surveying the room with an edge of self-consciousness that's almost endearing. Her eyes crinkle and spark when she directs them to Mark. She looks like she wants to reach for his hand but doesn't. But she wants to. It's all over her soft-featured face.

Fuck.

Fuck, fuck, fuck.

"Hi, Ellie." A voice jolts me out of this new plot twist in the story of my sad, pathetic life. A woman in a wheelchair wearing a colorful headscarf greets me with a sweet smile. Her skin is sallow, her cheeks sunken. The hollows of her eyes are covered in shadow, but they gleam bright blue and wide.

Her name on my tongue takes my breath away.

"Emma?"

She nods and reaches up for a hug. She's so frail and thin that hugging her hurts my heart. Daggers slice through it, sending pain into every limb. Tears prick in my eyes, and I blink. When I pull back, I'm composed, but obviously not a very good actor.

She fiddles with the scarf where her Best Hair should be. Her little sister stands behind her, hands on the push handles of Emma's chair. She smiles at me. Her hair is long and looks spun from silk, just like Emma's used to be.

"We just wanted to tell you that we love your show. We watch it every Thursday night." Emma grins ear-to-ear. I have to swallow before I speak because my stomach goes tight, woozy. What is this feeling? Not pity. It's so much more complicated than that.

"Thank you!" I say it with too much enthusiasm. I am so busted.

Her—still lovely—lips twist into a smile. She reaches for her scarf again, but in my mind, she's reaching for that hair. "I know I must look pretty shocking."

"No, no. You look great." Damn it, Ellie. Why do you have to be such a rodeo clown all the time?

"Thanks, but...I look like hell." She laughs weakly and I have the sudden urge to cry. She's doing me a favor. Trying to play off my stupid, blinking awkwardness as no big deal. She's sweet as pie and whatever has happened to her is so fucking unfair, but she's trying to make *me* feel comfortable. My problems are tadpoles in comparison.

I choke back feelings. She doesn't look the same, but there's something so stunning about her still. Something that she'll always have, no matter what.

"You're beautiful," I say. And this time I mean it.

"I did finally find the perfect contour for my nonexistent cheekbones." She motions to her concave cheeks, and her sister and I exchange confused glances. "It's called leukemia. What do you think?" She turns her face from side to side so we can admire her cheekbones.

I'm too startled to laugh at first, but then her sister bursts into a fit of giggles and I relax into the moment. Emma chuckles.

"You should do stand-up," I say finally. "Cancer comedy is pretty popular these days."

"Well, who doesn't want to be popular?" She grins in a knowing way.

She was one of the most popular girls in high school. Easily one of the prettiest.

She still is.

We talk more and laugh because now the conversation is flowing. Laughter is release, and with it, the moment we're in expands beyond Emma's fight for her life or my encounter with Mark and his forest fairy. Beyond Best Hair or the high school hierarchy or that stupid list that might lead to a meaningless promotion.

As we talk, I'm reminded how kind she always was and is. I wish high school wasn't so focused on appearances. Who cares who has the best hair? Why wasn't there a senior superlative for

Biggest Heart instead? Surely, that category would have gone to Emma Lovett and her kind eyes and warm, sunny smile.

Our conversation is interrupted by a tap on my shoulder. Reality tapping back into the ring.

I don't need to look to know who it is.

My eyes find Emma's. She can tell something's up because she lifts her eyebrow and then paints on a wide, toothy grin. I slap on my crinkliest smile and turn on my heel coming eye-to-eye with worried chocolate brown eyes and a tiny, smiley, strawberry-haired woodland sprite.

CHAPTER 11

The woodland sprite has a name. It takes a second for that name to register and for the tiny black dots in my peripheral vision to clear. My eyes have to refocus. They go wide and then zoom in, right back on Mark's lips as they twist around her name. I feign interest, but it's as futile as pretending I care about Soul Cycle or hiking Runyon Canyon when trying to make small talk at parties in LA.

"It's Liz, actually," she says, her voice high, clear, like the chime of a church bell. "I don't know why he always introduces me as Elizabeth. Only my mom calls me that."

"You look familiar," Emma says, tilting her head to one side.

"I went to school here," Liz explains. "Class of 2013."

She smiles. Her teeth are perfectly straight, gleaming white, and her smile is angelic and symmetrical. It's not the smile of a girl you hate: twisty and judgy—okay, like my smile on occasion, if I'm being totally honest. This smile is sweet, and I know without knowing her that she has the saintly personality to back it up.

"I'm Ellie," I say. Did Mark already introduce us? I hope not, but in my momentary fugue state, I wouldn't know. I think I smile. I can't be sure at this point. "Class of 2013..." I rack my brain.

"I was a freshman when you all were seniors," Woodland Sprite Liz answers my question for me. I try to remember her, but it's unlikely we ever met. Senior schedules don't overlap much with freshmen, academically or socially.

"What are you doing here then?" The words tumble out of my mouth without permission from my brain. My tone is more biting than it should be.

Her brows snatch together. Fuck, is she his girlfriend?

Emma raises her voice behind me, rescuing the awkward trajectory of this convo. "I saw your dad at the hospital the other day, Mark. He looks great."

I sidestep so Emma has the floor. My face heats up, and I pray they can't see how red I am. Damn this sober gymnasium. I need a drink. A real drink, not this Welch's sparkling grape juice crap.

Mark's face twists into a grimace, almost like he's in pain. "Yeah, he's doing okay."

Mark's dad is a doctor, and I can tell there's a story behind his tormented look and noncommittal reply, but I'm desperately focused on getting a read on his relationship status with Liz. Girlfriend? More? If she were more provocative, I'd even be willing to entertain the idea of her being one of those escorts Tina seems to think people bring to reunions. But she's the kind of squeaky clean they cast in commercials for Campbell's. Wholesome, just like a can of chicken noodle soup.

Mark's eyes flick to mine and then quickly away. Suddenly I feel like a jerk. Something is going on between Mark and his dad, and all I can do is flick my eyes back and forth between him and Liz, trying to read their body language and criticize her genuine adorableness.

Emma cuts the tension again without even knowing it. "The reunion committee sent me flowers and a card that said '*Wish you were here.*'" She rolls her eyes. "Might as well have said '*Stay home. Your battle with mortality doesn't match the reunion aesthetic.*'"

I love her. She's my favorite person at this reunion. It sucks that this is the first time I realize she could have been my friend in high school. I was too busy judging her pretty hair and social status, assuming that she was nothing more than that, to notice the secretly devilish sense of humor hiding inside.

Liz bites her lip. Glances at Mark. Travels over me and lands back on Emma.

"Well, your headscarf matches the table linens," Liz finally says.

Oh. Wow.

Emma grins. "Go Wildcats!"

We all laugh—mine admittedly a little thin. My eyes trail to Mark, and he's looking at me again. I see the muscle in his jaw tense, and two tiny lines appear between his brows. Fast, there and gone, and then Liz is back on us.

"So, you and Mark were friends in high school?" she asks.

"We bumped into each other a few times." I pause, flick my eyes at him. "He was way more popular than me."

"I wasn't popular," he says, rubbing his hand along the nape of his neck.

"You had a crowd," I say.

"I knew your name," Emma adds. "That's saying something."

"I did too, even as a freshman," Liz says. Her freckled, peaches and cream complexion can't hide her blush.

"Mark got invited to all the parties," I add. Our eyes meet again. I don't know if he remembers the one I'm thinking of. The one where he was tipsy or maybe even drunk. The one that ended in a dark room with him embracing Roxy, and me in tears.

"Like the one we met at," Liz says, as she nudges him with her elbow. Playful, but awkward, like it's not the physical contact she wants, but she'll settle for anything at all. He immediately tucks the hand closest to her in his pocket and presses that arm flush against his body.

"That was a college party," he says, his tone curt.

Okay, this has gone on long enough.

"How long have you two been dating?" I spit out. I'm an unstoppable train of socially inappropriate.

Mark is looking so hard into my eyes that it feels almost too aggressive, but I don't hate it, either. "We're not dating."

And simultaneously, Liz says, "We were engaged."

"But not anymore," he explains. His eyes don't leave mine.

"We're taking a break."

"I'm looking for a place."

"But we're still living together," Liz says. I can tell she's frustrated and holding on to him with both hands. "It's only been a week."

Whoa. What the fuck. Yikes.

Mark winces and breaks eye contact with me. This is too fresh, and he knows it.

"Stonybrook isn't exactly the rental capital of America," he says. "It's going to take a minute."

"I'm not the one pressuring you to find a new place." There's more to that statement. Something subtle, directed only at Mark. He shakes his head and suppresses an eyeroll. He's trying not to embarrass her, but she's clearly not over him.

"Why did you even bring me?" I hear her whisper. She's trying to say it quietly enough so that we can't hear it over "Disturbia" by Rihanna currently blasting over the speakers. Unluckily for her, I have wolf ears. All those years of getting made fun of for wearing earplugs to concerts have paid off.

"You begged to come," Mark whispers back. She squares her jaw and turns away from him to watch the embarrassing gyrations happening on the dance floor. Her lips are pressed together in a perfect pout.

One week.

I've been a writer for long enough to know that that makes for one complicated love interest.

My heart sinks. I'm not about to be somebody's kiss-and-discard rebound. Especially not Mark's. I've waited half my life to get up the courage to even *smile* at this man. My heart can't take it if I'm just here to get the taste of this incarnated cherub out of his mouth.

There's a slight sheen in Liz's eyes when she turns her attention back to me. I would almost feel sorry for her if I didn't already feel sorrier for me. "What do you do, Ellie?"

Clearly Mark hasn't told her about our late-night All-Star Special at Waffle House, or the deal we made, or that he wasn't just the boy I bumped into in high school but my one and only crush and he knows it. I bet he hasn't told her about his script, either. If they're really over, like dead and buried in the ground, why wouldn't he tell her the truth? I glare in his direction to convey my displeasure, but it's a fatal mistake. I can't help but notice the complete desperation constricting his every feature, like he's begging me to keep his secret, like he needs just a little more time and space to figure it all out.

I shouldn't care about what he needs—or wants. But I do.

And I hate that.

"I write for TV," I say, pinched. I'm sick of saying it at this point. "I'm visiting from LA." Mark's shoulders relax ever so slightly.

"LA?" she asks, knitting her brows together. "That's so cool. Mark lived in New York for a while, but I'm just not a city girl."

Mark's jaw tenses, there and gone. I'm the master of reading micro expressions. A writer's blessing-slash-curse. Knowing about his secret-but-not-to-me dream of becoming a screenwriter-director makes me wonder if Liz's dislike of big cities had something to do with the demise of their would-be marriage.

"It's not really about the city for me," I say. "I moved to LA to be a screenwriter."

"Oh, that's so cool!" I can't help but notice that the redundant use of *that's so cool* must be code for *we have nothing in common*. She tucks a thick, silky strand of stray hair behind her ear and glances up at Mark. She must know something of his big Hollywood dreams. She's chewing the lipstick off her lower lip, so definitely not Camp Hollywood, and possibly feeling the pangs of insecurity associated with my close proximity to his dream.

She's small-town, apple-pie. Content to live and die in Stonybrook, and I really can't fault her for it. A lot of people are like Liz, and there's nothing wrong with that life. I could have had that life given a different set of variables and circumstances. Maybe, if I'd acted on my crush on Mark instead of pretending it didn't exist, he and I would have settled in Stonybrook, too. Had kids, gotten jobs. On weekends we'd take our kids to soccer practice in the park and have Sunday lunch with Abigail Smart and her brood of smarties.

The thought makes my skin prickle and the inside of my throat feel tight, dry. And then I realize: Mark is still here, trapped of his own design, sure, but longing—gasping—working—to escape. Suddenly, his quiet desperation doesn't feel so totally foreign. He almost married his very own BLW, and the fact that he didn't—that he figured out just in the nick of time it wasn't right for him—or fair to her—to tie them both into something that would make them unhappy—sends prickles of electricity through me.

Mark is trying his hardest to get unstuck, and I showed up on my very own quest to break out just in time to witness his worthy struggle.

"Sorry." I cough, trying to swallow but my mouth is bone dry, like it's filled with cotton. "I need a refill."

Without waiting for them to give me a socially acceptable release from the conversation, I bail. Behind me, I hear Emma gracefully filling the gap I left with pleasant small talk, forever the social butterfly.

I shoot from the darkened gym, where the DJ has just switched over to a slow song, "Make You Feel My Love" by Adele. It's a good song, great even, but *vomit*, everyone is actually pairing off with their spouses-slash-dates to slow dance. I pass the reception table, now empty, and burst through the front doors into the crisp Ohio air.

I'm immediately smacked in the face with a puff of cigarette smoke.

"Suffocating, isn't it?" Roxy asks, drawing her cigarette to her lips again. She leaves a rim of plum lipstick around the filter.

"Why are you always lurking in the shadows?" I bite back at her, but it's halfhearted. "It's shady as hell."

Her lips twist, but there's a flash of doubt in her eyes. "I am who I am."

"No, you are who you choose to be," I say, coughing and waving away the smoke that is assaulting my airways. "And I guess you choose lung cancer, huh?"

Roxy takes another drag before stomping her cigarette out under the edge of her patent leather porn star boots.

"I'm trying something," she says. She twirls her lighter. "Habit replacement." She isn't looking at me as she talks. She can't see that I'm examining her under the halo of streetlight, and she still looks like my Roxy, only with harder, sharper edges. And her edges were pretty jagged to begin with.

"It isn't working," she adds. Her eyes slide to mine and she grins.

I look away, but I can still feel her watching, and it pisses me off.

Roxy always had a knack for seeing right through the bull-shit to the core—rotten, worm-eaten, or moldy. If she keeps looking, she'll unearth my inner turmoil, plus discover the truth about why I'm here without even breaking a sweat. I swallow, about to say something I probably shouldn't, when

Kyle Temple runs up in just his underwear, holding the tiger-striped head of a school mascot costume, somehow already drunk off his ass. He plops the head on his shoulders and fist pumps the air. "Go Wildcats!"

He streaks past us, screaming into the night.

Roxy and I exchange a look before doubling over with cackling laughter.

"What the hell was that?!" she says, wiping a tear away.

The doors fly open. A few people I don't immediately recognize trickle out, followed by Emma and her sister.

"Roxy, hi!" Emma says, her eyes sparkly. Roxy leans over and hugs Emma. When she stands back up, her eyes glisten in the streetlights. I lean forward. Is she emotional? No way.

"Love the new 'do," Roxy says. It should be offensive. It's not.

"Chemo chic," Emma grins and pats her headscarf.

The doors open. Mark and Liz wander out, talking easily with Brock Crawley and his wife, Christine. Mark's scanning the parking lot, the sidewalk, and when his eyes land on me, my stomach does a flip.

One week.

Fuck.

Brock walks over, a few steps in front of Christine and Liz, who are deep in conversation. Mark trails, looking out of place and a little sick to his stomach.

"It's starting to die down in there," Mark says. It takes all of two seconds for his glance to travel from me to Roxy. Some recognition, emotion even, registers. His expression flattens.

"Sparkling grape juice was lame in high school," Brock says. "We're taking this show on the road."

He winks at Roxy, who rolls her eyes and turns away from him. A suspicious swipe across her lower lids confirms my suspicion that she *does* have a heart, even if it is only operating at half capacity.

BEFRI STENDS.

I shake the thought out of my head.

Christine gives Roxy a once-over with undisguised judgment: pinched lips; a cocked, perfectly manicured brow; that vein in her forehead a little bulgy. It's ugly, not because she's ugly—because she's indisputably gorgeous—but because it's so clear that she thinks she's better than Roxy.

It's a full minute before she notices I've caught her in the act of being a mean girl. She stands up a little straighter.

"You guys should come," Christine squeezes out with sugar sweet–coated bitterness. "One thousand Whispering Pines. Everyone else is coming."

I guess you can too. That's what that means.

But wow, even the street name sounds idyllic.

A party at Brock and Christine Crawley's house. The list flutters to the front of my mind.

Number Six: Finally get invited to a party with all the "popular kids."

Check.

Though this technically isn't my first invite to Brock's house. Though the last one came through Roxy. And what a disaster *that* was.

My eyes trail from horrible Christine to Emma to Roxy (who looks like she's about to scream), over to Liz (who looks pint-sized next to the towering Christine, especially with their arms linked like a perfect pair of Stepford besties), and finally to

Mark. He's already fixed his eyes on me, searching my face. He looks concerned. Is he trying to figure out where we stand?

I look away from his intense gaze. My cheeks flush yet again, but thank God no one can see in this light.

No one except Roxy, who was watching Mark and me while everyone else was listening to Brock. She's wearing an all-knowing Roxy smile. A nothing-gets-past-me Roxy stare. It all adds up to a your-secret-is-safe-with-me Roxy promise. And I hate that she is still like this, that she still knows me so well, after all these years.

"Who's in?" Brock asks.

I don't want to go to Brock's reunion after-party, not really. I remember Brock's graduation party and how two of the people in this parking lot broke my heart that night. One who knew it, and one who didn't. I don't want history to repeat itself, and it's already started to, just in new, agonizing ways.

One week.

Ugh.

But I think again of the list on my phone and how most of the popular kids from high school will likely be there. I realize that I have no choice, that tonight might be one of my only chances to knock out so many superlative birds with one beer pong ball.

Cue my sigh of defeat.

Let the *Ellie Is Cool Now* games begin.

CHAPTER 12

The who's-riding-with-who debacle of Brock Crawley's reunion after-party was as awkward as when Lena Dunham tried to full-on kiss Brad Pitt on the red carpet and he turned away to escape. I felt like the paparazzi watching it go down through a lens, helpless, but unable to look away from the indignity.

It started because Mark asked if I needed a ride, a thinly veiled attempt to get me alone for some damage control. Liz assumed she'd have a ride with him since they came together—*because they are still living together, fuck*—or maybe she decided I, a personification of Mark's big LA dreams, shouldn't get free access to her freshly minted ex-fiancé. So she tagged along even after Mark said, "Oh, I thought you were riding with Christine." Gulp.

Since they've just broken up it felt super weird to take shotgun, so I'm sitting in the back like a third wheel. Liz doesn't let our silence linger long, breaking it with mundane, but polite, inquiry into my life. I don't know how many more questions I can handle. I know she's trying to fill the weird, tense air with the pleasant sound of inane chatter, but I hate small talk more than I hate awkward silence.

But I have to hand it to her, she's doing a good job endearing herself to me. I want to hate her—if she were awful, or snotty, or even saccharine sweet, then she'd be easier to dismiss. It was my go-to tactic in high school: assume the worst, never be disappointed. But everything about her feels genuine and easy. Open. She's happy. Content. This suburban life suits her. And even though she's not exactly a dynamic conversationalist, there's something almost refreshing about her. She's not like my friends in LA, not like Roxy, or me, not even like her former boo Mark Wright.

It makes me hate Mark a little bit for lying to her, even if it's just by omission. It makes it easier to understand why he would lie to her. Liz isn't thinking beyond Stonybrook, but Mark is. He wants out. He wants more.

He must, or he wouldn't be helping me with the list, and he probably wouldn't have ended things between him and Liz, either.

When she's run through her list of twenty questions (which feels like twenty thousand), I finally edge my own not-so-innocent inquiry into her backstory.

She was a football cheerleader, popular in her own high school class, and went to a local four-year college to get a teaching degree. She's close with a lot of the class of '10 alumni and coaches cheerleading with Christine, which is one reason why she came tonight. Although, I sneakily believe her motives for shadowing Mark at his reunion aren't just because she was feeling social.

Mark flicks on his blinker to turn through the gate into Brock's neighborhood, and his eyes find mine in the rearview mirror. We briefly hold each other's gaze before his eyes slide back to the road. Mine trail to the window, watching huge cookie-cutter houses pass in a blur.

Winding Ridge Estates is a new development of mini mansions that backs up to one of Stonybrook's many golf courses. It's the newer, sexier version of the neighborhood Brock grew up in with his mother the mayor and his father the pervy attorney. I never met his dad, but I heard stories about him walking in on girls changing in their pool house during their who's who of Stonybrook summer barbecues. I imagine Stonybrook will be the last town in the country to join the Me Too movement.

For some reason, I did not imagine that Brock Crawley would have grown up to become his mother in home-buying taste or occupation. But he definitely did.

I need to get focused. Mark's problems aren't my problems. I didn't come here to hook up with my high school crush—actually, I came here to hook up with the prom king.

Yuck.

The thought makes my stomach turn a little. But, as we established at the bar back in LA, just a kiss. That's it. And, I mean, no one said it had to involve tongue. It will absolutely *not* involve tongue. I will bite Kyle Temple's tongue in half before I willingly allow it to enter my mouth.

Oh, God. I'm going to throw up just thinking about it.

Mark parks the car, and I unbuckle, hop out the door, slam it closed.

My goal is to avoid close contact with him as long as

possible. Mark is fresh off a broken engagement. My relationship experience is admittedly slim. Like, a boyfriend in college who I never slept with and one semi-long-term thing (three months, does that count?) that ended amicably. I just don't feel equipped to get in the middle of something this complicated—especially when I can barely admit to myself that I might like him at all.

I click up the sidewalk to Brock's house. The door is cracked open, the universal sign for "We're having a party, come on in." I push inside. We're somehow not the first ones here. Even though Crest 3DWhitestrips Brock and Christine left only minutes before us, there's already a handful of my high school classmates here. Women I vaguely recognize thanks to Brie's reunion badges. Dudes I only sort of recall.

I wind through the den and into the kitchen. It's palatial. Gray marble counters. Recessed lighting. Copper sink. Designer range. There are velvet upholstered barstools tucked under the island, where, right now, catering staff are putting the final touches on a fancy spread. They don't look up at me.

There's a drink station at the far side of the kitchen, where a breakfast table would normally be. They've set up a bar and hired a bartender. I bet it's not a cash bar, either. This whole thing is a show. A big, shining spotlight on Brock and Christine's *nepo-tastic* success. Brock didn't have a hard climb; we all know it.

He's on city council. He's running for mayor. His mother groomed him for this life. He's chatting up a gaggle of dudes and their wives, who are all a little starry-eyed. Brock is easily the best-looking of all of them—in a sort of slick, too-polished way.

Waxed, tanned, and bleached.

I make a mad dash for the bar. There are more liquor bottles here than at a Western saloon. I scan for my boo Captain Morgan and spot him right away, no Sailor Jerry in sight.

"Captain and Coke, please," I say to the bartender. I spot the tentacles of Kraken Black Spiced Rum on the bar behind him. Oh em gee. "Just kidding, Kraken me up. That's my fave."

The bartender smiles politely and gets to pouring.

Boy, Brock and Christine really know how to throw a party. Always did, always will, I guess.

From here, I can see the den, pristinely decorated and dimly lit. It's starting to fill up. They've set up another bar on the far wall, and that's where Mark stands, tapping the mouth of his beer bottle against his lips and talking to someone I don't readily recognize. Liz is nearby chatting with Brie, whose hair has started to come out of its updo and now sticks out in tiny pieces that look electrified. Brie seems to be in desperate need of a stiff drink. I make a mental note to circle back to her when she's not having her ear bent by Liz.

Grabbing my signature drink (now with more pizzazz), I thank the bartender, and gingerly take a step into the party room. I need to find Kyle Temple. No doubt he's fully wasted already—he was well on his way back at the reunion when he streaked past in the mascot uniform. I need to find him, and corner him, and I don't know…

God, I'm *so* not good at this.

I need to find Kyle and all the other superlatives on my list. Figure out if they are here or went home or didn't show at all. Maybe Brie can give me a master list of everyone who RSVP'd to the reunion so I can follow up and make sure the superlatives I need are still in town, now that the main event is over. I really should have planned this out better. I definitely could use some help.

My eyes automatically trail to Mark, but I scold them back to casually scanning the room. Kyle must be outside. The back door is open to the yard and the golf course beyond. I make my way toward it, step out into the brisk air.

A hand, broad—a man's—splays across my shoulder.

"Ellie, hold up," Brock says. He's pulled away from his flock of adoring fans to follow me outside. My eyebrows involuntarily raise. I never got a close look at Brock in high school. We ran in the exact opposite kind of crowd—him, the center of the in crowd, and me, the outskirts of the in-between crowd. Class president Brock Crawley was at the center of every party, every school event. The only person more popular was Kyle, and we can see which one of them got better with age.

"Hey, Brock," I say, and I smile, because he's smiling at me. All those perfect teeth, all in a row. It's hard to resist smiling back.

"Needed some fresh air?" he asks, taking a careful sip of his champagne. What kind of dude drinks champagne at a party? Jay Gatsby, that's what kind. Brock so clearly believes his own press. I don't laugh at the thought, but I want to.

"I get it," he adds. I never said yes to his previous question.

"I may choke on all the memories," I say.

"The party was Christine's idea," he says. His eyes travel over my face. "You didn't come to my parties in high school." There's a question beneath the surface, but he doesn't ask it.

"You never invited me," I say.

"My bad," he replies, his voice low and growly, his eyes sensual, almost swoony. His lips twist again, but this time it's less a smile, and more a knowing smirk. All of a sudden I realize that he is *very* close to me.

Um. What the fuck. Is Brock Crawley flirting with me? With his wife less than ten feet away drinking and chatting with their friends—totally oblivious?

Over his shoulder, I spot Kyle at the bar. Inside. Damn it. I shrug at Brock.

"Yeah, your loss, I guess," I say dismissively. "Oh, there's Brie. She looks like she needs a drink."

I beeline around him, but I can feel him watching me as I walk away. Brie is nowhere near Kyle, so Brock will definitely know I was blowing him off. He'll know I'm not interested, and hopefully he won't make bedroom eyes at me again.

I shudder.

As I'm downing my drink and sliding through the crowd with determined precision, I hear my name. Quiet, almost a whisper, and in a voice I actually like.

"Hey, can I talk to you for a sec?" Mark asks. I spin, doing a quick survey of the space around us. Liz is out of sight. My eyes snap to Mark's, and his eyes are burning with so much emotion I almost crumble right there. Out of sight, out of mind too, apparently.

"We don't have anything to talk about, unless you want to discuss how you're going to help me hook up with Kyle Temple," I say. It's like I slapped him. It feels a little too good to see the smack of hurt contort his face. "Didn't think so."

I move away. He reaches for my wrist, grabs it. Light but firm.

"Let go, Mark," I say, stern. He does, and for the second time in less than ten minutes, I feel unwanted eyes watch me walk away.

Kyle keeps moving. I watch him lumber down the hallway and hear him yell something about beer pong. I need to get to him before he's so wasted that he passes out or starts puking.

I follow him down the hall toward what must be a game room—like everything else in Brock's house, it's decadent and classy, yet somehow almost tacky. There's a pool table, a few sets of lounge chairs, and moody lamps. One wall is fitted with ornate wood cabinets and bookcases full of serious-looking tomes. Knowing Brock, they are for decoration only.

Kyle is solo, setting up a game of beer pong on the Ping-Pong table. I scoff at the whole display until I realize that a few of the guys milling around are actively watching him. They must be planning to join. Jesus, they really never grew up. I snap my shoulders back.

Ellie Jenkins, co-executive producer of Cooler Than You.

I approach Kyle with a smile.

"Can I play?" I ask. Beer pong is my actual worst nightmare, but I need to engage him somehow, and right now, he's got the hots for beer pong.

Kyle offers me his trademark lazy grin, and then looks me up and down for good measure. "Little Miss Hollywood," he hoots, and almost spills a row of full red Solo cups. "Sure thing, you can be on my team."

I grimace. "Great, let me just go grab a shot. To get me in the mood."

We make shifting, probably blurry for him, eye contact. He grins.

"*Yessss.* Grab me one too." I nod. Exiting the same way I came in.

And bumping right into Brock. His champagne glass spills onto his stiff button-down, sloshing over into my hair and across my chest. It drips down into my cleavage.

"Oh my God," I exclaim. We're both looking down at my wet chest. "Sorry." I don't know why I say it, since we bumped into each other and I'm the one who got soaked.

"No biggie. Here, let me get you a towel," he says. He takes a step back, opening a door to reveal a bathroom. He flicks on the light.

"Thanks," I say, stepping inside to grab a hand towel.

I'm dabbing my chest, wringing out my hair, when I hear the door click closed behind me.

My eyes meet themselves in the mirror. Then glance up to meet Brock's. He's standing behind me. Towering over me. His eyes are almost black, like a cat stalking its prey.

What. The. Hell.

"You're like a fine wine, Ellie," he says. His tongue unwraps my name like it's a gift. I squeeze the towel, letting it drop to my side. "You've gotten better with age."

What is that *line*? He sounds like a cheesy movie villain. I've written similar dialogue for baddie arcs on *Cooler Than You*, but never dreamed I'd hear something that diabolical in real life.

I turn to face him. He's blocking the door. He's a big guy, not like Kyle, sure, but broad-shouldered, kind of ripped, tall. He looms.

"We're fucking twenty-eight, dude," I say, still cringing at his cliché-as-fuck come-on.

He eases away from the door, coming way too close for

comfort. His eyes search my face like they're looking for clues to a riddle. He's a really good-looking guy, but I've never been into him, not even a little bit.

"I think we should rejoin the party," I say.

His hand slides to my hair like he's going to tuck it behind my ear. Like I would let him. I jerk away, smacking it and pressing my hand to his chest to push him back. He smirks.

"What the hell do you think you're doing?" I ask.

"Come on, we can have a little fun. Rewrite the past," he whispers. His breath is hot and smells of champagne and salmon patties.

I give his chest another good shove.

"Come on," he spits. Visibly pissed. "We're just having a little fun. I thought a girl like you would be into that."

"A girl like me?" *What the hell is that supposed to mean?*

"Former goody-two-shoes nobody—"

I throw the towel in his face. "Thanks, but I don't like small-town dick." The implication is clear. I shove past him to reach for the door. My hand connects with the handle right as it twists.

Kyle Temple falls into the bathroom, yelling toward the room behind him, "Gotta take a piss." When he turns back to face the bathroom, he sees me in a huff, eyes blazing, and Brock, jaw clenched, as he straightens his shirt. Not ashamed at all.

Brock is out the door in a flash. Hopefully far away from me.

Kyle's eyes meet mine.

"You have great timing," I say.

"What?" His mouth kicks up into a lazy smile. He'll happily take any compliment. I let out a laugh, tension leaving my body with it. "Were you just in here with . . . Brock Crawley?"

"His dick is the tiniest," I say. I'm not even thinking about consequences. Just that it's payback time. All these years I thought charming Brock took after his mom. But like father, like creepo son.

Kyle's eyes bug out of his head before he doubles over in laughter.

"Someone should tell Christine."

"I'm pretty sure she knows," Kyle says. "About his dick and his douchebaggery."

I reach up to hug Kyle around the neck and plant a kiss on his cheek. When I pull away, he's grinning, but he doesn't say anything asinine or creepy.

I go for the door.

"I like Jameson," he says. "If you're on the way to grab our shots. Game starts after I pee."

Hook up with the prom king.

Sorry, team, looks like that's as close as I'm going to get. But as I meander down the hallway, I pull out my phone, checking the list. Three items down.

Sure, kissing him on the cheek might not be what they meant by *hook up*, but I wouldn't share a straw with Kyle Temple.

A hand snatches my phone from my grip. I jolt, looking up to find Roxy fondling my phone.

"*Ellie Is Cool Now*?" she reads. Her eyes meet mine. "Funny, you look the same to me."

She grins and points to *Hook up with the prom king*.

One dark eyebrow kicks up. "Check?"

CHAPTER 13

I snatch the phone back from Roxy.

"It's really none of your business," I snap at her. "But it's a work thing."

She purses her lips, pops a hip to one side. "I knew Hollywood was kinky, but I didn't think you'd go *that* far." She crosses her arms over her chest. "I'm impressed."

"Can you lay off being the antagonist in my life just this once?" She's good at hiding her feelings, but I'm better at reading people. Hurt flickers like a tiny flame in her eyes. She stamps it out with a sneer.

"So you hooked up with Kyle." She glances over at the former hotshot. He looks back at us and waves before he makes a *V* with his fingers and darts his tongue between them. We both shudder.

"I kissed him on the cheek."

"I think that's cheating." She winks at me.

"I prefer to remain STD-free."

She shrugs. "Didn't I see something on there about your high school crush? Isn't that Mark Wright?"

Oh, dear God. I do *not* want to go there with her right now.

"I don't actually remember," I say. I start to walk away from her, but she steps in front of me so I can't move.

"No, I remember now. I got super wasted at a party and hooked up with him, and you never spoke to me again even though I had no fucking clue you liked him."

"You did so know," I tell her. My cheeks are on fire, but this time it's from anger. I hate her fucking guts.

"I think I maybe sort of knew that you thought he was cute, but you were never going to make a move." She shrugs with her whole body. "You treated him like trash."

"Because I liked him, Roxy," I yell at her. "And if you were an actual good friend, you would've known that when I like someone, I pretend they don't exist, because I'm terrified. I was terrified of what might happen if he knew how much I liked him."

The thought of him knowing, even now, makes me feel naked and vulnerable. Like a tiger with no teeth, or a turtle with no shell. Helpless and defenseless. It's like I can't imagine anything worse, like it's a fate worse than death.

"You should've helped me," I continue because she looks like she's ready to fire off another arrow. "Instead, you got drunk off your ass and hooked up with him, just like you did with every other fuckwad in school."

At this point I realize the room has dissolved into complete silence.

Everyone is looking at us.

I glance around at the sea of wide, unblinking eyes until I spot a familiar pair of brown irises. Mark looks from me to Roxy and then back to me.

"You think you're so morally superior." Roxy's voice is sharp and low, for my ears only. "But your little high school problems were fucking child's play." When I look back, her eyes cut through me before she adds, "You have no idea what it was like for me back then."

Fuck me, I'm an ass. And just slut-shamed her in front of our entire graduating class.

"Roxy," I say her name once, but she holds a hand up to silence me.

Her eyes are glassy, and she swipes a hand underneath one eye before shouldering past me toward the kitchen.

"Where's the vodka?" I hear her demand from the other room.

I stand still, completely frozen, wishing I could disappear into the ether.

BEFRI STENDS.

No more. Or ever again.

One by one, other conversations pick up and everyone forgets that anything ever happened. Everyone except Mark, who is still staring right at me from his place on the couch. He sets down his beer and crosses the room. For me. Outwardly, I'm not shaking, or I don't think I am, but inwardly everything vibrates and pulses. This is a horrible feeling—what the hell is happening to me?

I need to get out of here.

I fidget with the lock on the sliding glass door until it opens and releases me from this blast from the past. I slide it shut behind me and march over to the neighbor's swing set. I hear the door slide open and shut again and footsteps follow me, leaving crunched leaves in their wake.

"Ellie?" It's both a question and a command. *Talk to me.*

I sit down on the squeaky swing and start to pump my feet. He walks around and sits down on the swing next to me, facing the opposite way.

Squeak.

I swing forward.

Squeak.

I swing back.

"I just don't get it," he says.

Squeak.

"Why didn't you tell me? Talk to me, flirt with me, look at me, *something*?"

Squeak.

"I don't know what you think happened, but Roxy and I didn't hook up."

Squeak.

"We were drunk. We kissed. That was it."

Sque-eak.

My feet hit the dirt.

"I just don't understand why you didn't say anything," he says, exasperated.

My feet hit the dirt again, and I stop swinging completely.

Mark leans over and grabs my swing, wrapping one hand around the chain closest to him. The weight of his body in his swing pulls me toward him. Startled, I turn to look at him. His dark eyes are puzzled, searching.

"I liked you," he says softly. His voice is deep and as husky as his voice ever gets. "I just—I couldn't tell if you liked me."

For a second, I worry that I'm going to pass out. The weight of his confession presses heavily on my chest, leaving me short of air. I'm breathless and lightheaded, like I might just float away. Shit, am I swooning? I think I'm swooning.

But a single star twinkles, and I'm reminded of other twinkling things recently removed.

"Where's the woodland sprite?" I ask him without thinking. He blinks at me, the magic of the moment sliced in two.

"The what?"

I feel my cheeks heat up. It's a good nickname, but it's kind of an inside joke. Just for myself. Too late.

"Sorry, that's what I've been calling her in my head," I confess. "Your ex."

He lets go of my swing and stands up too straight. "I don't know. She's my *ex*, Ellie."

"She doesn't want to be."

"It's not up to her—" he starts, and then he cuts himself off. "I love her, but we're not meant for each other."

"Then how did you end up together?" I ask him.

He leans against the metal frame of the swing set. We both settle in for story time.

"I came home from New York with a degree in biology, when what I really wanted was . . . well, you know."

He can't even say it.

"I was bored and depressed and my dad was disappointed— is *still* disappointed in me because I scored low on my MCAT and didn't get into med school."

"I'm sorry," I say. *I thought you were one of the brave ones.* My insensitive words replay over and over inside my head. Mark wanted to be brave, but it's so much harder when you don't have the support of the people around you. When the people you love are pressuring you to be something you're not. I'm so lucky my parents told me I could do anything, be anything.

"Don't be sorry," he says to me. "I've never wanted anything less in my life than I wanted med school."

I nod thoughtfully. He continues: "Anyway, plan A became plan B became plan...nothing. So I got a job at Stonybrook Market and started driving to college campuses with my buddies to party on my weekends off...and that's where I met Liz. She was...sunny. And I was sad. She was a breath of fresh air. Once she graduated, we moved in together. Her parents did not love that we were *living in sin*, so eventually she gave me an ultimatum, and I got her a ring."

"All the best marriages are born from ultimatums." He huffs out a laugh in response to my sarcasm.

"The ring was a Band-Aid. She kept trying to get me to set a date, and I kept putting it off. We were Pam and Roy from *The Office*, and I felt like a complete and utter ass."

"So what changed a week ago?" I ask him.

"I remembered that the reunion was this weekend, and it hit me that a decade has passed since high school and I'm still here. With no direction, no new plan, working at a grocery store."

"There's nothing wrong with that," I point out. "In TV, you usually spend the first few years fetching coffees anyway. The pay is shit, and even those jobs are hard to come by."

"Let me guess, you skipped that part." He shakes his head in disbelief in response to my embarrassed shrug. "Jesus, Ellie."

"Finish the story," I whine.

"Sorry," he says. "The end of the story is just that I told her how I was feeling and she freaked out. She threw her ring at me, and that was the end. At least, it was for me."

"For her?" I ask.

He shakes his head. "I don't think she believes it's over yet."

I let my eyes trail over his face. Even though he seems like his mind is all the way made up, no turning back, I can tell he's still warring with himself about the way things ended. Are ending. There's guilt behind those dark brown eyes. It's eating him up inside.

He looks back at the house. "It's way past her bedtime. She's probably back at the condo already."

"Wait, walked back? Alone?" I stand up, suddenly worried about her. Even though I hardly know her.

"It's Stonybrook, not Skid Row. She takes a lot of long walks at night," he assures me. "She *likes* to walk."

I scoff. "If she watched as much *Dateline* as I do, she wouldn't even take out the *trash* by herself."

Mark laughs and shoves his hands in his pockets. "You're paranoid."

"Oh, really?" I put my hands on my hips. He watches me with laughter in his eyes, but I'm *dead serious*. "At any one time in the United States, there are as many as two hundred active serial killers at large. Killing people. Actively."

"Wow. That's a lot." Mark digs his phone out of his back pocket.

"Some forensic experts believe there could be thousands."

He's not paying attention. His screen lights up, and he turns it to face me so that I can read the message. He has her in his phone as *Lizard*.

All talk of serial killer stats evaporates from my mind as I burst into a fit of giggles. Involuntary and uncontrolled. In the illumination of his phone screen, I can see him blush.

"I need to change the name."

"I'm shocked she didn't dump you immediately after you gave her a pet name like *Lizard*."

He checks it, like a reflex, and turns it around to show me. *Back door is unlocked. Going to bed.* "She's still texting me to check in when she gets home," he says in a low voice. He slips the phone back into his pocket without replying, scrubbing his hands through his hair in an exasperated motion.

She's still Lizard in his phone, too—*barf.*

"How long were you engaged to her?" I ask him.

He moves behind me, hands sliding around the chain and applying some pressure to swing me forward gently.

"Two years."

"Wow, and you just ended it a week ago. The corpse is barely cold."

I have a sudden awareness of how close he's standing to me. I could just lean back and our bodies would touch. I can feel his warmth pulsing toward me, reaching out even though he is firmly in his own space. My fingers twitch, longing to reach up to where his fingers clutch the metal of the swing. To touch him.

"Speaking of serial killers," he says, breaking the silence, "shouldn't we get back to Brock's party?"

I giggle. It lasts too long. I sound like an idiot. This is why I do not—should not—talk to guys I like.

Mark smiles at me, and I feel lightheaded.

"I think I've got to get out of here," I say. At this moment I can't even imagine going back to that stupid party. Facing Roxy, who is no doubt drunk as a skunk again. *Morally superior.* I hope she pukes her guts up all night and falls asleep on a toilet.

"I can take you," he says.

No. Not this again.

"No, that's okay, I'll call an Uber."

"An Uber? In Stonybrook? Are you nuts?"

Sometimes I forget that everywhere is not LA. Sure, we're close to Dayton and a stone's throw away from Cincinnati, but Stonybrook is too suburban to attract Uber drivers. Here, our DDs promise to drink just the one and our two-lane highways are lined with rumble strips in case a driver falls asleep at the wheel or forgets their designation.

Seriously, Stonybrook police pass out DUIs like Halloween candy.

"It's okay. I'll get your coat," he says as he runs inside. "Meet me out front."

My sigh is deep as I shiver and walk toward the street.

The ride home is quiet. Mark plays some easy listening hits on the radio. I look out the window and bob my head up and down to a Carpenters song. You don't really bob to the Carpenters, but I'm bobbing. I must bob.

"Turn right up here," I tell him. He turns onto my street. My heart beats faster as we approach my house. I don't know why. It's like it knows something I don't.

"It's the first house on the right."

He turns into my parents' winding driveway and pulls in front of the garage.

"Thanks for taking me home." I pick my purse off the floor and open the door. One foot is out of the car when he says it.

"Ellie." My name. His voice is deep and crackly again.

I hesitate.

"I wish I'd kissed you instead of Roxy at that party."

I slowly turn to look at him, still with one foot out the door. His eyes are pleading with the past, wishing things could be different. Between us back then, between us now.

"You do?" I ask. My voice sounds far away, even to my own ears.

He nods. "I wish I'd known then what I know now."

I stare at my hands on the door. "I was...scared."

"Who isn't?" His grin is lopsided. His eyes trail down to my lips. "Are you scared now?"

"Are you going to murder me and wear my skin as an outfit?" His laugh is a burst of bright sound in the darkness of his car.

My brain screams at me to get out of there, to be the morally superior goody-goody that Roxy thinks I am.

But when one of his hands takes hold of my wrist and pulls me closer, I don't resist.

When his other hand buries itself in my hair, I don't pull away.

And when his lips touch mine, I kiss him back.

CHAPTER 14

Now I'm the villain in a rom-com starring Liz as the sweet unassuming ingénue.

She's living in the aftermath of a romantic explosion. One week. They've been broken up for one fucking week. I've had take-out leftovers in my fridge longer than they've been broken up.

And then here I come. The pleather-skirt-wearing c-word who sucks the face off the guy she was supposed to marry. Total anti-feminist homewrecker—well, condowrecker.

Though I'm not quite the trope—no pleather on me today.

I put my hand on Mark's chest and pull away from the kiss. This is not right. I am not this person. I avoid messy. I sidestep icky.

My lips tingle, buzzing with the feeling of Mark's pressed against them.

"I can't do this," I say out loud. Mark's eyes are wide. He turns away from me and gazes at the steering wheel.

"I'm sorry," he says after a long, slow sigh.

"You're still living with her," I say. "You were going to marry her."

"I know." He says it quickly. Like he doesn't want to hear it right now.

"Liz is not ready. You're not ready."

He blinks, fast, because I'm right. He's just as stunned as I am.

I used to dream about this moment. And *this* isn't the way I wanted it to feel. In the dream, my mind wasn't racing toward all the reasons this wouldn't work, and I wasn't shivering with trepidation. Instead, I leaned in and let our lips touch, and the whole world and everything in it melted away until it was just me and him, me and Fantasy Mark.

But this Mark is the real deal. He's a real person with real feelings and real flaws. He just went through a very real breakup with a very heartbroken woman who is not yet over him.

And that was a real kiss.

The fantasy was always so easy. Real is so much harder.

I know I should get out of the car, but I don't. I don't want to. I want to know more about what just happened.

"You're fucking with my head, Ellie." He digs his fingers into his forehead.

"I am? You just kissed *me*, asshole."

"You know what I mean." He's all bound up nerves and energy on a collision course for me. Messy. Messy. Messy.

"No, I don't. I actually don't. Why did you do that?"

"You kissed me back," he says.

"I'm not still living with my former fiancée who I still have in my phone as her *pet name*."

He smiles. "Touché."

"Answer me."

"I don't know!" He runs a hand through his hair in frustration. "I just don't know, okay? All I know is I *needed* to. I had to know what it feels like to kiss you."

It's like my jaw has been wired shut. I'm speechless. No one's ever said anything like that to me. It's hot, and all I can think about is wanting to kiss him again.

I can't resist. "And? What's the verdict?"

He doesn't say anything, and I feel my stomach twist up in knots. Stupid, stupid, stupid.

"Never mind, I don't want to know." I open the car door again. I don't remember closing it. I'm out of the car before I hear my name again. I hesitate and lean down to peer in at him one more time.

His eyes are big and brown, like a puppy's. Pleading with me. *Go back in time. Tell me. Show me. Something. Anything.*

"Good night, Mark" is all I say before I slam the door shut and run into the house.

I lie in bed, wide awake. I'm filled with mixed emotions, but don't know how to express them. I'm mad at Mark, mad at myself, mad at teenage Ellie for not having the balls to confront her feelings head-on. Sad for Liz, who is at home in the shell of her former life while her ex-fiancé kisses me in his car. They're over, but their lives are still intertwined, and she was still wearing his ring *a week ago*.

Shit.

Why do I care, though? Liz's fragile feelings aren't my problem.

My problem is kissing the man—the once-upon-a-time boy I pined after for *years*—under less-than-ideal circumstances. And I liked it more than I should have.

I toss and turn. My phone buzzes. Vic and Tina have sent texts requesting updates all night long. I've ignored every single buzz. They must know that something is up, but I can't bring myself to unlock my phone and respond. They wouldn't give two shits about Lizard's feelings or the ick factor of kissing a guy still living with his ex-fiancée. Tina went to Cabo with a man the night he finalized his divorce. Ink wasn't even dry. But they're big-city folk, and while I'm an LA convert, my romantic sensibilities are a little more homegrown than Hollywood's.

My phone screen is now a cesspool of unanswered texts I am fully committed to ignoring until I've worked through my feelings of grossness.

I remember overhearing all the typical high school gossip. Girls making out with other girls' boyfriends, boys hooking up with their best friends' girlfriends, and that one guy who cheated on his girlfriend with a dude. Always drama central, and I prided myself on not playing a part in it. Ever. I always kept myself separate from the high school shitshow.

They're not together. My logic center screams at me.

They just were. Their clothes are still hanging in the closet next to each other's. She's still sleeping in the bed they shared, and unless they have two bathrooms, they're still using the same toilet, the same shower, the same sink to brush their teeth.

It doesn't matter how I slice it. At twenty-eight years old, I signed up to take center stage in the exact saga I had always avoided. Unrequited love. A missed opportunity. An unlikely reunion and then...

BOOM.

I shoved my tongue down the throat of a guy who was *this close* to getting hitched.

Liz probably couldn't wait to pick out her dress or ask her best friends to be bridesmaids. She was probably dreaming of crying at the bridal shop into a glass of champagne with her mom when she found the one dress to put all others to shame.

And now that will never happen.

The only real solace I have is that I wasn't here when they ended it—the ending isn't on me. I may have just become the reason they'll never fix it, sure. Shit. Not that Mark wants to fix it, but people act weird when they're in the middle of a crisis. They kiss women they have no business kissing, and they make rash decisions they'll wind up regretting.

My phone buzzes again from the floor. I don't know when it fell off my bed. I poke my head over the side to peer at it where it lies.

I nearly throw up.

It's Mark.

I'm really sorry, Ellie.

And another.

I can't sleep.

Ignore, ignore, ignore.

I throw off the covers and slide off the bed to pick up my phone. I quickly unlock it and stare at his messages.

I take a deep breath and blow out a sigh.

Me either.

I lock my phone quickly and drop it back on the floor. I don't know how my phone survives being my punching bag, but I've had it for a year and a half, and it's survived every blow. I lay my head back down on my pillow and stare at the ceiling.

Another buzz.

My stomach jolts. I close my eyes, but sleep is not happening. And what am I, fifteen?

I reach over the side of the bed and unlock my phone again.

We could talk about it. If you want...

I hesitate before I text him back.

You mean like, on the phone?

My phone buzzes instantly.

For fuck's sake, Ellie, yes. Can I call you?

Teenage Ellie is screaming.

Yes?

My phone rings. Mark Wright is calling. It's a weird feeling. I pick up.

"Buddy the Elf. What's your favorite color?"

Mark hesitates, and then laughs. "What the hell?"

I'm a raving lunatic. "Sorry, I'm more ready for Christmas than I thought."

"I love *Elf*, but it has third act problems."

I sigh with relief. "Agreed."

"Clap your hands if you believe!" His voice is all exhausted rasp and *trying*, and I can't help but imagine him lying in his own bed, wearing pajama pants, lit from above like an angel.

"Biggest plot cop-out ever."

We each chuckle softly, filling the awkward silence we know is coming. Mark clears his throat. His voice is quiet when he speaks.

"I want to apologize. What I did—I shouldn't put you in the middle of my breakup."

"No, don't do the thing." I pause, grabbing my ancient Hello Kitty plushie and squeezing it. "Don't do the thing where you take it back. It's so overdone."

"I'm not *taking it back*." His voice is defensive. "It's just...we probably shouldn't do it again."

"Probably?"

"Definitely. We should just be friends."

That's presumptuous.

"Who says I want to be friends?" I ask with a little bite. Even being friends with Mark will complicate things. I don't live here. I can't get attached no matter how much High School Ellie would have loved the prospect. Current Ellie is very committed to her life and future in Los Angeles.

Mark blows out a long, frustrated sigh. "I still want to help you with your list."

"So that I'll read your script?" I say, eyeing it sitting on top of my childhood desk.

"No! Jesus, Ellie, no. Because I want to help. I said I would, and I want to. Regardless of what it may seem, I'm a man of my word. And...I want to be..." He pauses, and it's full of *so much*. "Friends."

Why the hell am I suddenly smiling?

"Friends." I try out the word and let it dangle between us. Friends with my high school crush. Who just kissed me in his car. What could go wrong? "Okay, friends it is."

"Good, perfect." I imagine him nodding a little too adamantly. "Everyone's meeting for brunch at Murphy's tomorrow at eleven."

"I just have my parents' car," I say. Because it's true, and my dad still doesn't like to let me drive since I'm not on their insurance. "I need to check—"

"I'll come pick you up."

If a pause could be weighed, this one would be hefty.

"Pick me up?"

"Liz is coming, too."

Silence on my end.

"She and Christine are attached at the hip, thanks to cheer-leading, and Brie's daughter is on the team—"

"I get it, she's entrenched in the crew." My brain fills with images of perfect Christine, all legs and tits, standing next to pint-sized Liz saying *rah-rah-rah* to a bunch of eight-year-olds. "Fun."

My nose scrunches in mild disgust and I'm really glad he can't see my face right now.

"You're trying not to be snotty about it. I applaud the

effort." I grunt. "We'll just be three casual acquaintances car-pooling. Easy."

"Absolutely." I'm sure that's true. "No big deal."

"It was just a kiss," he says, pausing, breathing. My skin begins to prickle with heat. "It's not like we had wild monkey sex in the back seat of my car."

It's a joke, but all the blood in my body rushes to my cheeks…and other places. I try to stop it because no. No, no, we did not do that. But everything flushes, and I wrap my legs around the pillow, closing my eyes for a single, snap, second.

"Right." I try to laugh it off, but I sound like I'm being strangled.

"See you tomorrow," he says abruptly. Then he's gone.

I pull my comforter up to my ears, closing my eyes to banish the thoughts, but that only makes me imagine what sex with Mark in the back seat of his car would be like. Frenzied kisses. Shirts unbuttoned, skirt sliding over thighs. Heavy petting and heavy panting, him saying my name as he—

I throw off the comforter, fall out of bed, and decide that what this night needs is a good long cold shower.

CHAPTER 15

When I wake up, my hair is a mess of kinky waves and fuzz from falling asleep with it wet. I'm starving because I realize—to my horror—that I didn't really eat dinner last night. It's well after nine a.m., and Mark (and Liz) will be here in a little over an hour to get me for brunch at Murphy's. My stomach grumbles, and I scowl into the mirror above my vanity. That rat's nest masquerading as hair isn't going to tame itself.

But first, coffee—just like the memes and the T-shirt Vic wears on laundry day assert.

My mom is in the kitchen, already dressed in khakis and a flouncy blouse, reading one of her trade paperback thrillers and eating a piece of toast. Her eyes travel from the page to me as I bumble through the door.

"You didn't use eye cream," she says, squinting at me over her glasses. How can she tell? Mom spidey senses. "You should never go to bed without eye cream. I don't care how tipsy you are."

"I wasn't tipsy." Unless you count being drunk on kisses and bad behavior.

I still haven't texted Vic and Tina back, which makes me feel even shittier, since I'm avoiding them on purpose and from shame. They will ask about the list—and Mark, my crush who's supposed to be helping me with it—and I'll have to sit through their lewd comments and devilish encouragement to *get mine, screw Liz.*

Who I am determined not to be weird around. They're broken up. Mark isn't hers. He's not mine. We're all humans free to make choices with our own bodies—*It's not like we had wild monkey sex in the back seat of my car.* Mark's words from last night on the phone. Heat floods my cheeks, and I pour coffee in my Unicorns Are Real mug, slumping into the seat across from my mom. I am not doing a very good job of proving I'm not hungover.

She takes a micro bite of her toast. I can feel her silently judging my every move while simultaneously wanting to offer advice if only I'd just ask.

Last night was a disaster in all the ways. First, the whole Brock near-assault and vomit-inducing come-on. Then, I kinda sorta crossed number one off the list by giving Neanderthal Kyle Temple a kiss on the cheek, but couldn't even enjoy the tiny triumph because of what happened after with both Mark and Roxy. As much as I hate to admit it, Roxy still gets under my skin. I haven't forgotten what it was like to be friends with her, and even though she's a she-devil in patent leather, she still manages to look at me in that singular way that reminds me she was one of the only people who actually knew me in high school and who actually liked me.

"I saw Roxy at the reunion." I drop the bomb, and then take a sip of my coffee. Its effect on my head is immediate. Some of the fog clears so I can almost start to think coherent thoughts.

My mom closes her book and sets it to the side. I can see her settling in for some shit talk.

"Was she drunk?"

"Very."

Judgment settles over my mother's face like a dark cloud. Oh, so that's where I get it from. I smirk just a little.

"Did she say how her mother is doing?"

My mom and Maureen were friends through most of our adolescence. Not best friends per se, but they talked on the phone, met up for games of euchre, and even occasionally went to dinner and a show at the local community theater. As things fell apart between Roxy and me, Mom let her bond with Maureen shrivel and die. She wasn't sure how to deal with my anger and disappointment, even if I think she did very much want to be there for Maureen, who was in the thick of a new, bewildering health crisis. I know that the way all this went down bothers my mom, and I can't help but wonder if she blames me for their severed friendship, even if I never told her she had to sever it at all.

"I asked, but…" I shrug off the end of that statement. "She said she was sober for six months before this reunion weekend."

My mom shakes her head. "Yeah, right."

"No, she was. She had the medallion and everything," I explain. The memory of the clang of the medallion hitting the bottom of the trash can rattles my brain. Roxy may be a lot of things, but liar isn't one of them. "I think something happened. Maybe something with her mom."

"Maureen did look just awful when I saw her a few weeks ago," she says, then adds: "I can't believe she didn't even say hello." She shakes her head and takes a long swig of coffee.

"You could have said hello first," I say. Mom pretends like she doesn't hear me.

We sit there quietly for a long time staring off into space before my mom fills the silence with a loaded question:

"Are you going to talk to Roxy?"

"Are you going to call Maureen?"

Her lips purse. I roll my eyes.

"We aren't friends anymore." I say it too quickly and with too much venom, and I can tell I've hurt my mom's feelings. I can almost see the feathers ruffle up on her back.

"Do what you want," she says, her eyes a little misty.

"Sorry, Mom, it's just... It's complicated."

My initial thought is an adamant *hell no*. I do not need more Roxy drama on top of everything else. Roxy was *never* easy to be around, and if last night's run-in was any indication, it's not going to get any easier with her.

It will never be my responsibility to stop her from hitting the point of no return. It never was. So why can't I stop thinking about her?

I should be panicking about Mark and Liz. I should be looking over my list to plan my attack. I should be getting my ass up and straightening these untamed Medusa tendrils.

"Roxy needs a therapist," I say, standing to pour myself more coffee before I head back upstairs.

"She needs a friend."

So does Maureen.

My mom and I may both be hard on people and, okay, sure, overcritical at times, but at the end of the day, we have bleeding motherfucking hearts.

I sigh and set the coffee pot back on the burner.

"I'll talk to her."

Taming my hair would have gone a lot smoother if I wasn't fuming about my mom and Roxy, while also freaking out about being in a small confined space with Mark and not thinking about kissing him. Or worried about Liz feeling the tension between us and it breaking her already broken heart into smaller, more jagged pieces. Or daydreaming about catching the next flight back to LA, which only prompted me to worry about facing Vic and Tina and all their unanswered text messages.

I throw on my favorite jeans, tuck in my dusty pink silk button-down, slip on my boots, and apply a coat of lipstick. Tucking a few unruly strands of hair behind my left ear, I walk downstairs just as Mark sends me a text.

Out front.

Thank God I haven't eaten anything yet, or I might throw up.

Great!!

Those two exclamation points are better liars than me.

My dad is in the den watching a rerun of *Who Wants to*

Be a Millionaire from when Regis Philbin was still hosting. I wave and mumble something about being home later, but he doesn't hear me over a contestant incorrectly answering the three-thousand-dollar question.

Liz is in the front passenger seat, her hair braided and slung over one of her tiny shoulders. She smiles, offering me a wave through the window. Mark stares over her shoulder at me, and even from here I can see a small smile playing on his lips.

Someone shoot me now so I don't have to get in that car. I brace, walking and wishing. No shots are fired, and I open the back door and slide inside.

"I love your top," Liz says. "I wish I could pull off that color."

"Thanks, but I bet you'd look great in it." Okay, contact established, and I didn't die.

"I doubt it. My mom always says redheads shouldn't wear pink."

And I bet she's the type of girl who always takes her mom's advice. Unlike me, who hates to admit when my mom might be right.

"Thanks for picking me up," I say to the whole car, but my eyes land momentarily on Mark's ear, his jawline, the nape of his neck.

"Sure thing," he says, his voice strained. He puts the car in gear.

"Murphy's has the best crepes. I'm pre-regretting how much I'm going to eat at breakfast," Liz says. I chuckle.

Too bad thinking about breakfast food makes me think of another restaurant, in the dead of night, where the flames of my crush on Mark Wright were reignited. Friends *do not* daydream about the shape of their friend's lips, the tiny uptick when they're amused but trying not to show it, the way their hands would feel sliding around my waist to cup my ass. I roll the back window down a smidge. Mark's eyes find mine in the rearview mirror.

"Stuffy," I choke out. His eyebrows lift only slightly and the corners of his eyes crinkle to make room for a small smile.

I am absolutely, positively going to suck at being his friend. I'm going to fail miserably, and I never fail at anything.

The drive is short. I manage not to throw up or scream *Your ex-fiancé kissed me while you were fast asleep!* before we pull into Murphy's parking lot and Mark cuts the engine. It doesn't cut the tension simmering between Mark and me or do anything to alleviate the balloon of pressure expanding in my chest that is threatening to pop, but at least I'll be out of his car in a second. Liz hops out first, crepes on the brain apparently, leaving Mark and me alone for a heartbeat.

"Brie organized this brunch meetup, correct?" I ask, before he can speak. I do not meet his eyes in the rearview mirror, but I feel them searching my face, trying to figure out what I'm thinking. "I need you to help me convince her to have a cocktail at eleven a.m. on a Sunday morning."

"Operation Booze is a go," he replies.

I scoot out of the car, biting back my traitorous grin.

Murphy's is a local favorite, with oodles of charm, and brunch food up to the standard of any LA joint. I step inside the well-lit, warm interior and am immediately accosted by the smell of sweet breakfast breads, syrup, and coffee brewing somewhere nearby. We are some of the first to arrive. Apparently, as part of this reunion weekend, the planning committee reserved a whole section of the restaurant. There are Wildcats centerpieces instead of the usual understated daisies in clear glass vases.

Brie is straightening one now, her hair pulled up in a high ponytail that even Betty Cooper would envy. I'm about to head for her when Mark walks in behind me, running bodily into me. His hands curve light and sudden around the small of my waist as we jostle to break apart.

"Watch out," I snap under my breath. I want to lean back and press my ass into him just to see how it feels.

"Maybe don't block the doorway?" he says through a tight smile.

"Or you could pay attention to where you're walking."

His hands slide away, leaving behind a trail of heat.

Liz looks up from the table next to Brie's, her eyes flicking between us. I elbow away from Mark, passing her as I say "Klutz" and thumb toward her ex. She presses her lips together in a toothless smile.

I am not sitting with Liz or Mark. The quiet torture of the car ride was enough. Besides, I need Brie for more than just a checkmark on my list. I need to ask her about the other superlatives. In all the soap opera drama, I never confirmed whether they were all actually here.

I start walking, Mark hot on my heels. "She likes champagne and vodka, not together," he pauses, smiling a little. The dimple pops, and I want to lick it. *Ellie! Jesus.* Who am I?

"It's a place to start. Thanks," I say, and I return his smile.

Friends smile at each other. That is an appropriately friendly gesture of goodwill. We're going to get the hang of it. We'll be friendly enough to serve both of our needs, and then I'll get the hell back to LA, where I belong. His expression shifts ever so slightly when my lips move, eyes landing briefly on them. *I had to know what it feels like to kiss you.*

We split off, him toward Kyle, Brock, and a guy who must be Brie's husband. They've formed a pack near the bar while the tables get set up. I'm making a beeline for Brie when the bell on the door dings. My eyes slide toward it, responding to the signal that someone new has entered, and I almost trip on a chair pulled out from a table.

Roxy. Eyes covered by dark sunglasses. Hair twirled into a messy bun on top of her head. Wearing jeans and a simple black T-shirt with a fitted leather jacket over it. Even before she removes the glasses, I know she's looking at me.

She hooks a finger around the frames and pulls them down. Her sharp green eyes stare into mine. Dark circles rim her makeup-free lashes. The corners of her lips tick up.

I suddenly have second thoughts about propositioning Brie for a drink in front of Roxy. It's a mental war I engage in briefly before I decide that, oh hell no, I said I'd talk to her, not sponsor her sobriety at AA.

I slide into the chair across from Brie and force a smile. She has finally pulled her attention away from the center-piece. She mouths the word *perfect* so fast that anyone else might miss it.

"You deserve a drink after all the hard work you've done this weekend," I say. "Maybe a champagne—mimosa, Bloody Mary?"

Roxy slides into the seat beside me, and my skin immediately prickles.

"Bloody Mary, double vodka," Roxy says. "If you're buying."

Brie's eyes light up and she plants her butt in a chair. "Ooh, count me in." She does an awkward little cheer in her seat.

Roxy shifts her eyes to mine, smirking. Her expression says *Number three: Grab a beer with Best All-Around*. A Bloody Mary counts. Her pointy, chipped fingernail glides through the air to form a checkmark.

I get the waiter's attention to order, but I don't understand what just happened.

Roxy helped me with the list.

And worse, I *let* her.

CHAPTER 16

I do the right thing and order a fuck-ton of pancakes, bacon (extra crispy), eggs over medium, and deluxe potatoes with cheese, bacon crumbles, and microscopic veggies. Apparently making out with someone else's significant other really fires up the appetite.

That, and accidentally skipping dinner the night before. Oops.

As I slide my menu over to the waiter, Brie watches me with a question in her eyes.

"Can I help you?" I ask Brie as the waiter moves on to Roxy's order. A double order of bacon to go with her second double vodka Bloody Mary.

"I'm just surprised, that's all," Brie says. Her smile is too wide and too white. It's blinding.

"Out with it, Patty Simcox," Roxy says, taking the celery stick out of her glass. She throws back the rest with a satisfied gulp. I smile at the *Grease* reference. Brie frowns and cocks her head to one side, obviously *not* getting it. But her recovery is quick and her smile is like a rubber band that snaps back into place.

"You've been in LA for so long, I thought for sure you'd be vegan."

My answering laugh is ironic. "Oh, *hell* no."

"Yeah, Ellie, where's your hemp necklace and Lululemon camel toe?" Roxy returns her celery stick to gather up what's left at the bottom of her glass, soaking up every last drop.

"LA is a truly divided city," I say, trying and failing to keep up with Roxy on the Bloody Mary front. "Vegans and those who are sick of hearing about veganism."

"And you, miss?" the waiter asks Brie finally.

"I'll have the fruit plate," she says with a dimmed smile before she hands the waiter her own menu. Roxy snorts, and I kick her under the table.

When Brie turns around, her smile is strained. There is word vomit just dying to be hurled into the air between us. Vic once posted a meme on his Facebook wall of a giant piece of broccoli that said: *How can you tell if someone is vegan? Don't worry, they'll fucking tell you.*

Tina, good vegan that she is, didn't speak to him for a week after she saw it. They fought in alternating comments on the picture instead. I stayed far, far away from all of it.

I can tell Brie doesn't want to be one of *those* vegans, but she might also go into cardiac arrest if she doesn't get to say it, so I opt to save her life.

"Are you vegan?" I ask. It's Roxy's turn to kick me.

The floodgates open and suddenly Brie is regaling us with stories of numerous horrifying internet searches about how smart pigs are and how chickens love hugs, and when my plate of eggs and bacon arrive, all I can do is stare at my plate of dead animal friends.

Roxy uses one of her bacon slices to slowly stir her brand-new Bloody Mary before she holds it up to her lips. "Bon appé-fucking-tit," she says with a gentle pig snort before she takes a giant bloody bite.

It's times like these that Roxy reminds me of why she was once my favorite human on the planet. She. Does. Not. Give. A. Shit. And when I was with her, I could almost not give a shit either. She had a way with turning off the chatter in my mind and making it a little bit easier for me to simply live in the moment.

The spell would always inevitably break, though, and I'd go back to my usual, insecure, hyper-perfectionist, judgy self. But right now, with her elbow nudging my rib cage in a sneaky, conspiratorial way, I remember the feeling.

And I've missed it.

"How's round two treating you, Rox?" Brie asks, eyeing Roxy's already half-empty second drink. I glance over at Roxy. Her cheeks aren't even flushed. I'm not done with drink *numero uno* and my tongue is numb.

Roxy ignores Brie's not-so-subtle dig and points at my plate.

"If you don't want your bacon, E, I'll take it," she says to me over a mouthful of smarter-than-dogs meat. I push my plate over to her, and she dumps my extra crispy onto the pile. I decide to fork-attack my stack of pancakes instead.

Brie strikes up a new boring conversation with Sharon Digby and her beefy husband. Sharon is neck-deep in one of those fitness MLMs and she immediately starts to sell Brie on the merits of Metabocraze, a combination workout program and nutritional shake supplement.

My eyes glaze over mid-bite, and too much time passes before I realize I'm staring at Mark. He's at the other end of the table. Christine is between him and Liz, who nods profusely at something Christine just said. On the other side of the table, Brock and Kyle watch some kind of game on Brock's phone, occasionally making sports-lover *oh!* and *ah!* sounds when something exciting happens in the game. Two gross peas in a clichéd pod. I kind of pity Brie's husband, who got pulled away to sit next to her like the perfect pair they are.

When I come out of my bored stupor, Mark's eyebrows are raised at me in a *What?* face.

I shrug, shake my head, and look away. A minute later, my phone lights up on the table. Mark's name pops up on my phone.

Zzzzz.

I try to hide my smile.

I pick up my phone to text him back and say something platonic—"You got that, buddy," and not "Please kiss me again and maybe let's explore this wild monkey sex thing?"—when Roxy grabs my texting hand.

"You need to come with me to the bathroom," she says quietly.

"What? No, I don't," I fire back.

"Yes, you do," she says, yanking me. "You need to hold my hair back while I puke."

She bolts for the bathroom, and I heave a heavy sigh and follow her. Everyone at the table watches me go, pity etched onto their hungover, pancake-stuffed faces. I decide that helping Roxy during an alcoholic purge is infinitely more interesting than staying here with these hypocrites.

When I get to the bathroom, Roxy is not doubled over a toilet as expected. Instead she is leaning against the wall, waiting for me.

"Did I miss the puking part?" I ask.

Roxy's eyes roll. "Please, you really think two drinks is enough to put me under?"

"Two doubles, so it's really more like four."

Roxy shakes her head and snatches my phone.

"What the fuck is this?" she asks with a shit-eating grin, pointing at Mark's message on my screen.

I try to get my phone back, but she holds it away from me. She's taller and in heels, so my efforts to retrieve it are in vain. "Come on, Rox. It's none of your business."

"Didn't he just pull out of Liz like a hot minute ago?" She makes an *O* shape with one hand and inserts her pointer finger from the other, pulling it out for the full effect.

"We're just friends." I sound like the inexperienced former high school nobody that I am deep down inside.

"Nuh-uh, nope, you're not feeding me that line of bullshit." She waits and studies my face. I feel my cheeks flush and I look away. She gasps. "You guys fucked, didn't you?"

"Oh my God, Roxy, no!" My brain flashes an image of kicking her into a stall and shoving her head in a toilet to keep her quiet. Jesus, brain, psychotic much? "We've spent a handful of minutes together. Not enough time for...that." I blush and hate the way her eyes latch onto the new color in my cheeks. "Especially for me."

"Okay, so you didn't fuck, but you did...suck face?"

"No, please, just stop." My voice sounds far away inside my head, and I know that she's got me cornered.

"Aha! You did!" She beams in triumph. "I fucking knew it. I knew there was something going on here."

"I swear to God—"

"Calm down, babe. Your secret is safe with me." Roxy knows me too well for me to deny it now. She walks over to the counter and pulls herself up to sit on it. She leans forward eagerly, because apparently it's story time. "Was it just face sucking, or did you do other stuff, too?"

"Wow, can we *not* call it that? We kissed. Briefly. That's it."

"Okay, but you both *want* to do other stuff, right?" She waggles her eyebrows at me, and I shake my head as hard as I can.

"We're friends. We agreed. End of story."

Roxy snorts. "He's not looking at you like you're friends."

I smile in a coy way, my head all light and full of air, and she shakes her head, snorting. Another conspiracy just the two of us are a part of.

"You're dirty dancing on the fresh grave of Liz's love story." Roxy whistles. "And you love it."

It's at that moment that the woodland sprite, lovely Liz, walks through the door.

CHAPTER 17

Roxy and I both go quiet. Liz pushes through the door, her slingback heels clip-clopping against the tile as she enters the bathroom.

We both stare at her. She stops in her tracks. One eyebrow shoots up.

A slow smile spreads across her face. "Talking about me?"

I am Rizzo and she is Sandy from *Grease*. How did this happen? In high school I was the quiet, shy, naïve type. Adorable, sweater-set-wearing, doe-eyed Ellie. Now I'm the vixen with the wobbly morals, out for blood.

Roxy laughs and out-*Rizzos* me. "What we *need* to talk about are those bubble bangs."

Liz sighs and touches her forehead. "I gave my stylist a picture of Taylor Swift and came out looking like Zooey Deschanel."

"I think it's cute," I counter. She touches the puff of her bangs, her hand running down the length of her side braid to pinch the end. A twinkle glints in her eye—gratitude I *so* don't deserve.

She disappears into a stall. A hard knot of guilt forms in my gut. I look at Roxy with my best deer-in-headlights face, and she rolls her eyes.

"How long were you and Marky Mark together before you called it quits?" Roxy asks with a raised voice, leaning back against the sink and examining her nails. She has no shame. The tiny bathroom echoes with a steady stream of pee. Kill me now. I widen my eyes at Roxy, but she isn't looking at me. She's picking a chip of polish and flicking it onto the tile floor.

"Um, we were engaged for a little under two years." Liz's voice is soft when she replies. "We've been—I mean, we got together during my senior year of college."

"Since college!" Roxy exclaims, her expression a study in hyperbolic shock. "Wow. How'd you meet?"

I have to gulp back a laugh. I can't help it.

The toilet finally flushes, and Liz emerges from the stall. Roxy turns on the faucet for her. She looks appreciative as she rinses her hands.

"At college," she says with a shrug, like it's the most boring, typical meet-cute ever. And it is. "At this trashy bar called Jimmy's on Green Street. It was my twenty-first birthday and I was really drunk or else I probably wouldn't have said anything—but I spotted him from across the bar, and it felt like destiny."

Roxy hands Liz a towel to dry off, but she looks ready to actually barf now.

Liz nods her thanks as she accepts the towel and continues her story: "I walked right up to him and told him I'd had a crush on him in high school. He had no clue who I was, but he bought me a drink and we talked for a long time, and then he walked me back to my dorm after my friends bailed on me. And I kind of...instantly fell in love."

Her eyes sparkle with tears, and I mentally kick Roxy for making Liz take this trip down memory lane when the road is already closed.

"Wow, you fell hard," Roxy says, trying not to sound bored.

"Maybe too hard," Liz says, a sad smile playing across her face. She pretends to fix her eyeliner in the mirror, but I can see her catch a tear under her eye before it falls.

My stomach twists with guilt. Even though they're technically broken up, Liz isn't even *trying* to pretend she's not still head over heels. I think about the kiss between me and Mark last night, and how he went home after to a house he shares with a girl who's still in love with him. With a girl who last week at this time still had a ring on her finger.

For fuck's sake.

Roxy's eyes sparkle with mischief. What is she up to? "You know how guys are right before taking the plunge. Cold feet and all that. Maybe this split isn't permanent."

Liz bites a tiny lip. Her eyes are big, glassy, and hopeful, like maybe there's still a chance. I remember the way she looked at him at the reunion, with so much unrequited longing.

Roxy is the literal worst for stoking the suffocating flames of her affection. I glare daggers at her. Her tongue is swift, in and out, like the snake she can be.

"I mean, you're still living together." Stoke, stoke, stoke. "Maybe he's just getting something out of his system."

She's the worst, and she lives for it. Only she and I know

the *something* he may need to get out of his system is tongue tangling with me.

I decide to chime in. "Should we rejoin the group?"

"Hold on." Roxy puts a hand out. *Wait.* "But do you *really* want to get back together with this douchebag?"

I watch as Liz's doe eyes stare up at Roxy, the Big Bad Wolf. Roxy has a way of hypnotizing her prey. Those eyes, sharp green and wide. The way her voice rasps, rough and husky. You adore her even as you're bleeding and gasping for air, her claws sinking deeper and deeper into your back.

"He's not a...douchebag," Liz chokes out the word like she might go to hell for saying it. She's so pure. "He's just a little lost. His dad still hasn't forgiven him for bailing on med school. They had a really big fight about it last Christmas, and they're still not on speaking terms."

Whoa, hold up. Mark's not talking to his dad?

That certainly explains the quarter-life crisis.

"I think I've had one too many," she says. She holds up the back of her hand to her flushed cheeks. "I probably shouldn't be telling you all of this."

"Mark's secret is safe with us." Roxy mimes locking her mouth and tossing the key over her shoulder. Liz smiles gratefully.

"He's just going through something right now," Liz says. Her eyes flick to mine and away. Barely detectable, but notable nonetheless. "I just hope he knows that when the dust settles and he finds what he's looking for, I'll still be here."

She's failed, or maybe refused, to acknowledge the crux of the issue—that Mark doesn't seem to want to be *here*, in Stonybrook, at all. He's not fulfilled by his life here or the choices he's already made. He can't change the past, but knowing what you don't want is the first step in knowing what you *do* want.

And Liz doesn't seem to be on board with what he *doesn't* want.

It's dismissive, and to be honest, it kind of pisses me off.

"What if that's not what he wants?" I ask. The question is sharp, like a razor blade, and her head snaps to look at me. *Wee-oo-wee-oo*, we need damage control. I compose myself, and add: "To stay here, I mean."

"Then he and I can sort that out," she says, her eyes narrowed, possessive. "Together." The meaning is clear.

There's a long, loaded pause among us, and Roxy's eyes dart back and forth between me and Liz. It's a standoff, and she's waiting with bated breath to see who lands the final blow.

After a few tense seconds, Liz finally stands down. "I should go back," she says.

Roxy opens the door to let her out. She waits for the door to swing shut behind Liz before clapping a hand over her mouth and ducking into a stall.

I spin around to face her with my arms crossed over my chest. She sits fully clothed on the toilet, trying and failing to muffle maniacal laughter.

"Could you please?" I ask, worried that Liz will hear.

"She is delusional with a capital *D*."

I ignore the fluttering of hope in my chest. *Bad heart. Bad.*

"They're *never* getting back together," Roxy adds, in case I didn't already put two and two together.

"They've only been broken up for a week," I say. "Plenty of people get back together after a breakup. Get married. Churn out a brood of strawberry-headed children."

"Psh. If I was a betting woman"—Roxy raises her brows—"and I am, I'd bet you two will bump uglies before the end of the weekend." She stands up, places her hands on my shoulders, and squeezes. It's a surprisingly gentle form of affection that catches me off guard. "Strike while the iron is hot."

I run my hands through my hair. "I'm not really a striker."

She waits.

"You know I'm not." The words are a whisper, but she hears them, and instead of gutting my vulnerable underbelly, she winks, offering a swift smile of reassurance.

"But you could be."

I don't let my lips form the words, but I think them.

BEFRI STENDS, two fucking weirdos who somehow get each other no matter how much time goes by. I don't know how, but I think she wants to say it too.

She pinches my chin, before snapping back into her usual brazen self, and throwing the door open, strutting through it dramatically. "Garçon," she says with a quick snap of her fingers. I'm sure there will be a giant loogie in Roxy's next drink, and I'm sure she doesn't even care.

After brunch is over, Brock Crawley attempts to pick up the bill for the whole table, but I manage to intercept the waiter and grab mine and Brie's. It's more than just paying for drinks, but it still does the trick. Number three on the list is done. I'm going to check off these items, come hell or high water.

Roxy's finally had enough Bloody Marys to start slurring her words. She digs through her purse to find her keys, and as soon as she has them in hand, Brock snatches them away from her.

"Come on, Foxy," Brock says, putting an arm around Roxy's shoulder. I take note that he's just a little too friendly with the gross nickname, and Christine exchanges a look with Liz, who's also riding with the Crawleys since she and Christine have to coach cheer practice this afternoon.

I'm just glad Roxy is going on with them; otherwise, I'd feel responsible for getting her home. And frankly, I don't need any more guilt to add to the pot.

Roxy's slightly dilated eyes find mine. For some reason, I know this isn't goodbye.

Not yet.

Liz gives me a polite hug goodbye, and her eyes trail to Mark, my ride, before climbing in beside Roxy. Mark and I are the only ones left standing in the parking lot.

I climb into the front seat and buckle up. He walks around the front of the car, scrubbing his hand through his hair, before yanking the door handle and sliding in. We drive in silence, my eyes on the fall colors passing by us in a blur of red, orange, fading brown.

"I always miss Ohio this time of year," I say quietly.

"It's the best part about being here."

That single sentence says so much, but I don't tell him. I don't think I've earned that kind of assessment. But when I look at him, written on his every feature I can see the knowledge of all he's not saying out loud.

I have to look away.

When I was a kid, I waited for the bus in the morning with my dad and a few other kids who lived on my dead-end street. As the school year progressed, each morning would get cooler and cooler, and to distract us while we waited, Dad would use a stick to rip open the silk cocoons tucked into the neighbor's gate. We'd gather around him and watch in awe as a frustrated spider crawled out and immediately went back to work repairing the damage to his winter home.

I imagine Mark must feel like the spider in my memory, like his life was just ripped open, leaving behind a gaping hole. And he has to decide whether he wants to crawl back in and repair the mess or start over and settle somewhere else entirely.

"Sorry about your dad," I say finally. He looks over at me, surprised. "Roxy coaxed it out of Liz with her claws."

Mark's jaw clenches, and he doesn't respond right away.

"He's still not over me deciding not to go to medical school," Mark finally says, almost in a whisper. "He thinks I'm a loser."

"He doesn't think that," I say. I can't pull my eyes away from his face. "Did he actually say 'You're a loser'?" I cut him a skeptical side-eye.

"He might as well have." His lips twist into a grimace. "He still brings up med school every time I see him, and it's been almost six years. I've told him one hundred times that it's what *he* wanted for me, not what *I* wanted. But he thinks film is a joke, and he doesn't even own a TV."

I huff. "I hate that. People who brag about not owning a TV drive me nuts."

"He is *that* person. Self-righteous, always knows best. Unless you're saving people's lives, you're not worthy."

Yikes. Mark's dad sounds like a hard-ass.

"There's no way he's that great of a doctor if he treats people like that," I say.

"Oh no, Dr. Rick Wright has an impeccable bedside manner," Mark says. "He saves all his unreasonable expectations and relentless disapproval for his kids."

"You're not a loser, Mark." I say it again. I wouldn't have a crush on a loser. But I don't add that part.

Mark's hands clench on the steering wheel. "Maybe I am."

"You're not," I say. "You're allowed to need time to figure out your life."

He doesn't respond, and I can't help but wonder what he's thinking, about his choices, his future. Marriage and all the stuff he once let himself believe were the right things to do, only to watch it all crumble like ruins in front of him. It's enough to make anyone question how they got where they are, and where they're heading. He clearly doesn't want to talk about any of it, and I really don't need or have the right to become more involved, so I lean back in my seat and close my eyes. The kaleidoscope of dying leaves outside my window and the tornado of emotion I want to repress are making me dizzy.

The car stops and my eyes open to a place that's unfamiliar and unexpected. We're parked in a driveway among a Stepford wives development of duplex condos.

I frown. "Is this the part where I end up on *Dateline*?"

Mark chuckles and unbuckles his seat belt. "What's with you and murder?" he asks before he gets out of the car.

I follow him, confused by this turn of events. "For one thing, there are over—"

"Two hundred active serial killers in the United States. I know."

I pout. "Maybe thousands. It's not like they include *serial killer* on the US Census."

He laughs and fumbles with his keychain until he lands on the house key. "How many items are left on the list?"

The vise around my stomach unclenches. Duh, the list. Mark wants me to read his script, and we agreed I'd read it *after* he helped me finish the *Ellie Is Cool Now* list.

Mark unlocks the front door to the home he shares with Liz. He pushes the door open and steps aside so I can go in first.

The inside is so Midwestern that it hurts my eyes. Everything is brown and cherry wood. The decor is an offensive mix of IKEA, Home Depot, and Grandma's hand-me-downs. There's even a pink floral chair they've tried to hide with a hand-knitted afghan beside the front living room window. The couch has a set of folded-up sheets and a pillow on it. It hits me that I'm standing in Mark Wright's current bedroom, and Teenage Ellie squeals from somewhere deep down inside.

I tell her to shut it. There are boxes shoved to one corner, closed and marked with various labels. Books. Dvds. Playstation Shit. This isn't exactly the stuff of young Ellie's wet dreams. This is the battleground of a breakup in progress.

"What do you think?" he asks. I hear the keys hit the counter before Mark takes off his coat. I nibble on my lip, trying to find something nice to say before remembering that I don't care.

"I hate it," I say.

"Good," he says behind me, too close. I'm sure I'm dead serial killer meat as his hands find my hips and spin me around to face him.

But instead of a knife, it's his lips. On mine. His hands. On my hips. His breath. On my cheek. I taste his tongue, laced with coffee and syrup, sharp and sweet, and heady with wanting. It slices through my resolve, killing every sensible thought in my head.

Not a knife, but a kiss that cuts just as deep. I will never recover.

It's only been two days, but I've been waiting fifteen years, and it's finally happening. He's finally here. Snarky, imperfect, sexy—and kissing me.

It washes over me like a tidal wave, slowly at first until suddenly I'm drowning.

I'm falling for Mark Wright. Not the teenage fantasy, but the man.

For real this time.

CHAPTER 18

I don't know how or when I ended up on a steel gray IKEA couch, my shirt coming untucked from my jeans, my skin flushed with the heat of Mark Wright's kisses edging over the line of my jaw, but here I am. Just a minute ago, his lips hit mine and shook my world like an eight-magnitude California earthquake.

It's the Big One.

Love?

I mentally shoo the word away, tuck it into the cushions of his couch, to be unearthed at a later date.

Cut to—my fingers burying themselves in his ruffled hair. His hands exploring the curves of my ass and thighs, trailing close, closer to the waistband of my jeans. Every touch is tentative, like we really are two teenagers just discovering each other for the first time. All stops and starts of heat-soaked friction. Curious hands and bated breath. It's all surreal, living out this Teenage Ellie fantasy in real time.

He fumbles when his hand reaches up under my blouse, his warmth spreading over the bare skin of my waist. For a split second, he pulls back. His lips are swollen and pink from kissing, his eyes dilated with desire. He presses his forehead to mine and exhales.

"You're a really good kisser," he breathes, searching my eyes. My blush is so strong, I have to bury my face in the side of the couch. He laughs and his lips trail down my bared neck. He gently bites my collarbone and it sends me...right into a moment of clarity.

We're in the house he shares with another woman.

A nice girl who would be crushed if she saw us together like this, even if she doesn't have a claim to his heart, or his lips, anymore.

"Mark," I say, then the tip of his tongue flicks the tender skin where my jaw meets my ear and my knees squeeze together, pushing back the flood of ache surging through my hips. He breathes my name into my collarbone and continues his downward spiral of kisses. Before I lose it completely, I touch his shoulder and push him away so I can look into his eyes.

"Liz," I say, pointing to a picture of them together in a silver frame on their mantel next to some faux flowers and Yankee candles. Liz flashes her sparkly smile to the camera. I can see every last pearly white tooth.

He looks behind me at the silver frame in question before hanging his head, his hair tickling my chin. He swears at my still fully covered boobs, and I'm glad he hasn't yet been made privy to my highly practical flesh-colored T-shirt bra.

He looks up and sighs before dipping his head back down. "I need to get rid of that," he whispers against the curve of my earlobe before he bites it. This biting thing—I could get very used to it.

I arch my back and my breasts press against his chest. He groans. "You could burn it," I say, breathless. "Give it a proper Viking burial."

Mark pushes himself into a sitting position, pulling me up with him. "We could cut them apart. Her disembodied hand on my shoulder, my floating arm around her waist."

He tugs at my blouse. "Can I take this off?"

Oooh, consent. We like a man who asks first. I reward him by taking it off for him, T-shirt bra be damned.

He looks at me then, taking in every inch he can see.

We both slowly turn to look at Liz smiling back at us from the mantel, haunting us.

"Damn it," I say, before picking up my shirt again. He watches me longingly; his sigh is deep with disappointment.

I look down at my state of disarray. Wait, when did my jeans come unzipped? I zip up the fly and finger comb the snarls out of my hair, and scoot back away from him. Mark takes a cue from me and resituates himself, running his hand through his own wildly disheveled hair.

"Why can't she be awful?" I pull my wrinkled pink top over my head. "This would still be weird, but I might enjoy it more."

A small smile plays on his lips as he watches me try to smooth the creases in my shirt before putting it back on. "In *The Parent Trap*," I say, "we don't care when their dad gets back together with his ex-wife, because his fiancée is a gold-digging C-U-next-Tuesday."

"Why can't real life be *just* like the movies?" He's being

sarcastic, but he scoots closer to me and touches my silky pink shoulder. I pull my shirt down and begin tucking it into my jeans as another line of defense.

"But you—*you* have to pick out the syrupy-sweetest ex-fiancée in the history of engagements, and she's still clinging to the hope that you'll come back around."

"Come on, she knows it's over between us," Mark says. "She's not as simple or sweet as you think."

I give him an *are-you-serious* look. "She's like a gummy bear personified. And she's definitely still in love with you."

"She'll get over me."

I didn't, I want to say, but that feels way too heavy. Too real, again, and more vulnerable than I am comfortable being today, maybe ever. He leans, fingers running along my collar to gingerly trace my collarbone. A shiver runs down my spine. His fingers slide up to my chin, thumb touching the edge of my lip. I want to melt into him like ice cream. Like warm hot fudge. With whipped cream and a cherry on top. Come to think of it—

"Do you have ice cream?" I ask him.

Mark's raises an eyebrow. "We just ate."

"Your point is?"

I freeze my complicated feelings with a bowl of chocolate ice cream drizzled with chocolate syrup (the more chocolate, the better) and continue to lament the awfulness of this situation.

We're sitting on Liz's couch. Eating from her bowl. Licking creamy chocolatey goodness from her spoon—and also her ex-fiancé's lips.

"You really are a horrible person," I say to Mark finally. "You were always kind of a dick, but now you've crossed the line and you are *definitely* going to hell."

He laughs outright.

"What about you?" he asks before he picks up my spoon and scoops a melty bite into his mouth. "You keep saying all these nice things about Liz, but you *definitely* kissed me back."

"I've been into you since the sixth grade."

His eyes go wide. Okay. So he didn't know that part.

Of course he didn't, Ellie. You mostly acted like he didn't exist.

My cheeks are on fire, but I decide to blow past it and play it cool. Like my ice cream.

"I was basically in a fantasy relationship with you inside my head for seven years." I stop, do the math. "Fully one-fourth of my life."

He blinks in shock.

I shrug and dig back in, sucking some now-chocolate-soup from the spoon. "As pathetic as it is, this is pretty much my lifelong dream, so yeah, I fucking kissed you back."

He says nothing, just stares. My resolve starts to crack.

Fucking Liz doesn't have a clue how much longer I have wanted this than she has.

Not that it gives me the right to swoop in and ruin any chance of her getting what she wants.

But *still*.

Words tumble from my lips. Mark is the priest, and this is my confession.

"I used to spend nights lying awake, imagining what it would be like to kiss you."

My walls are caving in, toppling down around me, and there's nothing I can do to hold them up.

"What it would be like to go to the movies with you and not watch the movie. To hold hands at football games and steal kisses in the hallways at school when the teachers weren't looking."

Years of pent-up emotions and well-kept secrets spill from my lips like Niagara Falls. If I'm drowning, he's drowning with me.

There's still a part of me, deep down, that wants to snuff out whatever this thing is, to show him what a weirdo I was, what a weirdo I *am*, so I can get back to LA and get on with my life. We can pretend none of this ever happened. The fantasy can live on inside my head where it belongs.

Unchanged and perfect.

But I keep telling him the truth, and he keeps looking at me like I'm more than just a former Miscellaneous kid who grew up and got a better wardrobe and a dream job. His eyes are on me, watching my every move. His lips are parted like he might launch forward and kiss me again. My secrets consume us like wildfire.

I double-down on the crazy.

"We'd take graduation photos together. Our parents would be so against it, but we'd apply to the same school, get into the same school, go to the same school. Maybe elope in Vegas when we're twenty-one. High school sweethearts from beginning to fucking end."

My shoulders drop, relief flooding my whole body because it's finally out there, and it feels *so* good to not be the only one who knows. I wait for an *oh, look at the time!*, but it never comes. Instead, Mark searches my eyes for a long time before he says, "You're *definitely* a writer."

His hand leaves a trail of heat as he traces down my shoulder, my arm, my wrist, until it reaches my hand. His fingers interlace with mine, and his thumb strokes over my knuckles with the lightest touch. I close my eyes as the heat from his hands travels all the way up my arm and through my chest until it finally drops and settles dangerously low in my belly.

When I open my eyes again, his eyes are closed. I examine his face, since I've never gotten this close to look at him before. His skin is pale olive and his eyelashes are long. A few well-placed moles dot his skin near his lips and his cheek. His cheeks are slim and his jaw is elegantly defined. He's not the most attractive man I've ever seen, but I've never met a man I've been more attracted to. It's a paradox I've never been able to shake.

When his eyes open again, he catches me staring. I don't even look away, because what's the point now? He knows everything. The deepest secret and weirdest obsession of my life is out of the closet and on the table.

His eyes stay locked with mine, but it takes me a full minute to realize he's not going to initiate this time.

The ball is in my court. It was always in my court. I spent my entire childhood keeping it locked away because I was afraid. Afraid of losing the game. Afraid of life not turning out like it does in the movies.

Fantasies are fantasy for a reason. They're not real. But this moment *is*, and it's my choice to seize it or lock it away forever.

I lean forward and touch my lips to his.

His lips are soft and cold and taste like chocolate ice cream. We warm them up fast.

He takes the bowl of now-liquid from my lap and sets it behind him so he can scoot closer to me. His hands touch my waist first and then circle around to my back.

The fire burns slow this time. Clothes don't fly off in a hurry to snuff it out. We let our kisses build to a blazing crescendo.

Right now Mark *is* mine. He was mine before he even met Liz; he just didn't know it.

We're both lost in space and time. I feel like I'm in high school all over again. I'm sixteen, kissing the boy of my dreams, falling in love for the first time. We'll go to school tomorrow, and he'll meet me at my locker and offer to carry my books. I won't let him because it's not 1950, but he'll kiss me on the cheek and everyone will know.

I have no idea how long we sit on the couch, slow kissing and time traveling, but when the door opens and something hits the floor like a bomb, I feel the whiplash as my brain snaps back to reality.

Liz stands in the doorway, a bag of groceries exploded at her feet, still wearing her red and gold cheer coach uniform. Milk leaks from one of the paper bags in a ring around her shoes, but she doesn't move. She just stands there, staring at us in shock.

Mark leaps to his feet.

All traces of sweetness drain from her countenance and are instead replaced by the scariest expression I have ever seen on such a tiny human. Like a gremlin someone just fed after midnight.

I will never eat gummy bears again.

"What the fuck, Mark?"

CHAPTER 19

I thought you weren't going to be back until four," Mark spits out.

Stop talking.

Oh my God.

"We got done early." Her nose is red and her eyes are wet, but she's holding in the waterworks for now.

It's impossible to look away from the carnage.

Spilled milk spreads out in a pool, covering the entry room rug, splashing against the crushed bread bag, seeping into the slats of the wood floor. An egg carton flopped open and now sticky yellow yolk stains the side of Liz's white Keds.

It's a crime scene, and I'm a serial kisser.

Momentarily, my eyes flick to the back of Mark's head. He runs his fingers through his hair, yanking the sides so they stick out straight like a shot of electricity went through them. I can see the swirl of a cowlick at the crown, and suddenly I'm remembering all the times I sat staring at it in homeroom, all through high school, and I can't help it. I smile.

"Are you *smiling*?" Liz asks, her voice vibrating at a frequency of kill. She takes a single step closer to me, and Mark moves into her path. His hand stretches out to stop her, and she glares at it like her eyes can set it on fire.

"Wow." She laughs, but her lips twist like she has a bad taste in her mouth. "So all those questions about Mark in the bathroom at Murphy's—it wasn't encouragement. It was an interrogation." *Bang-bang-bang*, I shot the ex-fiancée right in the heart.

Her eyes are shiny with tears. My own eyes burn—just like the tip of my tongue—with all I'm not saying.

I'm sorry, but I'm not sorry—and—*if you want to take the island, you've got to burn the boats*. Their relationship is already dead, and this is the Viking funeral pyre.

We stare at each other for a blistering second.

I know I should feel bad. No matter what their relationship status is. No matter how much I've always wanted to make out with Mark Wright. We've defiled her couch with our make-out session. Not exactly role model behavior. Not even a little bit fair to anyone here, especially her.

I know I should feel bad, but I don't. Maybe I'm just a terrible person. Hopeless, incurable.

I think back to my initial conversation with Andy (a lifetime ago, it seems) and his nebulous explanation for why he was forcing me to go to my high school reunion.

A fresh perspective, my ass.

Liz flicks her eyes from me to Mark, beaming lasers of death through him. He doesn't turn to ash, but his cheeks burn red from the heat of her gaze.

"Fuck," he breathes. I get a sick feeling in my stomach.

She clutches her house keys in her hand so hard, I am one thousand percent sure she's going to draw blood.

"Fuck is right." Her voice sounds calm, but her eyes are murderous. She lunges at him. The keys are a weapon. He puts his hands up to shield himself from her wrath unleashed. "The least you could have done is get a cheap motel room to fuck her in so I don't have walk in on it."

Oh. Shit.

I slide behind the couch, hoping to use it as a shield should she maim him and then decide to come for me. The woodland sprite has become a screaming banshee. It's ferocious and personal. I'm embarrassed to be watching. She's saying things like *We were going to have kids in this house* and *We haven't even divided up our coffee mugs yet.*

"I asked you to pick which ones you wanted!" Mark's voice cuts through the screaming panic of Liz's. She stops shouting and goes eerily quiet, her lip quivering as tears stream down her face in anguish. "I'm sorry. I'm an asshole," he says. All his bullshit beliefs about Liz moving on were wrong. He's hurt her again, somehow, so much worse than when he took his ring back.

"You're a spineless *fucking asshole*," she edits. It might be the meanest thing she's ever said to anyone. "It's been *one week*."

Mark doesn't even flinch. He just watches her rage dissolve into sobs. She covers her face with her hands, and he says nothing else—just calmly wraps his arms around her, and she lets him.

Jesus. I don't want to watch this. I don't want to hear about how much he still cares about her. I don't want to see her wither in his arms and drink in the moment and know it's probably the last time. It's heartbreaking, but not just because it's the fiery wreckage to a would-be marriage, but because they still care about each other, and in this moment it's glaringly obvious.

He's not in love with her, but he loves her. There's history and baggage and familiarity. It's the most selfish I've ever been in my life, but I want to be the Mark Wright expert whose coffee cups mingle with his in our shared cabinet space. I want to go back to a time when there wasn't all this complicated life stuff in our way.

No *me* getting in our way.

I back away, my eyes darting around the room for another exit. There has to be more than one door. That's like a fire code violation or something. From my vantage point, I can see that the dining room connects to the kitchen, and I don't know, but I hope against hope that there is a back door.

I try to noiselessly scoot past the side table with all their framed photos on it. My eyes catch on one of those frames you get at Michaels with little ceramic hearts attached to the wood. The kind of kitschy shit girls in love usually adore. In the picture, Mark is holding Liz from behind, the side of his face pressed lightly against her hair. She looks so damn happy— laughing, the wind whipping her strawberry strands around her head. Then there's Mark, and he's much more subdued than she is, sunglasses hiding his eyes, but he's still smiling that signature smirk of his.

A smile I know is totally real.

Once upon a time, he did love her with his whole heart. He may not now, but he's still not totally free to fall for someone else. I'm so focused on the picture that I don't notice my foot slide too far to the left and hit the table leg.

Everything begins to topple like glass dominoes of their life together.

I spring forward, trying to stop them from breaking but making it so much worse. My purse hits the ceramic heart frame, and it crashes to the ground, shattering.

Not the smooth getaway I was hoping for.

I squint up at both of them. They've stopped talking to stare at me. Liz's face is now stained with tears, the hair in her side braid coming out in wavy tendrils. Mark's eyes lock with mine.

"Apparently, I'm not very good at sneaking out," I admit, uneasy under their gaze, especially Liz's.

"I can take you home," Mark says.

Liz's tear-stained face turns to stone. "No," she spits. She rips off her Keds and throws them across the room, slipping her feet into a pair of boots by the door. "I'll take her home."

Hold the fuck on—

Sadness mixes with rebellion in Mark's eyes. He knows what he's done—what we've done—is wrong, and there's no telling how long it'll take for them to resolve everything, but he doesn't want to let me walk out, either.

His inner conflict is clearly written all over his face.

Liz grabs the car keys. "Come on, Ellie."

Hell no.

I turn to Mark, panicked. Taking a car ride with the girl whose almost-husband I just made out with is a hard. Fuck-ing. Pass.

"That's a horrible—" Mark starts.

"My dad can totally come get me," I interrupt, fumbling in my purse for my phone.

"I have things to say," Liz says, stepping around the mess of destroyed groceries on the floor and opening the front door. Her voice is firm as she waves me forward. "Let's go."

I don't know why, but for a split second I think *This is a version of Liz I can get behind. Fierce. Resolved. A little bit mean.*

I still don't want to get in a car with her behind the wheel, but I feel like my hands are tied. I'm not a fast runner, and I don't think I can get away without her following me to mow me down with her car. With one more sideways glance at Mark, who looks like he's just had his stomach kicked in, I gingerly step away from their broken-picture-framed life and speed-walk through the door toward her car.

I climb into the passenger seat and slam the door, buckling and tightening my seat belt, sucking in a panicked breath. I can see Liz's lips moving, Mark tucking his hands in his jean pockets, and then she's walking, face all screwed up, across the tiny front lawn.

When she's inside the car, she cranks the ignition, hard, and slides it into gear. Backing out almost gives me whiplash. I clutch my purse to my chest for protection. For how fast she zipped out of the driveway, she takes the road out of their neighborhood at a glacial pace. Slow and unnerving. Her face cold as ice.

I stare out the window at a mom walking her napping baby in a stroller, her eyes on her phone, paying no attention to the woman who's about to be brutally murdered.

The mom easily passes us.

Liz should just get on with it. Whatever she wants to

say to me, she should just lay it all out. When she eases to a stop before turning left out of the neighborhood, her hands slide from the wheel. She just sits there, looking out the front windshield, mom and baby crossing the street and ambling away.

Is she waiting for her to be gone so there will be no witnesses?

"He could have gotten you a room at the Marriott," Liz finally says. "You don't seem like a cheap motel kind of girl."

"I prefer a Hilton," I say, but it's more of a croak.

"I'm not sorry I said it." She cuts her eyes across me, turning on her completely unnecessary blinker. The tick-tick-tick fills the car. "But you aren't the problem."

She turns, accelerating at an almost normal rate. We overtake the walking mom, pass her, and turn onto the main road through town.

"It takes two to make out on a couch," I finally say to the inside of my purse. Liz's lips twitch and she nods. I'm not the problem, but I'm not off the hook, either.

"He's not the same guy I fell in love with," Liz says, her eyes a little hazy, like she's remembering. "We used to love all the same things. Same movies, same pizza toppings. We liked to take long walks in the park, eat breakfast for dinner."

If all this is true, the Mark and Liz union was so quaint it makes me almost want to barf. Definitely dangerously close to Boring Life Wife—no, just Boring Life—territory.

"I really noticed the distance after what happened between him and his dad. We fought about everything to do with the wedding—I could tell he wasn't into it. He was pulling away from me. Maybe he was struggling with how it made him feel—I don't know. I just wanted things to be normal, and he wanted everything in our life to be different. Then he didn't want our life anymore at all."

Her words are almost a stream of consciousness. She's trying to understand, trying to get to a place of closure, but she's been holding on for so long she's not sure how.

"I just didn't expect him to make out with some random girl in our living room before our relationship was even cold in the ground."

Wow. Random? I guess it looks random to her. Little does she know…

I bite down on my lip before replying.

"I wasn't planning on any of this happening. I just needed his help with a list."

From her side profile, I can see Liz's brows fold in like she's furrowing them. She stops at a red light, and looks over, raising both eyebrows in question. I pull my phone from my purse. It's full of new texts from Vic and Tina, but there are a couple of missed calls from a number I don't recognize. Whoever it was didn't leave a voicemail. Nothing from Mark. Thankfully. He knows I'm still in the car with Liz, and while I'm sure he's flipping out, he would be a complete idiot to text me right now.

Salt in this gaping wound.

I unlock the phone, scroll to my photo of the list, and show her. After a second, she looks up, straight into my eyes, and asks, "High school crush?"

Her voice cracks on the word.

I pull my hand back, nodding. "Since middle school."

Fuck. Somehow Liz actually looks sorry for me.

Oh hell no.

"I thought I was over him," I say, quickly. "For *years* I thought I was. I hadn't even thought about Mark Wright, or high school, since I walked out the front doors and never looked back."

Well, that's not exactly true. But Liz doesn't need to know about the Facebook message of doom.

I continue: "Not until my stupid showrunner forced me to complete this ridiculous list and promised me a promotion if I came to this godforsaken reunion."

Thanks again, Andy. I'll have to remember to send him cyanide chocolates when all this is over.

The light turns green. Liz starts driving again, but I can tell she's mulling the whole thing over.

"And Mark is helping you?" She sounds almost hopeful. Like she wants Mark to still be the guy she wanted to marry, the same guy who loved Stonybrook and wanted to grow old here. That guy might have helped me out of the goodness of his heart, and might still come back to her at the end of all this.

That guy isn't the Mark I made out with on the couch.

Maybe he never really was.

"He is." She deserves to know the truth, but Mark should be the one to tell her.

She turns down my street. Dad is out front doing some early fall pruning in the flower bed. As she pulls up, letting the car idle, he looks over, grins, and waves when he sees me in the passenger seat. I give him a tight smile, tiny wave.

We sit in awkward silence for another overlong beat. Can I get out? Is it rude to just...bolt? Cut and fucking run?

My hand hovers at the door handle. She doesn't stop me. So I pull it, flicking my eyes to her once before climbing out and letting the door slam shut. She peels out before I even take the step up to the sidewalk. My phone buzzes, that unfamiliar number calling again. I roll my eyes and answer. It's probably a robocall.

"Hello?" I say, pressing the phone lightly to my ear, ready to hang up. I wave again to my dad as I pass him on my way to the front door.

"Meet me at the school tonight at five." I immediately recognize the voice. When Roxy Draper is happy she sounds like an evil villain who just vanquished the king and seized the kingdom. I feel my lips twitch with a smile at the sound.

Roxy. Happy.

On the phone with me.

"How did you get my number?" I ask, curiosity piqued.

"I have connections." I hear the smirk in her voice. "Five. Outside the school gymnasium."

"Why?" I ask, a fool taking her bait.

"Wear something spirited."

Then she's gone.

CHAPTER 20

I have nothing "spirited" to wear, and I also don't know what Roxy actually means by *spirited*.

School colors?

A rented cheerleader costume?

My face painted like a tiger with little *W*s on my cheeks?

I fall back against my bed, yanking my *Hello Kitty* pillow over my head. Everything goes blissfully dark, momentarily peaceful. Except for my thoughts, which bounce back and forth like a Ping-Pong ball during a pro tournament.

From Mark's hands brushing under my shirt, rough fingertips against soft skin—

To the crash, splash of the milk carton—

To the way his skin smelled like fresh soap and his mouth tasted like syrup—

To the crack of their perfect picture frame, from their formerly perfect life—

My phone buzzes incessantly somewhere beside me on the bed.

I reach over, feeling around for it until my hand lands on the smooth surface. Lifting it to my ear, I say: "Ellie Jenkins, life-ruiner, destroyer of wedding fantasies, queen of avoidance—at your service."

"You forgot to say future co-EP of *Cooler Than You*," Vic chirps on the other line. My lips wobble at the sound of his voice.

"And Greta's honorary auntie," Tina adds. "Why can't we see your face?"

I sit up, hugging the pillow as I blink into the light. I hold out the phone, watching them vie for space in Vic's computer webcam. Tina fluffs her hair and puckers, which receives an eye roll from Vic, who then looks at me straight on, his nose nearly pressing into the camera.

"You've been dodging us," he says.

"I've been busy."

"Busy. Every flake's go-to excuse."

"He's right." Tina nods, winking into the camera. "And flake is *my* shtick, thunder stealer. So what gives?"

They both wait, watching me in the camera like I'm prime time TV.

"You know number ten on the list?" I ask, crossing my legs and slumping down over my pillow.

"Get your high school crush to help with at least one item on the list," Vic says with a shrug and a smirk. "My favorite."

"He helped me." I suck in a breath. "Like, a lot."

Vic and Tina lean forward into the camera, eyes bulging.

"Tell me more, tell me more," Tina sings in a high-pitched voice, doing her best impression of the Pink Ladies from *Grease*.

"Like does he have a car," Vic finishes in falsetto.

They both start to snap and sing in unison. "Uh-huh, uh-huh…" and I really must stop them before they start dancing.

"We kissed."

Their karaoke dissolves into squeals. I turn the volume down on my phone so my parents don't think I smuggled two stuck pigs home from brunch.

"Also, he just got out of an engagement and still lives with his ex." I face-palm as squeals turn into gasps and expletives.

"You dirty dog!" Vic puts a hand over his heart in shock. "Did she walk in on you two swapping spit?"

"This is better than *The Kardashians*," Tina says. "Hold on, I need to freshen my rosé." She sets Greta on Vic's lap. He begins aggressively scratching behind Greta's ears.

"Andy asked us for an update, by the way," Vic says. "So…" We lock eyes in the camera. He wants the whole story, but I know he'll give Andy the edited-for-TV version. I wish I could reach through the phone and tackle-hug him for his loyalty.

When Tina's back, I weave a Daytime Emmy–worthy tale based on my own ridiculous real life. I omit nothing, and even include the twist with Roxy showing up and inserting herself into my quest without my permission. When I finish, Tina leans back and lets out a substantial sigh. Vic taps his lips, thinking and absently stroking Greta's head while she sleeps.

"So what you're saying is, thanks to Andy—"

"And Vic and me—" Tina interjects.

"And Tina and me. You're living out your high school fantasy with the one who got away?"

"This wasn't exactly how my fantasy was supposed to play out," I reply.

"Come the fuck on." Vic waves me off. "They're broken up. Sure it's not good form to make out in their shared living space, but we're grading on a curve here. *Lizard* will deal."

Vic simply cannot handle Mark's pet name for Liz. He thinks she should have thrown the ring at him the first time he used it.

Tina smiles, tying her hair up in a messy bun. "Do you love him?"

My nose scrunches at the word. I've written big, swoony monologues for characters in the romantic climax of their stories. I've dabbled with the L-word to describe how I feel about Mark—just a few hours ago even—before burying it in the couch he shares with his ex-fiancée. I've imagined what it could have been like to love him when we were in high school. But I've never said it out loud. Not to anyone. I'm not sure I've ever been with a guy long enough to even consider it.

"She does." Tina wiggles.

"You do," Vic agrees.

Do I? Should I? And if so, to what end?

It's not like Mark can just up and move to LA. And I sure as hell am not moving back to Stonybrook. So if this *is* love, if that possibility even *exists*—where is it all headed?

Nowhere, because it's not love.

Is it?

I'm so confused.

Not just about what I should do with my rekindled feelings for Mark, but also what being back in Stonybrook is dredging up about Past Ellie and all the people she tried to leave behind forever.

My mind immediately shows me the faces of the superlatives I've already encountered on this whirlwind weekend trip, before getting permanently stuck on my former best friend, current uninvited co-conspirator, Roxy Draper.

I'm supposed to fly back tomorrow night, but with all these distractions, I've checked off less than half my list.

It's time to buckle down and get the job done, so I can get the hell out of Dodge and get back to my *real* life in LA. The life I built for myself far, far away from this horrible place.

Away from Mark, away from Roxy.

Two thousand miles away from the person I used to be.

It's Sunday, but I happen to know that Andy is permanently attached to his phone.

"How's my little Wildcat?" Andy asks when he answers my call.

I scoff. "I need an extension," I say, before he can ask any questions. "I got distracted, but now I've got my head back in the game, and I'm ready to finish this list and get the fuck out of here."

"Sounds complicated," he says, delighted. Yep, still hate him. "You have until the end of the week. Send Susie the new date so she can extend your ticket."

I sigh, relieved. Determined. It's go time. Go-so-I-can-get-out time. "Thanks, Andy."

"And Ellie?"

"What?"

"Slow down a little. Enjoy it." He hangs up.

Fat chance.

I wonder what will happen if I go back to LA without the fresh perspective Andy assigned to me for this trip. What if Andy's wrong about what this trip is going to do to me, and I show up to the writers' room more cynical than ever?

I set the phone on my vanity counter and look up into the mirror. Mom had an old red sweatshirt in the closet. I've paired it with some leggings and a half-up ponytail tied with a gold ribbon I found in a drawer that my dad must have saved from a long-gone box of Godiva chocolates,

Go Wildcats?

Mark still hasn't called or messaged. I think about texting him to see if he's still alive, to make sure Liz hasn't cooked him into gummy bear stew. I have a feeling their still interwoven lives are going to start unraveling faster after today, and maybe it's for the best.

But that might be me trying to let myself off the hook.

I lean forward and touch a hand to my lips, scrutinizing myself in the mirror. A few days ago, if you'd bet me a million dollars that I would be here, living in the aftermath of a make-out session with my high school crush, in a house he still shares with his ex-fiancée, I would have taken that bet. It would have felt like a sure thing.

I don't *do* complicated. I don't do random hookups. I don't date men in relationships or guys who are fresh out of them. I'm nobody's side piece or rebound girl—my heart can't take it.

But Mark.

The boy-turned-man I fantasized about for *six years* in high school finally knows the bizarre truth of my long-ago feelings and reciprocated at least some of them. With his lips.

He kissed me, and I kissed him back. The kind of toe-curling kisses that might finally make me an advocate of the sport.

Now all bets are off. The odds have changed.

I couldn't predict how this was going to end if I tried.

I touch my phone and it lights up, revealing no new messages and also quarter till five.

I walk out of the bathroom, tuck my phone in my purse, and meet my dad at the front door. He's grinning, his big, kind blue eyes practically beaming.

"You know what? I don't think I ever saw you wear Stonybrook colors even when you were a student at Stonybrook."

"I didn't." I gag.

My dad chuckles. "They look good on you."

I just shake my head. There was a time when wearing Stonybrook High School–themed anything would have given me big, itchy purple hives of anxiety and would have felt like selling my soul. But I have to admit to myself that, for the first time ever, I only *ninety percent* hate the idea of showing a little school spirit.

Damn it, Andy.

I don't want to, but I'm starting to crack.

We pull up beside the high school, and the parking lot is full.

"Basketball game," Dad says, but he holds back his looming question: *Why are you here?*

"Oh, I almost forgot. I'm going to stay a few extra days. Hope that's okay," I say, opening the passenger door.

His smile is all the answer I need. For a second I wonder

what it would feel like to know my dad was disappointed in the choices I made, so much that he would rather ice me out than offer support. Having parents who are there for the ups and downs made the scary act of going for it a little bit less terrifying.

I lean over to give Dad a quick side hug, but I'm startled by someone yanking on the door. My foot slams to the ground just as the smell of cigarette smoke and whiskey accosts my senses. *Roxy.*

"Hey, Mr. J," Roxy says, leaning into the car, her trademark smirk slicing across her face.

"Roxy, nice to see you," Dad says, looking genuinely happy to see her, and not like he's revolted by the smell of alcohol and cigarettes on her breath.

"Nice to see you, too." She says it like it truly is nice.

I push her back and climb out of the car.

"Thanks for the ride, Dad." He nods as I shut the door.

Dad drives off with a honk and a wave goodbye. I turn to face Roxy, my eyes flicking to the lit-up gym windows and back to her.

"Follow me," Roxy says, sauntering toward the entrance, which hangs open and is manned by an exuberant mom in school colors.

"Go Wildcats!" the woman cheers as we walk up to the door. Roxy walks past her without acknowledging her existence. I smile at the woman apologetically and follow Roxy inside.

"What are you doing here?" I ask the back of Roxy's head. "You don't have to help me with the list."

We walk between a row of lockers, the hallway dimly lit.

From the end, light streams through the gym door windows. The sound of a raucous crowd groans through the closed doorway.

"While you were busy swapping spit with Mark, I got us courtside seats," she says, pulling open the gym doors. I rush to scoot inside before they close. Roxy leans back against the wall. Rows of bleachers line the walls in front of us, full of people, cheering and screaming. The game is in active play.

Roxy points to the area where the benched players and coach are watching the game.

It takes me an overlong minute to realize who it is.

"David Duncan coaches the high school basketball team?" I ask.

She nods. "Most Spirited—though not Most Athletic and now definitely *not* Hottest Bod—never even left Stonybrook High."

Does it count if I just watch the game from here?

"I know what you're thinking, and I'll take a crisp fifty for your gratitude," she says.

I scowl. "How many pint-size liquor bottles does fifty bucks get you these days?"

It's mean, but Roxy loves it. She laughs, raspy and full-bodied. I can't help the smile that creeps across my face at the sound. She's older, dirtier, with a host of bad habits, but that laugh takes me back to midnight giggle fests under my pink fluffy duvet, daydreaming about what we wanted to be when we grew up.

A tiny part of my heart breaks when I remember I wasn't the only one with big dreams.

"Come on, let's reintroduce ourselves," she says.

"I'll be just *introducing* myself," I say. "I didn't know David in high school."

"He was the best," she says. There's not a hint of malice when she says it. Unprompted, annoyingly, I wonder if Roxy and David were friends in high school, and if I was just too busy judging her wild spiral while obsessively worrying about my grades, my nonexistent love life, and my Miscellaneous status to notice.

I slide up beside Roxy just as she taps David on the shoulder. A boy sitting on the bench elbows his teammate to take a look at Roxy's ass in her jeans. I give them my best death glare. Eviscerated, they turn back to watch the game, and I mentally pat myself on the back—the power of deterring unwanted male attention is alive and well with me.

"Roxy Draper," David cheers when he turns around, grabbing her into a bear hug.

Roxy introduces us, and David thrills at the mention of *Cooler Than You*. He invites us to watch the game from the court sideline and chats us up while simultaneously yelling out plays and hustling boys in and out of the game. Roxy and David have an easy back and forth, like not only were they definitely friends in high school, but they still might be friends now.

David is in the middle of telling us about the unsolved vandalism that happened at the homecoming dance this year (someone spray-painted over the school sign so it read "Sucky-brook High"—I have to pinch my lips together to keep from laughing) when his assistant coach approaches and hands him a water bottle. "You need to hydrate with all the not-coaching you're doing."

"Always taking care of me," David says, and his eyes linger

for a second, full of warmth, before he shifts them away, bust-ing out a shout of encouragement to the kids on the court.

Hey, I saw that.

David stayed at Stonybrook High, and he stayed in the closet, too.

I bite down on my tongue. Jesus, Ellie.

Old habits die hard.

Maybe he just wants to keep his private life private, which is something I totally understand he would want to do in Stonybrook. This conservative slice of Americana still has a lot of opening up to do.

I got out of here as fast as I could, and not just for the opportunities only Hollywood could give me, but because of outdated beliefs that stifled lives, along with my own budding creativity. Even in high school I hated the closed-minded preju-dice of the extremely white, wealthy little suburb. I've always been a judgy, hypercritical jerk, but I'm not a bigot.

High School Ellie either blended into the background, happily counting the days to graduation, or stuck her foot in her mouth with her (often correct) judgments of the kids she went to school with. But she still knew that everyone should be allowed to be who they are and love who they love, and not be afraid to show it.

David seems happy, but then he always seemed happy and never failed to get everyone around him to feel the same way. Whether it was during a pep rally or a bake sale, the home-coming dance or selling concessions at a football game. Even though I didn't know him well, if I'd had even one ounce of school spirit, I might have actually liked him. We might even have been friends.

I want to kick myself a little. What would high school have been like if I hadn't been so closed off to the possibilities? Maybe I would have had a better time. Maybe I wouldn't have been so miserable.

But the past is in the past, and the truth about David—and the secret he's probably keeping from the tiny conservative town's school parents—doesn't change the fact that his smile is infectious and his stories about the moms of Stonybrook are hilarious. He's making me feel like I belong here, at this basketball game, next to my former best friend, eating fundraiser popcorn and sipping an ice-cold Coke. And he's doing all of that while also coaching a winning game.

Most spirited, then and now.

One of the boys playing for Stonybrook steals the ball, taking it all the way down the court to score. The room goes wild cheering—everyone, including me. I stand up, clapping and hooting like a weirdo, congratulating David.

When I sit back down, I notice the pounding in my heart, the way my cheeks flush. Is that excitement? At a basketball game?

Roxy leans over and whispers, "Cross another one off your list, babe."

7. Go to a basketball game and out-spirit Most Spirited.

In my glow of triumph, I glance down at my phone to see a single missed call notification:

Mark Wright.

CHAPTER 21

The phone nearly drops from my hand like a hot fucking potato.

It buzzes with a voicemail from Mark.

Roxy digs a bony elbow into my rib cage. I scowl at her, but she's looking at my lit-up phone screen, reading the notification, a peculiar expression on her face. Like curiosity and annoyance are dueling it out inside her brain.

Whatever. I should just tell her. Save us both the time of her prying it out of me or stealing my phone again to find out for herself.

"Mark and I made out," I say quietly. Roxy's eyebrow quirks like *big fucking whoop, Ellie*. "Like, hot and heavy. On his couch. In the townhouse he still shares with Liz."

She cackles. "Jesus, I hope you at least laid their engagement photos facedown while you defiled their suburban oasis."

I snort. "Actually, I broke the one with little ceramic hearts after Liz walked in on us."

Roxy's smile slices her face open. "I don't know if I should clap or buy you a drink."

"It's a disaster," I say. The guilt is still all-consuming, and I'm not feeling celebratory. Not one bit. "She was so upset. I feel like a homewrecker, even though they technically don't have a home for me to wreck."

"Well, *technically* they do," Roxy points out.

"Shut up."

She grunts, shrugs, and stands in one fluid motion.

The gym is starting to clear out. Parents and younger siblings, grandparents and proud girlfriends pass us as they congratulate David and the team. David turns to face us, joy beaming from his eyes and momentarily catching both of us in the rays of his sunny disposition.

"Stephen and I are heading to Cooper Corn Maze," he says, grinning, looking from Roxy to me and back. "Wanna come with?"

Roxy's lips purse. "If you're driving. Ellie is grounded—"

"My parents only have one car," I explain. Mom doesn't like to drive, and I took my car with me when I drove it across the country for the big move five years ago.

"And I don't have a license," Roxy admits. The subtext is thick with that statement.

He agrees to drive us and makes a *whoop* sound before telling us to meet him around front in a few minutes. When we push through the school doors, the parking lot is already starting to clear out, but a few cars, probably parents waiting for their players, idle in the dark. The temperature has dropped, and my breath smokes out from my lips like a cloud.

Roxy lights up a cigarette, turning her breath to literal smoke.

"I'm pretty sure school grounds are a smoke-free zone," I say.

"You gonna listen to that voicemail or what?" Roxy asks, blowing smoke in my direction. I dodge it, and stare at my lock screen. The image is an inspirational Oprah quote: *The only courage you will ever need is the courage to live the life you are meant to.* Bah humbug.

I don't know why this matters to me so much. Three days ago, I was in LA worrying about the future of my career, the zit on my cheek, and whether the dialogue on page seven sounded forced. I was *not* thinking about the state of my love life or day-dreaming about my former high school crush, who now works at a bakery and just so happens to kiss like the tormented lead in a romance novel.

Whatever Mark has to say, I can and will deal with it.

I swipe the notification and hit the play button on the message.

Roxy leans over to listen. She shockingly has the decency to stamp out her cigarette first.

"Ellie." He says my name carefully, like he wants to protect it. "I drove to your parents' house and have been sitting outside. I can see through the downstairs window that your mom is watching a *Golden Girls* rerun."

Roxy raises an eyebrow. "Wow, stalker much?"

I shush her and try to push her away, but her hand clutches the phone to steady it, and suddenly we're huddled together listening.

Mark breathes into the receiver. "I thought about throwing stones at your window, like some kind of grand romantic gesture in a John Hughes movie, but then I remembered your whole serial killer thing and I'm afraid you'd come out and impale me with a stiletto. Also, it just occurred to me that I've never actually been inside your house before, so I have no clue which window belongs to your bedroom."

A smile creeps up my cheeks.

"I understand if you don't want anything to do with me. I'm mostly a fuck-up, and this mess with Liz makes me want to impale *myself* with your shoes. She deserves better, and so do you. But for the first time I'm starting to see things clearly. I know what I want—" He lets out a long breath. "And it's not in Stonybrook. At least, not for much longer."

Roxy makes a gagging motion. I shove her, and she stumbles a little. She chokes back a laugh.

"I hope you . . . decide to call me back."

The message ends.

David pulls up in his navy-blue hatchback, and Stephen climbs out the passenger side, pulling the front seat forward.

"Shit," I whisper. "What do I do with that?"

Roxy shrugs. "Call him—or not." She climbs into the back seat.

"Call who?" David asks.

Shut up, Roxy.

"Mark Wright," she answers, waggling her eyebrows.

"Oh, Mark is great. He got Stonybrook Market to donate eight dozen cookies to the soccer team's bake sale last year," David says, beaming.

"He's sucking face with Ellie," Roxy says.

I kick her in the shin as I slide into the car, and her face screws up in pain. She makes me crawl over her to sit behind David.

"Isn't he engaged?" David asks, confused eyes meeting mine in the rearview mirror.

"They broke up," I say, flustered. "A week ago."

"Yeowch," David says, almost like we burned him too.

"I get it, we're deplorable human beings," I say, trying not to sound as annoyed as I feel. They are *broken up*. It's not like anybody is actually cheating.

David notices my distress and shrugs. "The heart wants what it wants," he says. There's not a single hint of irony in his voice as Stephen climbs into the front seat and shuts the door. They smile brightly at each other before David takes Stephen's hand.

And there it is.

I smile at the reveal and David releases his boyfriend's hand to put the car in gear, while Roxy leans over the center console to turn up the radio. "Mad World" by Tears for Fears is on, Roxy's favorite song junior year during her eighties phase. She closes her eyes, humming even though she knows all the words. David drives, opening the sunroof to let the wind in. It whips our hair around, and strands get stuck on our lips. Roxy taps her fingers to the beat, singing softly now, and I'm overwhelmed by how totally *high school* this moment feels. Like an iconic montage in a teen movie, one they would use for the trailer to illustrate the whimsy and wistfulness of youth.

I'm struck by the fact that High School Ellie never did anything like this.

I wouldn't have sought out the back seat of David Duncan's car after a basketball game. And even though I heard this song a hundred times in Roxy's bedroom, turned all the way up, I don't think I've ever really listened to the words.

I lean back, clutching my phone to my chest. For a second, I'm just a girl with a crush on a boy who likes her back, riding with friends down an open road, and nothing that happened all those years ago—or didn't happen—matters at all. I'm getting a do-over. A second chance at something that, before this weekend, I didn't really know I missed out on.

And it feels nice.

David kills the engine and all three of them look at me.

The moment is over. Reality sets in.

I look down at my phone. "I'm going to call him."

My eyes meet Roxy's. Ten years ago, I stopped talking to her because of what happened between her and Mark. If I'm really honest, that was the final nail in the coffin of our friendship, and just like I wrote off my feelings for Mark, I always assumed that was it between us.

Now, I don't know. I'm not sure about anything. We ended our friendship in a spectacular crash of betrayal, but for a long time, Roxy was the one person in the world I told everything. Even now, I find myself drifting toward her magnetic pull. There is danger at the edge of her orbit, but there's also the promise of real, unstoppable adventure, the kind that pushes you out of your comfort zone and turns you into someone a little bit braver.

My thumb slides over my phone screen to unlock my phone.

"I need a cigarette," Roxy says, pushing on Stephen's seat. Her voice is thin, tension laced through it, and I don't know why or if I even want to know.

They climb out. Now it's just David and me in the car.

"It took me a long time to admit to myself that my feelings for Stephen were more than platonic," David says. I lift my eyes from my phone to meet his. "We keep it to ourselves around the school, but those who really matter in our lives know." He blushes. "When you find a person like that, who makes your palms sweaty and your heart beat faster, you do whatever it takes."

I don't argue. I don't have to know what my feelings for Mark mean to know that he does dangerous things to my pulse.

He clears his throat, swallowing back emotion. "You went after the life you wanted in LA. This is no different. If you know what you want, you should go for it."

"You two seem happy," I say.

"We're more than happy," he says, squeezing my hand. "Loving someone is the scariest feeling in the world. But it's also the best."

He gets out of the car, following Roxy and Stephen toward the entrance to Cooper Farms.

When I call Mark back, it rings once.

"I thought for sure you were *not* going to call," he says, rushed, breathless. He somehow sounds both panicked and relieved.

"Sorry, I was too busy out-screaming David Duncan at a basketball game. Rah-rah, go Wildcats and all that," I say in my own signature school spirit monotone.

Mark's laugh makes my stomach do flip-flops. "You crossed another one off the list," he says, with just a hint of FOMO. "How many is that now?"

"I don't know if we can count number ten yet," I say, grinning. "So far the only thing you've helped me with is unzipping my jeans." It's bold and flirty—at least for me it is. My cheeks heat up from embarrassment even though I'm alone. Mark hesitates, and I don't give him a chance to respond.

"Um, how's Liz?" I ask, trying to steamroll over my mortification with a question that I quickly realize is equally uncomfortable, maybe worse.

"She's staying with her parents in Rutledge," he says. They must have moved a few towns over. "I don't know what she's planning, but she's done sharing the condo with me. That much is clear."

"That's five so far." I change back to the original subject, realizing that I don't want to hear any more of his thoughts on Iz-Lay. "Five more to go."

"On your way to co-EP," he says, but there's a question in his voice, and it has nothing to do with *Cooler Than You*.

"We're at Cooper Corn Maze if you want to meet us. Unless..." I pause. I want to ask him more about what he's thinking re: Liz, but I also *don't* want to ask. I don't want any details, and also I want every last gory one. But I want it in person, where I can look in his eyes and try to figure out how he really feels. How *I* really feel. "Unless you can't."

"I'll be there in twenty," he replies, not missing a beat.

"Great." I try to sound breezy but my voice cracks like a teenage boy going through puberty.

"Ellie," he says. His voice deepens and my stomach flops over. "I think there's more to number ten than just *unzipping*."

He hangs up. My phone drops into my lap.

Who am I? Who is this person who is sneaking around, having clandestine meetings with men who just got out of long, *long*-term relationships? Is this some kind of high school phase that I missed out on and am just now catching up with? I feel like I'm playing out some kind of adolescent rebellion, something I didn't go through back then because I was too busy hating it to actually *experience* any of it. I didn't get to make mistakes, or test the boundaries of my own moral compass, or do something just because I wanted to and not care whether or not it was the *right* thing to do.

Now it's ten years later, and it feels like my teenage rebellious phase has just begun.

I've gotten myself tangled up in the middle of an unexpected, unpredictable mess.

And I think I like it.

CHAPTER 22

Cooper Corn Maze is a redneck mecca. It's muddy and patriotic with John Deere tractors (and hats) everywhere. Rows and rows of harvested corn weave around to form a labyrinth in the shape of an American flag, usually with "God Bless America" scrawled out in cornfield cursive. There's a dirty, ancient shanty that has barely survived at least four tornadoes. Inside, they brew cider and sell pumpkins. Everything's dirt and mud and manure, and the Midwest girl in me has died and gone straight to fall family fun heaven.

I make a beeline for the hot apple cider and don't care who follows.

When I return to the group with a steamy cup of basic bitch brew, Roxy shakes her head at me and flips off the whole place.

"Fuck fall," she says, shivering into her leather jacket. "And farms."

"I love it." I feel like a perfect smiling idiot. Live in *sunny and seventy-five degrees* LA for a few years, and you learn to cherish all four seasons.

She gags.

"Whatever," I say, but I can't suppress my smile. I try to calm the swarm of butterflies crescendoing inside my stomach with a too-long swig of steamy hot cider and end up choking.

Roxy slaps me a little too hard on the back as we walk toward the cluster of firepits.

"We should take a photo for the 'Gram," I hear David whisper to Stephen, who, even in the dim light, I can see is blushing. David's arm slides around Stephen, and they take a selfie in front of the corn maze entrance.

"Lover boy going to make an appearance?" Roxy asks me.

"He should be here any minute," I say, trying not to sound as breathless as I feel.

We sit on crudely carved log benches around the firepit and chat while we wait for Mark. Stephen and David are mega impressed by my TV job. Turns out they are both huge fans of the show. They're asking me for insider scoop on all the stars, eyes lit up like jack-o'-lanterns while I regale them with all the on-set drama.

I sneak peeks at the parking lot while they talk to me. Finally, I see a silver Honda pull in and wind around to find a spot. Suddenly, those butterflies have turned to pterodactyls.

I leap to my feet so fast that some of my apple cider spills into the grass. "I'll be right back."

"Ellie?" Roxy's voice sounds far away inside my head, like we're in a tunnel.

I speed-walk to the farmhouse and duck inside. The floor creaks with my weight. I try to hide myself behind a display of stacked pumpkins. I pick up a gourd and pretend to admire it—until I notice its phallic shape and drop it back into the pile like it's on fire.

"What is your problem?" I whisper out loud to myself.

But I know what my problem is. Up until now, Mark was just a fantasy. Now he's smiling at me, *for me*, sitting outside of my house like fucking modern Romeo and Juliet, but with a happy ending. A very happy ending, considering all the sexy things he's implying are gonna happen between us.

In a fantasy, everything turns out perfectly and exactly how I want it. In real life, I put my heart on the line, and I don't get to decide how it all turns out in the end. My heart could get chopped up into a million pieces by Mark's serial-heart-killer smile.

I'm just a co-writer in this love story, and that scares the shit out of me.

"Ellie." It's Roxy's voice again. Damn it.

She leans her hip against the display, picking up a tiny pumpkin by the stem with chipped black fingernails. She is the very portrait of Halloween chaos. "What the hell are you doing in here? Mark is looking for you."

"I'm sorry," I say. My voice sounds small, ashamed. Roxy softens, tosses the pumpkin back into the pile. She steps forward, closing the gap between us.

"Is this still about Liz?"

I shake my head.

Understanding dawns in her eyes. She puts a hand on my shoulder.

"You can't live in a fairytale world forever, Ellie Bellie," she says, a sincere smile shifting her features into something almost sweet. I try to relax, but my body tenses up even more.

Even before, in high school, when Roxy and I were thick as thieves, it never felt like this. This is new—a grown-up moment between the two of us. It feels...strange. Foreign.

"I know I can't," I say, my voice cracking. I hate this. I hate feeling this vulnerable. With her, with Mark, at this goddamn high school reunion.

She squeezes me once and lets go. "I can only take so much of the lovesick puppy dog eyes, so you need to tell him to cool it."

"Lovesick? No—"

She smirks. "Come on, befri—" She cuts herself off. Her surprise is clear, and a tinge of blush hits her cheeks.

"Stend," I reciprocate.

Her smile is a trophy, just like it always was.

"Come on, we have a cornfield to conquer." She twirls away.

I take in a single deep breath in and blow it out, watching Roxy walk ahead of me back toward the firepits, where I know Mark is waiting for me. Where the past and the present are forming a supercollider. I know I'm being overly dramatic and overthinking this—because of course I am and why would that surprise anyone? Relationships have never been easy for me. I can count on one hand the number of guys I've been on more than one date with.

Roxy stops walking and turns around, waiting for me to follow. I let go of the neck of a gourd I've been clutching unconsciously and follow her. She eyes me with amused suspicion.

"Practicing?" she asks with a smirk.

"You're disgusting," I breathe, but my cheeks are burning.

We weave through the firepits, surrounded by mostly teenagers from rural schools, too rowdy to be sober. Beer cans litter the ground, and an earthy skunk smell fills the air.

The guys are near the edge of the yard, close to the entrance of the maze. Next to them, a giant wooden sign is hand-painted with CORN MAZE ENTRANCE and Cooper's goofy (and slightly creepy) corn maze mascot beckoning its patrons to enter.

Mark stands by the fire, his hands in his pockets, talking to Stephen and David. His head keeps turning to look in our direction. When I get close enough, his dark brown eyes lock with mine. A slow smile spreads wide across his face.

My heart rate kicks up.

Stephen notices Mark's sudden lack of interest in their conversation and elbows David. They both make kissy faces behind Mark's back. I bite my lip to hold back a giggle.

Mark's holding a beer and wearing a burnished leather jacket. His hair is all mussed on top of his head from running his hands through it a thousand times, a quirk I remember from high school.

I walk up to him. "Hi," I say, not sure if I should hug him or kiss him or what.

"Hi," Mark says. He turns to face me but doesn't make any other moves.

"Oh dear God," Roxy groans. "Touch each other."

Next to her, Stephen snorts and tries to cover it up with a cough. David elbows him hard in the ribs but is also holding back laughter.

Before my brain can work out what's happening, Mark's hand touches mine. Our fingers interlace and he's drawing a tiny row of circles on my palm with his thumb. It's better than intoxicating and makes me wonder if that cider was secretly spiked.

"There you go," Roxy says, her eyes rolling up to the stars.

I can feel the heat of his gaze on me, and when I meet his eyes, there are all kinds of questions in them. Shyness kicks in, and I turn from him to face the rest of the group. Stephen motions to the entrance of the maze.

"Shall we?" Stephen asks.

Roxy stomps for the entrance, her Doc Martens trampling leaves, every step a loud crunch. "Let's get this over with."

"So, tell us about this list?" David asks, catching up with Stephen. As soon as the entrance is out of sight, their hands fuse together.

"Well, watching the game with you was on the list, as was hooking up with the prom king—"

"Please, dear God, tell me you're going to lie about that one," Stephen says over his shoulder with a shudder.

"I kissed Kyle on the cheek," I say. David and Stephen both nod and blow out sighs of relief.

"Was that before or after Brock Crawley tried to assault you in the bathroom?" Mark asks. I shoot Mark an aggravated sideways glance for bringing up the incident. Even in the dark I can see that his face is tense, serious.

"What the hell?" Stephen asks, alarmed. "Ellie!"

"I'm fine," I say. "Brock Crawley is the creep to end all creeps."

Everyone groans in agreement except Roxy, who walks ahead of me and Mark.

"Left or right?" David asks when we come to a crossroads. Cross-stalks, if you will.

Everyone looks at me for some reason.

"Um, left, I guess?" I say. I'm not sure why they're deferring to my judgment, but we all go left.

We navigate the twists, turns, and dead ends of the maze, taking turns calling the shots. While we walk, I tell them the whole story of the after-party, including Brock's sad impersonation of Jay Gatsby drinking champagne by the pool. Stephen and David are a riot of shock and laughter and apologies, applause and gagging. Everyone enjoys the Brock roast, except Roxy, who has gone completely quiet, acting even shiftier than usual.

"Where were *you* during all this, Mark?" David asks.

I'm watching Roxy, trying to figure out what all her sudden weirdness is about, when Mark says, "Ellie was avoiding me like the plague."

"Now she's infected." David winks at me.

Stephen groans. "She would've been if she'd hooked up with Kyle Temple."

David hisses for a sizzle effect. "Ouch!"

Mark's lips twitch, the little dimple near the corner tweaking. He isn't sure where we stand, and neither am I, but he likes the idea of me being afflicted, unable to shake my attraction to him.

My eyes have finally adjusted to the darkness, so it's blinding when Roxy's phone lights up in her hand. She holds it down by her hip and glances at it quickly.

With a sleight of hand, her phone is in her back pocket and out of sight, before I can get a good look at the screen. She's not bothering to respond to whoever texted her, like she doesn't want to risk anyone seeing.

Especially me.

I know I shouldn't be nosing around in her business, but Roxy is a puzzle I still stupidly want to solve even if only for my own peace of mind. She looks pale, even in the darkness, even for her.

"We're waiting," Stephen says, drawing my attention back to my captive audience.

Oh, right. The list.

I open up the photo on my phone and hand it up to Stephen and David. They each glance over it and hand it back to me.

"Five left to go," I say, trying to sound cheerful, even if the number still feels daunting.

We hit a dead end and have to turn around.

"Marky Mark over there is number ten on the list. But—" Roxy chimes back in, returning from whatever stupor she's been in for the last few minutes. She cranes her neck around to eye him with playful scrutiny. "Can you count fondling Ellie on the couch as *helping*?"

My face is on fire. Mark is unfazed. "I'm help with benefits," he says with an arrogant grin. He pulls me to him and puts an arm around my shoulders. Roxy's eyebrows pinch together. "And...I happen to know that Most Likely to Succeed flew in for the reunion and never showed."

"Look at that—lover boy *is* helpful," Roxy concedes.

"You didn't tell me," I say, leaning back to get a look at his face in the moonlight. I can see a faint shadow of stubble coming in, and all I can think about is reaching up to brush the back of my hand over his jaw. I resist the urge.

"Give us the tea, Marky Mark," Roxy says. From her purse she pulls out a travel-sized bottle of vodka, cracks the top, and swigs, emptying it halfway. David reaches his hand back for a sip and she reluctantly places it in his wiggling fingers.

"Ever heard of Rachel Rice?" Mark asks the group.

"The vegan chef?" I say. "The one who wrote *Vegasm: Cruelty-Free Foods to Spice Up Your Sex Life*?" Gag. My saga with veganism in every form continues.

"I'm sorry, what?" Roxy says. I can tell she's about to bust out laughing.

"There's an eggplant on the cover," I tell her, matter-of-factly.

"You sure know a lot about it." Mark eyes me suspiciously.

"One of my best friends is vegan," I explain to him. "And also a little bit slutty."

"Well, *that* is Rachel Bumpass," Mark reveals.

The rest of us stop dead in our tracks. "*What?!*"

"No *way*," I exclaim.

"Yes, way," Mark says, proud of himself.

"Was Rachel Bumpass even vegetarian in high school?" I ask. Stephen and David are vigorously googling on their phones.

"She had an I LOVE MY DOG bumper sticker," David contributes. "I guess the feeling escalated?" He gasps, holds up his phone. "That *is* her."

Roxy squints at the Getty image of Rachel posing with her book at a Goop event. "A name change, a nose job—a new life."

The way she says it makes me wonder if Roxy secretly wishes she could have a new life too.

"Hollywood's magic wand is a scalpel," I say. "And Dr. Ruby is the wizard."

David crosses his arms. "What. A. Bitch. We basically spent four years together on the student council, and—let me just confirm—she did jack shit all senior year. Too busy fucking Robbie Bernstein. Not too busy, however, to show up and take all of the credit. For prom, for homecoming, for everything."

"You're definitely not still bitter about it though, are you, boo?" Stephen reaches up to pinch David's cheek playfully. David swats him away, huffing.

Mark clears his throat, preparing us for the big reveal.

"Last Wednesday, she ordered two dozen cookies from the bakery," Mark says.

"The vegan, gluten-free ones?" Stephen asks, hopeful.

Mark shakes his head slowly.

"Real. Butter."

CHAPTER 23

We all gasp.

Except Roxy, who has already lost interest in our conversation and has stepped away from the group to type something on her phone.

"Gwyneth Paltrow would be *so* disappointed," Stephen says, a dramatic hand over his heart.

David is still scrolling on his phone. "It says here that she just had a messy breakup with her boyfriend. There's a blind item that says he may have cheated on her."

Another gasp from Stephen. "Shame and scandal!"

"What's a blind item?" Mark asks, looking at me.

"Celebrity gossip columns," I say. "It's all unconfirmed. I used to read them all the time, but about half of the things they publish are bull."

David reads aloud: "This A-minus list chef-slash-author just found out that her fiancé has been cheating on her with her best friend."

A sharp pang of guilt twists my guts. I'm not Liz's friend, nor is Mark a cheating fiancé, but I really don't want to ruin her life. Mark's arm is still around me, and I duck out of his embrace, pretending to examine something on the ground until the wave of shame passes.

David doesn't notice and continues reading: "She left LA and is now living with her parents in her hometown that rhymes with Storybook."

"Well, that *is* pretty specific," I admit, standing upright again. Mark is looking at me with just a hint of torment in his eyes, and I can tell he knows something is up.

"My store manager made me deliver the cookies myself, since she's so high profile," Mark says, still looking at me. "So I do know where she lives."

"Can't you get fired for that?" I ask him.

He shrugs. "You're the one who's not gonna get promoted if you don't finish this list."

"Oh my God, Ellie, he's taking such big risks for you," Stephen says. He threads his arm through David's and sighs.

Mark still hasn't broken eye contact with me, and even though it's dark, the intensity of his gaze is like looking directly at the sun. I have to look away.

I hear Roxy's Docs crunching dried-up cornstalks as she stomps back over to us. "Are we going to finish this maze, or should I pitch a tent?"

"You go on," Mark says to the group. "I want to talk to Ellie about something."

"Ooooooh," David and Stephen say in unison.

"Come on," Roxy says to Stephen and David. "I have to pee."

She throws me a sideways glare, annoyed we are separating. They follow her and I hear David say, "It's a cornfield, just pee anywhere."

Once they're out of earshot, I look at Mark, wondering what he wants to talk to me about. He says nothing at first. Instead, his hands slide around my waist, pulling me closer.

He bends, and his lips are next to my ear when he whispers, "Is this okay?"

All I can do is nod.

I don't know what it is about Mark that makes me feel so nervous. There's just something about him being my once-upon-a-time, unrequited high school crush that melts me—from established career woman back into a shy schoolgirl.

Or maybe it's not about high school. Maybe this is just how it feels to really fall for someone, to be vulnerable and afraid of saying or doing the wrong thing. To be afraid of getting your heart broken after you're already in too deep.

Maybe I just wouldn't know because that's never happened to me before. Not like this.

"What are you thinking about?" he asks. His hand traces across my collarbone. I shiver.

"I feel like I'm in high school again," I admit. He smiles and lets his fingers slide up to my neck, tracing the line of my jaw down to my chin. His thumb brushes over my lips, parting them gently.

"That's just how it feels," he whispers, leaning forward. His lips are inches from mine.

"That's just how what feels?" I whisper back, wanting desperately to have all the answers before we go any further.

"This."

He closes the gap between our mouths, catching my lips in the gentlest kiss that two people have ever shared. It's like napalm, this kiss. Heat pools low in my belly, and I'm suddenly struck with the desire to be closer to him. I want skin to skin, lips and limbs, let's go.

Damn it, he's *so* good at this.

The kissing intensifies, and I forget where we are completely. His hands slide down to my butt, and before I know what's happening, he lifts me into the air so that my legs are straddling his hips.

I thank God, the universe, Zeus, and whoever else could possibly be involved that I chose to wear leggings on this outing. I can feel him wanting me, and I've never been so turned on in my entire life.

"Hey, come on—" A gruff male voice is a bucket of ice water dumped directly over our heads. "There are kids in here."

I jump away from Mark so fast that I tumble backward into the side of the maze, falling on my ass between crunchy brown corn stalks.

I hear Mark mutter a halfhearted apology to the guy before coming over and reaching out a hand to help me up.

"You okay?" he asks me.

"Are there any spiders on me?" I say, turning to have him inspect the back of me. He laughs and brushes a few leaves off me. His hand grazes my butt.

"Hey!"

"Sorry!" He laughs again and holds out his hand for me to take. "Spider-free."

I can feel my eyes sparkling at him as we walk. "I've never gotten in trouble for PDA before."

He smiles wide and shakes his head. "How are you twenty-eight and this innocent?"

"I am *not* that innocent!" I protest. Cue the Britney Spears song. *Oops, I*—Shut up, brain. "I've done all the things. It's just never been this fun before."

He grins and squeezes my hand, and a comfortable silence falls between us as we walk through what's left of the maze. After the angry middle-aged man catching us touching tongues in a dark corner, we don't meet anyone else on the path. The moon is high in the sky, the stars twinkling among a few wispy clouds.

"Ellie." Mark says my name so softly, I feel like I'm in a dream. "Have you been in a relationship before?"

"What?" The question startles me. I stare up at him with wide eyes. "Why are you asking me that?"

An interesting question, considering he *just* got out of one. A relationship that was supposed to end in *marriage*, and didn't.

His back stiffens, and I can tell he's on the defense. "I'm not asking you to be my girlfriend. I was just wondering."

Even though it's a good thing he's not jumping into something new, it's hard to hear him say the words. *I'm not asking you to be my girlfriend.* Ouch.

"I've dated, mostly in college," I say. "Nothing long-term or super serious. After college, I moved to LA, and then it was *all work and no play makes Jack a dull boy.*"

He smiles at my use of a quote from *The Shining*. "I love it when you talk film quote-y to me, Ellie."

We come to another dead end and turn around. Mark pulls me in a direction that feels familiar, and I wonder if he's purposely dragging out our alone time. I savor every sensation, every simple touch. We start by holding hands, and then suddenly his arm is around my shoulders. And then a sharp turn has his hand sliding down around my waist to guide me in the darkness.

His hand makes its final journey to the small of my back, the gentlest pressure, far enough away from my ass to not be pervy, but close enough to make me go wild. It's a subtle touch that is almost my undoing.

"I know a lot has happened in the last few days," he finally says after a few minutes of walking in silence. "I just want you to know—this didn't come out of nowhere for me."

"What do you mean?" I ask.

"When you sent me that DM." He trails off. I gulp.

Hi Mark it's me ellie.

No. No, no, no. I do *not* want to talk about that embarrassing-as-fuck message right now. I pull away from him to put some distance between us. He looks a little hurt and shoves his hands in his jacket pockets.

"I was drunk," I say, suddenly feeling desperate to be any-where but here. To just disappear. I eye the walls of the maze and imagine slipping between the stalks of corn. Mark notices the line of my gaze and grins.

"Spiders," he reminds me.

Damn it all.

I take a deep breath and hang my head, watching my feet as we walk. My shoes are caked in mud. "I'm really sorry."

"It was pretty mean," he admits.

My hands ball up into fists. I'm not great at admitting when I'm wrong. This one's pretty hard to deny though. "If it's any consolation, I woke up the next day hating myself—and puking my guts up."

"Karma," he points out.

I scowl at him. "Do you have a point in bringing this up, or are you trying to make me hate you?"

He smiles at my brutality. I think he's onto me—the meaner I am to him, the more it means I like him.

"You were *right*."

I am stunned into silence and can do nothing but stare at him and wait for an explanation.

"I applied to film school at NYU," he says. There's a long pause before he adds: "I didn't get in." He sucks in a breath, like it still hurts.

I clap a hand over my mouth. "Oh my God, Mark. I'm so sorry. God, why am I such a fucking asshole?"

"The point is, I could have applied to a different film school. I even went to NYU thinking I would just try again the next year. But I didn't. My dad was up my ass about med school, and I just...caved."

"You can't blame yourself for that," I tell him. I take one of his hands in mine. It's cold, so I cradle it between both my palms. "It's difficult to follow your dreams. It's a path of uncertainty. I'm lucky that my parents were supportive, but I've met plenty of people who don't have that kind of support. And I think it must be the hardest thing in the world."

When I look up at him, his eyes are shiny and filled with some emotion I can't place. He's very intense with his eye contact, especially right now. I don't break his gaze, though—

I can't—because I want him to know that I mean every word. I want to make up for the horrible, careless things I said years ago. I want to show him that it's okay to make choices that you regret.

"What's for you will not pass you," I say, quoting a bracelet my mom once got me for Christmas.

He chuckles and steps forward. "Okay, now you sound like a meme."

And then he kisses me.

This isn't the hungry, lust-fueled kiss from twenty minutes ago. This kiss is slow and deep and lovely. A sensual kiss I feel all the way to my bones and in my heart—shaking my soul.

When he pulls away, my eyes are wet with tears. He brushes one away with his thumb.

"You are something, Ellie" is all he says. And then I can tell there are more words he doesn't say, and I wonder what they are, but I'm too shy and dumbfounded after that earth-shattering kiss to inquire further.

We finally find the end of the maze, marked by a giant hand-painted sign with an elated ear of clipart corn and a talk bubble that says, *You did it!*

David and Stephen are cuddled up by the fire, waiting for us. We apologize to them for making them wait.

"Where's Roxy?" I ask, my eyes scanning the darkness.

David shrugs. "She said she was going to the bathroom."

"Like twenty minutes ago," Stephen adds. "Nobody spends *that* much time in a Porta-Potty."

The parking lot is almost empty, and the corn maze workers are making the rounds to close up shop and put out the fires in the firepits. I pull out my phone to text Roxy, but something catches my eye.

A sleek black Escalade swerves into the entrance of the parking lot, brights on, bass bumping—but doesn't park. I watch as a shadowy figure emerges from behind a tree to slip into the passenger side of the car. Before the mysterious person even has a chance to shut the door all the way, the Escalade peels out, and I can see its lit-up LED vanity plate clearly.

In all caps, it reads BCRAWL69.

I'm screaming on the inside because I would bet every penny that I have that I know exactly who that car belongs to and who just got inside of it.

A very *married* Brock fucking Crawley.

And a very drunk-off-her-ass RoxygoddamnDraper.

It hits me, and I nearly fall over with the weight of it.

"Ellie?" Mark's voice sounds far away. I feel his knuckles brush my cheek. I must look as dead as I feel inside.

"Oh my God" is all I can say.

Roxy is fucking Brock Crawley.

CHAPTER 24

W hat's wrong?" Mark's voice is low. His eyes search my face for answers.

I press my eyes closed and shake my head. "Can we go?" I whisper to him.

"Yeah, of course." He digs in his pocket to fish out his keys and tells a concerned Stephen and David that I'm feeling sick before he guides me to his car. His hand is on that place on my lower back that usually lights me on fire, but right now is just barely rooting me in reality, saving me from having a full-blown panic attack.

He opens the door for me, and I slide into the passenger seat. I press the heels of both my hands to my temples, fighting the sudden headache I feel coming on.

"Do you have Motrin or Advil or something?" I ask him as soon as he's in the car.

"I'll stop at a drugstore," he says. He turns to face me. "Can you tell me what's going on?"

"I saw her," I say. "I saw Roxy leave in Brock Crawley's car."

Mark's sigh is deep. He leans his head back on the headrest, his eyes rolling up to the sky. "You're sure it was him?"

"Unless you know someone else who goes by BCrawl69."

"Oh, God," he says. He turns the key in the ignition and starts the car, pulling out of the parking lot.

We drive in silence for a few minutes. My head pounds, and I massage pressure points in my temples.

What do I do? Do I text Roxy? Tell her that I can't believe she's knocking boots with the creep to end all creeps? He's the most disgusting human being alive. Does she really hate herself that much that she could resort to having an affair with that predatory, narcissistic prick?

I can't do it. I know I can't. For someone like Roxy, who's spent a lifetime being picked apart by her own mother, every criticism is an attack. Roxy is the Queen of Rebellion, and if you tell her to do one thing, she'll make sure to do the exact opposite.

BEFRI STENDS echoes in my head, aches in my heart.

I grunt in pain and rest my cheek on the window. It's cool to the touch and feels like heaven.

I feel Mark's hand slip into mine.

"Hang in there," he says softly.

We pull into the tiny parking lot of a store that is literally called Drug Store. Mark ducks in alone and comes out with a bag full of headache-fighting goodies. I dig out the ibuprofen, bust through the childproof cap, foil, and cotton ball, and throw back four orange pills with a giant swig of the water he got me.

"Wow," he says. In awe.

"Professional TV writer, remember?" I'm still holding my head, squeezing my eyes shut. "Professional procrastinator too. All-nighters and migraines galore."

It takes about twenty minutes for the pain meds to kick in, and I can feel my body start to relax. The light doesn't bother my eyes so much anymore, and when I open them, I realize we are still in the janky Drug Store parking lot. An ancient streetlamp flickers uncertainly above us. When I look over at Mark, he's leaning back on the headrest, staring straight ahead. My hand is in his and he's absentmindedly playing with my fingers.

Any thoughts about Roxy trigger stabbing pains behind my eyes, so I decide to put a pin in it, for now. After all, it's her business, not mine. She's a grown-ass woman, and if she wants to have sex with a bloodsucking worm, that's her prerogative.

I give myself the *ick* and shudder.

"Hey," he says when he realizes I'm coming back to life. "How are you feeling?"

"It's a dull roar," I say, leaning my head back to get a better look at him. In this light, his skin is a soft tan, his eyes dark orbs of chocolate brown. His expression is faraway, like he's thinking and he's forgotten he has me for an audience. "What were you thinking about?"

He hesitates, as if he can't decide whether or not he should share his private thoughts with me.

"Brock Crawley's graduation party," he finally admits.

I shift uncomfortably in my seat.

"You're just digging up all the ancient history tonight," I say, rolling my eyes.

"You asked," he says with a shrug. "We don't have to talk about it."

"No, we do," I say, sitting up. We should. "What the hell were you thinking?"

"The kitten's claws come out."

"I'm a tiger, not a kitten," I correct him. "Seriously though—Roxy? My best friend in the whole world? And you can't say you didn't know. Everyone knew."

"I knew." Two little words. The truth, touched with melancholy. He continues: "I don't know, Ellie. I was eighteen. I was drunk. It was the end of the year. I'd gotten rejected by the one school I wanted to go to more than anywhere else. And on top of all that, the girl I had a crush on did not seem to like me back."

"You had a crush on me?" I say, my voice getting small and squeaky.

"I think I made that clear," he says. He throws his hands up in the air in frustration. "I still do. The second I saw you at work. The rest of the day, I couldn't stop thinking about you."

My heart flutters and I run away from it, scared. "You hooked up with Roxy."

"Okay, whoa, I just kissed Roxy. Let's not rewrite history."

"Kissing her with a hand up her shirt," I say, pouting.

"What you saw was as far as it got," he says to me. "I'm sorry it happened. I really thought you didn't like me."

"I liked you," I tell him. "But you know that now."

"Why couldn't you tell me then?" he asks. He takes my hand and pulls me closer to him. The flickering streetlight outside has finally given up, and his dark brown eyes are almost black in the darkness of his car. Even in the dark I can feel the intensity of his eyes on me, and I shiver.

"I was scared," I say finally.

"Of what?"

"There's a reason I'm a writer, Mark. Fantasy is easier than reality. In the fantasy of you, happily ever after is all there is. There's no rejection or you kissing another girl or you deciding one day that you've changed your mind about us, about me. Reality is painful. Fairy tales are safe."

"Are they? Are they really?" It's a challenge.

"Why don't you ask Liz?" I say, the challenge accepted.

He frowns and pulls back, looks away from me.

Oops.

Awkward silence hangs between us, but I don't apologize or take it back. I know I should, but I can't help it. I have to test it. I have to test him.

I have to test *us*.

"Wow, that sucks." It comes out as almost a whisper.

He puts both hands on the steering wheel and for a second, I think he's about to drive away. To take me home. To tell me that's it, this is over. This is too hard, and you're too difficult. We're done here.

But he doesn't. Not yet anyway.

Instead he turns back to me and takes both my hands. I refuse to look him in the eyes. It's too much, too intense.

But he doesn't let me off the hook.

"Look at me," he says. I don't, I can't. He lets go of one of my hands and reaches up to tilt my chin until I'm staring directly into his eyes. Black eyes that are like looking into the sun. Or maybe getting sucked into a black hole. I can't decide which.

"I'm sorry I kissed Roxy," he says. "I shouldn't have done it. It is one of my greatest regrets."

I suck in a deep breath and sigh.

"But if it's any consolation, I was pretending it was you the whole time."

My jaw drops. Mark smirks.

"You could have led with that," I say, my eyes rolling back.

His grin is full of mischief as he leans forward to kiss me, lingering to nibble on my bottom lip.

I groan and glance longingly at his back seat. He laughs.

"As much as I would like to get naked with you in the back seat of my Honda Accord in the Drug Store parking lot, don't you have a list to check off?"

I tense up at the thought of getting naked with Mark. I want it, and I'm terrified of it. But more than that, I want it.

"Can't it wait?" I whine.

"It's your job," he says with a shrug.

"Fine, fine," I say. "But it's ten o'clock at night. You really think Rachel Rice is going to answer the door?"

He starts the engine. "I guess there's only one way to find out."

We drive to the address Mark remembers from the cookie delivery. We park the car outside the house—presumably her parents' house—one street over from Brock's not-so-humble abode. Roxy and Brock could be parked somewhere in this neighborhood getting their rocks off to some porno pop or freaky hip-hop.

The thought makes me shiver.

We get out of the car and shuffle up the driveway. At the same time, a dingy red Corolla with a light-up Pizza Hut roof topper pulls up in front of the house. Mark and I exchange a look as we watch the pizza guy get out of his car and grab his insulated delivery bag out of the back seat.

All three of us walk up to the front door, and Mark rings the doorbell.

The door opens, and Rachel appears in sweatpants and a stained T-shirt.

"One large extra cheese for Rachel Bumpass?" The pizza guy gulps back a snort as *ass* leaves his lips.

Rachel looks like a deer in headlights. Her eyes cut over to the pizza guy, and then back to us, back to him and his pizza box filled with delicious real-cheesy goodness. Her face screws up into a snarling scowl that would melt the polar ice caps.

The poor guy takes a step back, but it's too late.

Rachel's hand shoots out, the box flies from his grasp, and a massive, extra-cheesy cheese pizza hurtles through the air, meeting its fate on the walkway next to the porch.

Mark and I could never have predicted what comes next.

Rachel Rice, cruelty-free chef and Goop darling, winds her fist back like a UFC champion and makes knuckle contact with the pizza dude's acne-ridden face.

CHAPTER 25

I gasp, and my hands fly to my mouth.

"Oh, shit." Mark gets between Rachel and the pizza boy. I'm frozen in place while Mark holds her back as she spits a string of expletives. Her eyes trail from the teenager on the ground to the warm slices of gooey pizza splattered on the sidewalk. She takes one look at me, and I watch her face contort into an Oscar Award–winning mask of rage.

This is the performance of a lifetime.

The pizza box, now crumpled, is turned over on the ground. She yanks it open and looks longingly at the dirt-covered slices of pizza, before throwing them at Mark, who is now helping the pizza guy to his feet.

Holy shit. She is in the middle of a full-blown nervous breakdown.

I pull out my phone and punch in 9-1-1, my thumb hovering over the send button. Should I call? I have no clue what to do. I've never attended a pseudo-celebrity's semi-public meltdown before. This is all very Charlie Sheen circa 2011.

Mark shields the frazzled pizza guy with one arm and drags him to his car. Rachel flies past me and walks barefoot toward the driveway. "Who called you? Who fucking called you?"

"You did!" the teen says in a nerdy high-pitched voice before Mark slams his driver's side door shut and motions for him to get out of there fast.

Rachel starts to pound on the passenger side window of his car.

"Was it the stalkerazzi?" Her eyes are fully dilated with murderous intensity. They scan the street for potential witnesses and land on me, still standing on the front porch. I try to hide behind a potted plant, but it's no use.

New target identified.

I am going to die now.

Mark looks completely helpless as Rachel powers up, dropping the piece of pizza she had crumpled in her fist, and makes a beeline for me. He tries to get around the Pizza Hut car to stop her but has to jump out of the way as the pizza guy nopes out of there so fast that he rams the back of his car into a neighbor's mailbox. There's a horrible metallic crash before he peels out, busted up bumper scraping the asphalt and sending tiny sparks into the air.

I hear a chorus of curses and fear the worst until everything goes quiet. Either I'm dead or Rachel Rice has finally succumbed to a bovine-induced apoplexy.

"Ellie Jenkins?"

I peek through my fingers. Rachel's face has transformed

completely. It's a face I know well. It's the you-might-know-someone-who-knows-someone face I've often encountered when I tell people I write for *Cooler Than You*.

Usually, it annoys me. Today, it's my saving grace.

I'm afraid to break eye contact with her, like I'm a lion trainer trying to subdue a rabid beast. I slowly lift my hands in surrender, hoping to woo her out of her cheese-induced rage with encouraging phrases like "I love your book!" and "We should bring you on the show for a guest appearance."

No one can bullshit like a Hollywood producer.

Co-executive producer, but close enough.

That moment never comes, because I watch Rachel Bumpass aka Rachel Rice get smacked in the face by a soccer ball. She stumbles backward, and I'm grateful it's onto grass and not concrete.

"Mark!" I shout.

"Still got it," he says with a fist pump.

Rachel groans and sits up. I fall to my knees in the grass beside her.

"Can you help me, please?" I say to Mark, exasperated.

"I just knocked her down. Why are we helping her get back up?"

I sigh and turn back to her. "Are your parents here?"

Rachel shakes her head, rubbing her cheek. It's then that I smell the alcohol on her breath and realize she must have been drinking. Why does everyone from this godforsaken town have a drinking problem?

Mark reluctantly helps me get her to her feet. She is sore, but unbroken—at least on the outside. We help her into the house, which is decorated in floral wallpaper and pink plush carpet.

We sit her down on her mother's overstuffed rose-covered couch with a cup of collagen tea Mark reheats in the microwave. I fish a bag of peas out of the freezer and try to hand them to her, but she waves them away with a barfy face, and I wonder if she understands they're for reducing swelling, not for eating. *The Great British Baking Show* plays on the TV, joyous and polite, in stark contrast to the violent pizza carnage we just witnessed outside.

"It's just that the soccer ball might leave a mark," I say. She crumples, flopping her head back so her stringy, unkempt mane splays out in a wave across her parents' floral couch cushions.

"Maybe I can spin this," she says. Her eyes snap open with horror movie precision. They fix on me. "I could claim my ex came to Stonybrook—caused a whole scene. Chance still owes me five fucking K for our trip to the Hamptons." She dissolves into a weepy grimace as the name of her ex-fiancé leaves her mouth.

I have my phone in my hand, and as soon as she spots it, any trace of teary eyes evaporates from her expression. Rachel's eyes narrow on me like a viper, sharp and hard and ready to strike. "No pics. This ends up on TMZ, and I will sue you for everything you don't fucking have."

I pull away, stunned, and she yanks the peas from my hand and smacks them against her cheek.

Mark is behind me, reheated collagen tea in hand. He holds it out for her to take, his eyes flicking to mine briefly. A look that shares the thoughts he can't speak out loud—like *What the fuck?* and *Let's get the hell out of here.*

"Thanks," she says sweetly. She takes the mug from him and

blows on it gently. Steam rises from the microwaved liquid. "You guys are really great," she says in a garble of hiccups and sobs, before slurping her tea like a child.

I blink at her. It's like Dr. Jekyll and Mr. Hyde.

Her feelings are giving me whiplash.

We sit on either side of her, unsure of what comes next. I'm supposed to compare lives with Most Likely to Succeed, but I'm not sure that comparing a high point of my life with an obvious low point of hers is exactly what Vic and Tina had in mind when they concocted this list.

Mark mimes a checkmark at me. I suck in a deep breath and pull my knees up to my chest.

"So, Rachel—"

"I ordered the pizza," Rachel blurts out.

Mark and I look at each other, not exactly surprised, but also stunned that she's admitting it to us.

"I've been vegan for almost a third of my life, but when Chance broke up with me, I just—I needed cheese. Mac and cheese, grilled cheese, cheese quesadillas..." She buries her head in her hands. "Cheesecake!" She bursts into tears.

"You're making me hungry," I hear Mark say under his breath. I tell him to shut up with my eyes and put a hand on her shoulder.

"You're allowed to eat cheese," I tell her.

"No, I'm not!" She sniffs and wipes snot away from her nose. "If the tabloids find out about this, I'm ruined. Everything I've achieved, everything I've built...It will all be for nothing. I will be a lamb to the vegan slaughter."

"Ironic," Mark says.

"I can just *see* the opinion pieces now," she says. "Hot takes for days. Hit pieces galore. I'm an utter failure. A dairy-eating hypocrite."

"I think maybe assaulting a teenager is the bigger deal here?" Mark points out.

She rolls her eyes, her tone changing completely, the remorseful dramatics over. "I'll give him a couple grand if he signs an NDA."

"Generous," he says. I can tell by his tone he's being sarcastic.

"You two have to sign NDAs too," she says.

"Have your people call our people," Mark says. "Ellie's a big-shot TV producer."

I open my mouth to correct him—because I'm not yet—but before I get the words out Rachel grabs my hand and turns her big watery eyes directly on me. I recognize that hungry look. It's the *You scratch my back…* A Hollywood classic. "I think I heard something about that."

Oh no. Mark, what have you done?

I can tell she's racking her brain for some way she can take advantage of this shiny new connection when Mark reaches over and pats my leg.

"Okay!" he says as he stands up and exaggerates a stretch. "Well, good luck with the cheese situation, and we look forward to signing our NDAs."

He takes my hand and pulls me to the front door. My chronic rule-following kicks in, and I wonder if I've done enough to check this item off the list.

Rachel stands up to wave goodbye. She leaves us with "If this ends up in the tabloids, I will see you in court!"

"Do you really think this one counts?" I ask him.

"Are you kidding?" he says as he opens the passenger-side door. "This one should count as two. She was awful."

"I kind of feel sorry for her," I say.

"I don't," he says and gets in the car. He locks the doors. "I hope she chokes on a cheese ball."

I gasp. And then snort with laughter.

"Kidding," he says. "Kind of."

He fires up the ignition.

"Let's get out of here."

CHAPTER 26

Mark drops me off at my parents' house, planting a kiss on my cheek. We're too tired to linger in our goodbye, so we say good night, and he promises to call me in the morning.

I step out of the car and head for the front door. Out of the corner of my eye I spot a figure lurking in the shadows, slumped in one of my parents' ancient floral patio chairs.

"Hey!" I shout. I thrust my house key in front of me like a weapon, ready to key-knife the shit out of whoever has decided to sneak attack this *Dateline*-watching damsel in defense.

I'm about to throw my purse at him when I notice the long dark hair and hear the feminine groan. This is not a physical ambush, but more likely an emotional one.

"Roxy?" I say, lowering my purse.

She holds her head in both hands. "Hiya" is all she can manage.

"Damn it, Roxy, I thought you were going to abduct me," I

say, sagging into the chair next to her. I dig in my purse for the painkillers Mark got for me.

She drunkenly mimics the shrieking violins from the *Psycho* shower scene and stabs the air with her fist. I roll my eyes and hand her the ibuprofen Mark picked up at the drugstore for me.

She waves the bottle away and stands up to lean over the porch railing and hurl. I close my eyes and plug my ears. I may love true crime, but I have a weak stomach for bodily functions.

When she's done she stands up and wipes her mouth with the back of her hand. She turns around to lean against the railing, steadier on her feet now that she's emptied the contents of her stomach.

"That's better," she says.

"My dad's going to love that in the morning," I say, standing up and heading for the front door.

Roxy pouts her lip out in the closest thing we'll ever get to an apology and follows me, assuming she's coming inside.

We enter the house, and I motion for her to take her shoes off so she doesn't clomp all over the hardwood floors and wake my parents. She reluctantly slips out of her shoes and follows me up to my room. I'm thankful that heaving her guts out seems to have sobered her up—at least a little. She's walking in a mostly straight line and manages to make less noise than a bull in a china shop, so I decide to count my blessings.

When we get to my room, I shut the door behind us. Roxy flops down on my pristinely made bed. I don't make my bed, but my mom does when I'm home. She'll use any tiny gesture of taking care of me to persuade me to try to come home more often.

"Please don't barf on my bed," I beg her.

She sits up. "I won't. I'll just barf on this Holiday Barbie collection instead." She points to the shelf on the far wall where they all sit displayed with pride. I can't wait for her to notice the Beanie Babies. She looks around my room and sighs, half nostalgic and half disapproving. "It looks just like it did. It's like you never left."

"My mom won't let my dad touch it," I say. "He, of course, wanted to use it for storage...aka hoarding."

Roxy chuckles. "Remember that one time we went to your grandparents' house to paint Easter eggs? We didn't want to leave, so we hid in the basement behind billions of boxes."

"They looked for us for a full hour," I say, laughing.

"Until we tried to kill that centipede and started screaming," Roxy adds.

I shudder. "Oh my God, that thing was so gross."

"It was *huge.*" Roxy uses her index fingers to remember the length of it.

"We were determined, though. Remember? We struck a deal: you could use my shoe, but you had to kill it."

"Yeah, except you cheated!" Roxy raises her voice. I shush her, and she whispers, "You wrapped your shoe in toilet paper."

"Just because I'm resourceful that doesn't make me a cheater." I stick my tongue out at her.

She tips her hand in a *comme ci, comme ça* gesture, indicating that it's a gray area.

"Hey, speaking of cheaters..." I say.

Roxy stands up and starts going through my things. I know it's a defense mechanism, her way of trying to ignore me and avoid the truth.

The first item on the chopping block is my Humphrey the Camel Beanie Baby, which I did not have the forethought to preserve in a plastic display case.

"He's worth over one K," I say.

"Not mint condition," she counters, pointing a sharp nail at his crumpled Ty tag.

She will not distract me.

"I saw you get in the car with Brock Crawley."

She ignores me and starts pulling open drawers. Some are stuffed with junk—old Halloween decorations, some toys that haven't yet made it to Goodwill, plus a few items of clothing that are sentimental but don't fit anymore.

"Roxy," I say, trying not to sound too accusatory. Admittedly, it's not my strong suit.

She pulls out a vintage shrieking ghost toy and flips it on. It makes a horrible noise like its battery is dying.

I grab it from her and click the battery off. "Come on, you'll wake up my parents," I say, shoving it back in the drawer.

As if on cue, my mom knocks on the door, her voice groggy. "Ellie? What was that?"

"Nothing, it's fine," I reply, but she opens the door anyway and pokes her head inside. She squints at Roxy, her eyes trying to adjust to the light.

"Roxy?" she says in a surprised croaky voice. "Hi, honey!"

"Hi, Mrs. Jenkins," Roxy says, standing up straight and trying to sound sober.

"How's your mom?" she asks. Her good-to-see-you tone drops to serious and solemn.

"She's fine," Roxy says. It's a blow-off. My mom knows it. I know it. We're both used to it. It's Roxy avoiding the pain of reality. Always avoiding, always numbing, always keeping herself far, far away from anything that could break her heart.

"Okay," my mom says. I can tell she's a little offended by Roxy's lack of response. "Try to keep it down, okay? I don't want you to wake up your dad."

We both nod like we're twelve again, and my mom's head disappears. She shuts the door silently behind her.

Always up for a rebellion, Roxy continues to rummage through my things.

"So, you're not going to tell me anything about your life?" I ask her.

Roxy slams a drawer shut and spins around. She shouts at me in whispers. "What's there to tell, Ellie? What do you want to know? My life's a mess. Is that what you want to hear? I've failed at getting sober more times than I can count. My mom is sicker and meaner than ever. And for some reason, the only thing that gives me some tiny modicum of joy is sitting on Brock Crawley's face."

"Okay, okay, wow," I say, not ready for this outburst of truth. But it is the truth, and the last thing I want to do is punish her for opening up to me. Even if I don't agree with the choices she's making, it doesn't mean it's going to help to admonish her. She doesn't need my commentary. She needs to be loved, and somewhere circa 2010, I lost sight of that. I made what happened between us all about me, and I made everything that happened in high school all about how much I hated it, instead of seeing it for what it was: a time to learn and grow and make mistakes...with your befri stend.

So I bite my tongue and shut my stupid mouth and slide a drawer open that Roxy has so far skipped in her snooping.

I pull out the necklace I shoved in there on the first day of this trip and hold it out in front of her. It's tarnished, but still legible and unmistakably half-heart-shaped.

She sucks in a breath and reaches out to take the necklace from me. She runs her thumb across the engraved letters and chipped pink paint.

"Befri stends," she whispers. "You kept it."

"I know our friendship has always been..." I take a beat, searching for the right word. "Complicated," I say carefully. We wince, but we both know it's the truth. "But I will always be here for you. No matter what."

Roxy's chin quivers, and for a second, I think she's going to cry, but she doesn't. She does, however, put her arms around me and hug me for a long time.

We lie on top of my childhood bed and talk until late in the early morning. I tell her about LA and my TV job, and she tells me about her mom and how much she hates AA. At some point during our conversation, I drift off to sleep.

When I wake up, Roxy is gone.

Mark is standing on my parents' porch.

I look through the sidelight of the front door, and a thousand butterflies take flight inside my stomach. I hate that feeling. I have actually spent most of my life so far trying to avoid that feeling.

I eye him again through the window. He looks tired, but not sad or distressed. Not like he's rethinking this whole thing between us. Whatever this thing is.

I don't pretend to know the endgame; I only know that right now this is the only place I want to be. Falling into lust with Mark Wright.

His wet hair glistens. He's freshly shaven, and he didn't miss a single spot. Once again, I'm surprised by how good-looking I think he is. How unbearable it is when I'm not touching him, when he's not kissing me, and when we're not laughing together about something only the two of us get.

It's strange, but I want that part more than anything else.

The inside jokes. The shared memories. The communicating with just a look.

I don't want a fling that fizzles.

But what if that's all he wants?

I close my eyes, steeling myself for whatever he's going to say. I'm Ellie Jenkins, co-fucking-EP of *Cooler Than You*. Master of character development. Go-getter. I can handle anything.

I twist the door handle, opening my eyes as I do.

They meet his. Warm brown and kind.

"You look like you're about to throw up," Mark says.

I spit out a laugh. "You really know how to deliver a romantic opening line."

He grins, and that dimple pops, the one that only comes out for his biggest smiles.

"Wanna take a walk with me?" he asks.

I grab my coat. He's wearing a thermal shirt under his trim corduroy jacket—the mocha brown color matches his eyes and brings out the warmth of his olive skin.

It's a perfect fall day. Crisp and dewy, trees on fire with color, leaves falling to the ground like snowflakes. We walk to the soundtrack of crunching leaves playing in the background, but we don't say anything right away. At first, I'm waiting for Mark to speak, but then I don't know why I'm doing that. I don't need to wait for an invitation, but I do anyway.

"I met Liz for coffee." He shoves his hands in his pockets, like he's trying to make himself small. He looks like he's still all twisted up inside. Every move, every motion is strained.

"And?" I ask, eager for him to get to the point.

"She's hurt."

"Well, duh," I say. Fuck. Spit it out, Mark.

A guy whizzes by on his bike, sending leaves flying into the air beside us. Mark sidesteps to get out of his way and presses into me. His hand goes around to the small of my back, steadying himself and me. Our eyes lock.

"But she's moving out for good." His breath puffs against the side of my cheek. "It's not a clean break if we're living in the same house."

"Makes sense," I say. His expression is unreadable. Is this what he wants? I don't know why I feel so unsure. "Are you okay with that?" I ask him. My voice sounds squeaky to my own ears. I try to put some distance between us, tucking my hands in my jacket pockets.

His eyebrows scrunch together, and he pulls me closer to him. He takes my hand and holds it up to his chest. His thumb brushes the knuckles, his gaze careful but determined.

"I found Liz at a time in my life when I needed sunshine and safety. She is…a really good person. And I hate that I hurt her, that I keep hurting her." He hesitates. Is there a *but*? There's got to be a *but*. Where is it? I feel panicky.

"But?" I ask, my impatience overriding reasonable thought.

"Liz deserves better than being someone else's safe place to land. It's why I ended things with her, even though I still have *no* fucking clue what I'm going to do or how I'm going to do it. I just wanted to do the right thing in the meantime." He's looking at me now, with eyes that burn. "I don't want to live scared, even if I feel that way all the time. I want to be brave. Like you."

"Like me?" I'm shocked that he thinks of me as brave, when I feel like every decision I make comes with a hefty dose of overthinking and second guessing. "I liked you for six years, maybe longer, and rejected you so that I wouldn't get *rejected*. That's probably the most chickenshit thing anyone's ever done—ever!"

Mark laughs. I can tell I'm making him feel better. And it makes *me* feel better.

I keep going: "And when I finally *did* tell you, it was via drunk message. On Facebook." I bury my face in my hands with a frustrated groan full of self-loathing, but he laughs again, and pulls them away.

"You *truthbombed* me from your college dorm room right before you wrote a TV pilot that landed you an enviable position on a hit TV show. Maybe you're not always brave in love, but you're brave in life. And I think maybe the first one needs the second to survive."

I nearly choke on my own spit. Did he just say *love*?

"So, I know we got off to a weird start here. I know it's not morally all that responsible or maybe even acceptable. But this thing between us—I want to see where it goes," he says, before quickly adding, "if you want."

I blush. I nod. No words come out. I'm afraid if I speak I'll sound like one of the Chipettes. *He just spilled out his guts to you, Ellie! Say something! Anything!*

"I'm hungry," I say. I'm mentally disgusted with myself. *That's the best we can do?!*

My brain is a bitch, even to me.

Mark's face falls just a little from disappointment. He leans back and lets go of my hand to fondle the back of his neck, thinking. "You're hungry?"

"If you're hungry?" I tuck my hands in my coat pockets.

"I could be hungry?" It comes out as a question. It's awkward. We're awkward.

"I don't want to make you eat if you don't want to," I say.

"I wanna eat with you."

His disappointment fades to a cheeky grin as he realizes what's happening. I still feel awkward as fuck.

"Okay, then it's decided. We're hungry and we're going to eat," I say, but my body buzzes with new excitement.

"I need to run by the bakery real quick. I'll be back here in about thirty minutes?"

We must stop speaking in questions.

"Yes. Perfect. Thirty minutes. I'll be ready. I mean, I'm ready right now, but I'll be more ready then. I'll have my purse and phone and house keys."

"All important things."

"Yeah."

We stand in place another minute before turning around to head back to my parents' house. As we walk, I run over the last few minutes in my head. Did I just ask Mark Wright on a date? He might have asked me. Whatever. The point is, I'm pretty damn sure we're about to go on a real-life, Technicolor, no-longer-a-fantasy-in-my-head date.

CHAPTER 27

I all but skip into the house. Mom and Dad watch me suffer with the side effects of full-blown lovesickness like I have an extra head growing out of my neck. I launch myself onto the couch and put my feet up on Dad, who is eating a salad on the couch and watching a *Frasier* rerun with Mom.

"Wasn't this guy still living with his ex-fiancée two days ago?" Mom asks with a raised eyebrow and voice filled with skeptical motherly concern.

I pull my purse off the coffee table and reach in for my lip gloss, using my cell phone as a mirror. "She's moving out," I say, smacking my lips together. I feel Mom staring at me intently, waiting for an explanation. I shrug. "They aren't together anymore. This is totally aboveboard."

"You know what they say about rebounds." Mom turns back to her show.

"It's not like that," I say, getting angry. "I'm not just some easy score, someone to distract him from his loneliness. He's not lonely. I'm not a distraction."

"You only live once," Dad chimes in with fatherly wisdom. He shoves a cherry tomato into his face.

"Exactly," I say, nodding at him. I'll take fatherly wisdom over motherly skepticism any day of the week.

"Well, just be careful. That's all I'm saying." Mom is relentless.

"What's the worst that can happen? He breaks my heart? That's better than the perpetual dry spell my love life has been until now."

"I don't want you to get hurt," Mom reiterates. I roll my eyes at her like an indignant teenager. I'm not proud of it.

"Then you shouldn't have had kids, Mom, because it comes with the heartbeat."

The doorbell rings and Dad pats my feet.

"Have fun, honey," he says, oblivious as always to the mother-daughter spat.

"I will." I sling my purse over one shoulder and shoot a tongue at Mom, who pretends to ignore me for the TV.

When I open the door, Mark is waiting with one hand in his pocket and the other holding a heart-shaped box of chocolates. My heart soars.

"You dog," I say, and take the chocolates, setting them inside on the entryway table. "That's why you went to Stonybrook Market?"

His grin is wicked, just the way I like it. He looks deliciously disheveled, and I resist the urge to grab his face between my hands and kiss him.

Oh, what the hell.

I grab his face and stand on my tippy toes to kiss him. He tastes like coffee.

When I pull back, he's smiling. Swear to God, he has the prettiest smile. All symmetry with lots of teeth, but not too many teeth. The perfect amount of teeth. His sparkly eyes lock with mine. It knocks the wind right out of me. "Should I come in and say hi to your parents?"

"Please don't." I push him a little too hard toward his car. "They might never let us leave."

"Where are we going?" I finally ask Mark after minutes of driving in silence across hilly country roads. What was once my favorite thing to do as a kid now makes me carsick, especially on an empty stomach that is simultaneously swarming with butterflies.

"If I'm doing a traditional Midwestern first date, it starts with Cheesecake Factory and then a movie, maybe ending with some over-the-clothes action in your driveway." Mark waggles his eyebrows at me.

I crinkle my nose at him. "Over-the-clothes is all you get for microwaved frozen food and stale popcorn at a crappy mall theater."

"I suspected as much, so that's not where we're going," he says.

I breathe a sigh of relief and sink down in my seat. "Thank God."

"We're going to the Renaissance Faire."

My head snaps to him, expecting a barely contained fit of laughter that reveals a joke. Instead, I'm greeted with a mischievous smirk.

"We're not," I say. "You're joking."

"Jousting and mud wrestling and fortune telling, oh my!"

"Cheesecake Factory doesn't sound half bad by comparison."

Mark puts a hand to his chest, pretending to be shocked. "Ellie! You don't mean it!"

"I do. I mean it. Let's go to the mothereffing Cheesecake Factory." My stomach growls in agreement, and I clap my hands together in pleading prayer. "Just please don't make me gnaw on a turkey leg like a goddamn barbarian. Not on our first official date."

"What if I told you that our Class Clown is now the Bawdy Buccaneer?" Mark asks. One eyebrow kicks up, anticipating my response.

A grin spreads wide across my face. Every inch of me is thrilling over the fact that Mark is still helping me with the list. That he wants me to win. I'm so used to dating men or watching my friends date men who couldn't give a shit about their girlfriends' careers. These guys care about *their* careers and *their* jobs and *their* promotions. And here's this man I've been with now for about twenty minutes who has thought through our very first date based on me *winning*.

I lean over the center console and kiss Mark on the cheek.

"What was that for?" he asks, touching his cheek where a smudge of lip gloss stayed behind.

"For taking me to the Renaissance Faire," I say with a sigh of surrender. "But I'm not eating a freaking turkey leg."

Cut to me ripping flesh off the boiled leg of a turkey with my teeth. It's sinfully delicious on my empty stomach. It has turned me into a wild, ravenous animal. This turkey leg has unlocked something primal within me, and I think I like it. Mark likes it too. He watches, lips slightly ajar, as I take another bite. Grease coats my lips, and I lick it up. He holds a turkey leg of his own, but seems not as enthusiastically carnivorous as I am. We take the gravel path through the fairgrounds, side-by-side.

"I warned you," I say with a mouthful of turkey, suddenly embarrassed. I try to switch to smaller bites, and his fingers intertwine with my one turkey-less hand.

"I could watch you eat that thing all day." His voice is lower, gravelly, like this look on me is fulfilling a fantasy he didn't even know he had. The implication ignites a different kind of hunger inside my belly. I swallow another bite before I finish chewing it completely. We stare at each other for a long time, suspended between insatiable turkey bites.

He clears his throat, jogging us both out of our sexy turkey haze. "So...what's our plan for when we spot Roy?"

Roy Willard was Class Clown for one reason and one reason only: motherfucker was *mean*. He made fun of anyone and everyone, and *nothing* was sacred. He once made our male gym teacher Mr. Hugo cry by repeatedly cracking jokes about the poor guy's "man titties." Rumor had it the principal was laughing so hard he could barely sign the detention slip.

"I'm supposed to pull a prank on him," I say with a shrug.

"That's a dangerous game." Mark's eyes spark with concern.

"Can't I just tap him on the opposite shoulder? Surprise, no one's there!"

Mark blinks at me. "*That's* the best you can do, Ellie Jenkins, co-EP of a hit TV show about mean girls?"

I sigh and throw out the rest of my turkey leg, suddenly feeling queasy again. First date with the man of my adolescent dreams *and* confront the biggest bully of my high school with a practical joke?

Thanks a lot, Andy Biermann.

If Andy taught me anything, it's that just when you think it can't get any worse for a character, you reveal a trapdoor below them. There's always a new level of hell to send them to.

"Mark Wright," I hear a familiar voice say behind us. When Mark and I turn around, Brock is standing there with arms crossed and a slanted, smug grin across his face. He's in leather pants and a long-sleeved white shirt with a suede leather vest. He looks good, and if it weren't for the thick layer of slime my eyes add to his person automatically, I'd say he's a solid 8.5 on the attractiveness scale, maybe even a 9.

Behind him, looking uncharacteristically sheepish, is none other than Roxy. She's got on her finest inauthentic wench outfit, complete with corset cleavage and hiked-up skirt revealing leather thigh-highs, totally embellished for added sex appeal.

"Did you finally ditch the cheer coach? She's a smoke show, but she probably only likes it missionary style." Brock's giant smirk begs for me to slap it off his face. He looks me up and down, insulting me with his eyes. I want to hold his glare, to send it back at him with one thousand times the force, but my eyes have a mind of their own. They shift without warning to Roxy. She's watching him, and the look on her face says it all. She's okay being treated like shit, but she doesn't want him to do the same thing to me.

Mark visibly bristles at both the vulgar comment and the degrading eye fuck. "I thought you were married?" He looks up, pretending to think about it. "Oh wait, you are."

Brock wraps an arm around Roxy's shoulders in a weirdly possessive way. There's a ring on that hand, and he makes zero effort to hide it. "Roxy and I are just friends. Right, Rox?"

Roxy's eyes meet mine. There's shame. Tons of it. Damn it, Roxy.

In this split second I see how vulnerable she is right now, and how much she needs a friend, an ally. Someone who knows she's more than just a hot piece of ass or a trainwreck in motion. Someone who always saw her potential and loved her for it, even when she let herself down.

No matter what I think about her decisions, the familiar tugging on my heart is unmistakable.

She nudges for him to move his hand off her shoulder. He squeezes.

"Sure you are." Mark takes my hand, possessing me in his own, very Mark way. Gentle possession. Possession that builds up instead of tears down. I watch Roxy's eyes flick down to our joined hands and then back up to meet mine.

"What are you even doing here?" I ask.

"Role playing," Brock says with a suggestive eyebrow waggle. "It's our thing."

"You mean hiding," Mark jabs. Brock shifts his attention back to Mark, who impressively doesn't flinch.

"So the cheer coach is up for grabs?" Brock asks.

"Fuck off, Brock," Roxy says with a giant eye roll, shoving him away from her. She's trying to downplay their proximity, her connection to him.

Brock puts up his hands in defense. "What? I've got some single friends who might want in on that."

"She's not a cow Mark is selling at auction, fuckface," I chime in.

Brock's eyes snap to mine. I shoot imaginary death beams out of my eyes into his disgusting lizard brain. "How's that list coming along, Ellie Bellie?" he says, using Roxy's childhood pet name for me.

My jaw drops. "How do you know about—" My eyes try to meet Roxy's, but she refuses to meet mine back. "You told him?"

Roxy rolls her eyes at me this time. "It's not a big deal."

"Yes, it's a big deal. Why the hell would you tell this flap-jawed scumbag about my list?"

"Like it's a secret?" Roxy shrugs.

"This is exactly why I didn't want you to know about it!" I'm shouting. People are looking. "If people *on* the list find out *about* the list, it could screw up the whole thing! It's not rocket science, *Roxy*!"

I'm so angry there's pressure building inside my head until it feels like it might explode. I haven't been this angry since I can remember. And it's not just about the list. It's about Roxy, here with this contemptible son-of-a-bitch, looking so unlike herself. I hate it so much I could cry.

But Roxy says nothing. She looks so small and weak next to Brock.

I'm seeing red. Anger rises in me like a tidal wave and I can't stop my words from overflowing.

"This isn't you—" I step up, closer to Roxy, my fingers sliding from Mark's grip. "You're not the girl who stoops to the level of side piece for the town molester. Look at him in his leather pants and his weird chest hair popping out of his V-neck. He's practically Gaston." My voice lowers and I speak only to her. "You're better than this."

When she looks at me this time, there's something so broken behind her eyes that my heart nearly cracks in two right there in front of the medieval sword shop. I feel tears threatening to spill over. I want to save her—to help her—but I don't know how. Or why. Or if she'd ever even want my help at all.

You can't save someone who doesn't think she's worth saving.

"And you're not?" Her eyes flick from me to Mark and back to me.

"It's different, and you know it," I say.

"Is it?" she asks, her eyebrows lifting in question. It stings just like she wants it to.

"Fuck you." I hold eye contact one more heartbeat before pivoting away and bolting for the exit sign.

The heart wants what the heart wants. I hear David's voice in my head as it throbs with the sting of Roxy's scorpion lips.

Is it?

CHAPTER 28

There is something completely satisfying about stomping off through the mud in expensive knee-high boots. Especially when you are stomping away from your ex–best friend and your almost-assaulter who just happen to be knocking boots (ba-dum-bum) in every outhouse, public restroom, back seat, and one-hour motel within a fifty-mile radius.

Is it? My cheeks flush when I think of Roxy's jab.

Is it? It is.

Is it? Welcome to Slutville. Free drinks on Thursdays if you put out.

Is it, is it, is it—

"Ellie." Mark's voice is a record scratch to my internal freak-out.

"I'm storming off," I say, without pausing or turning. "Join me."

"Hold up," he says, sounding calm and rational and totally in control. His hand clutches mine, tugging me backward until I give in. I turn, eyes flying to his, hoping to convey the absolute wildfire happening inside that cannot be contained.

"Talk to me," he pleads, somehow working his fingers between my vice grip of rage.

"What is there to talk about?"

"A lot, it seems," he says, those caramel-almost-molasses eyes twinkling with understanding.

"Roxy and I haven't been friends in over ten years. Anything we have to talk about was buried in a Stonybrook time capsule. Circa two thousand fucking ten," I say, wishing that I wanted to dislodge my fingers from his grip but not having the fortitude to follow through with it. Damn this romantic desire.

He considers me for an overlong moment. I stand firm. He rubs his thumb over the rise in my palm, that lopsided smile of his like water poured on the flame of my anger. Not that I tell him that. But as it ebbs, the feeling that rises up in its place is unmistakable. Regret. Soul-sucking, nauseating regret.

"I don't want to talk about the Roxy thing," I say, but I meet his eyes, and give him a one-shoulder shrug. "I don't know how I feel about it. What I feel. Or why I even care."

It's a lot to express to anyone, and even though it's not romantic feelings, I still ache with the stretch of all this new vulnerability. Mark responds to my exposed nerves by pulling me in and brushing the hair off my neck. His fingers tingle over my skin, and his lips touch lightly to the edge of my ear.

Everything else falls away.

I lean in, closing my eyes, wondering how I ever lived so many years without this. Without him.

"When you're ready to talk about it, let me know," Mark

whispers in my ear. He's so sweet, it actually physically hurts me. Like a toothache.

I know this is different. Mark is not Brock. I am not Roxy. But we still hurt someone. We're still jumping into something new just a day after she caught us on her couch. I can't help but feel like we don't deserve a good thing, this fast. To be happy together, holding hands, fairytale thriving. I feel like I'm waiting for the other shoe to drop.

"In the meantime, we still have a prank to pull on the most notorious bully of our high school class." His hand trails down to the small of my back. It's a simple touch that tingles all the way up my spine and then back down again to lower, unmentionable places. I tilt my head back to look at him, and it takes every ounce of my willpower not to jump him right here, right now, in the middle of this medieval dirt path. I clear my throat.

"Lead the way, Mr. Wright. We need to get a look at what has become of Roy Willard."

With a grin, Mark presents an arm and I take it, and we make our way through the fairgrounds to a stage built into a small grove of trees. The backdrop is of a windswept sea, and rising from the stage is the wooden façade of a ship. We're just in time to catch the end of the show—which Mark told me plays three times a day—about a violent brute of the sea and his pillaging crew.

Roy Willard, aka the Bawdy Buccaneer (aka number eight on my list of doom), twirls center stage in a horribly choreographed final fight.

Some people change so much in ten years that when you see them again, your brain refuses to believe they are the same person. Roy Willard is one of those people.

In high school, Roy was the kind of guy you only noticed because if you didn't, he'd coat tampons in fake blood and hang them from your locker. He was short for his age, with floppy brown hair and perpetually dirty fingernails—like some heavy-handed metaphor for him digging up dirt to use on his victims. He had a baby face that acted as a mask for the demon lurking at his core. Think *Children of the Corn* and Damien from *The Omen*, but maybe Roy was meaner than both.

Ten years later, he's still short, but his floppy hair has grown long, and his once deceptive smile has morphed into a devilish sneer that shines with a gold canine. When he turns his eyes to the crowd, stabbing his castmate a little too emphatically in the side, they're bloodshot, heavy with dark circles, and cold as ice.

They say you earn the face you deserve, and a decade later, Roy Willard looks like the bully that was always lurking deep down inside.

I glance at Mark, and I have to admit, I'm shaking in my knee-high boots. I managed to go four years of high school without ever getting crossways with Roy, but that doesn't mean he never hurt me. The week before senior superlatives were announced, photos of Roxy topless in a swimming pool were texted to every senior by an anonymous number. Rather than hide, Roxy did the most Roxy thing of all and responded by dropping a nude of Roy in the chain.

Roxy was the only person I'd ever known to stand up to Roy Willard. And it backfired.

Roy printed the pictures of her from the pool on poster-sized paper and hung them in the teachers' lounge over the weekend.

Roxy was suspended. She almost didn't graduate.

And she was awarded Most Likely to Brighten Your Day as punishment from her cowardly classmates.

Why Roxy was suspended and Roy wasn't expelled for committing a sex crime, I'll never understand. Hopefully, society has progressed since then.

There was nothing a Miscellaneous kid like me could do about it—or that was the excuse I used to get myself to sleep at night.

The crowd roars as Roy takes a bow.

I squeeze Mark's hand.

"I think I have an idea for how we can prank Roy Willard," I say, and I can't help it—my smile becomes a sneer.

Kyle Temple is more than happy to send us some incriminating photos of Roy from college, especially since Kyle got expelled for vandalizing the dorms and Roy evaded punishment in the usual way—by throwing Kyle all the way under the bus. For the promise of video footage and a case of Bud, Kyle texts pictures of College Roy that Mark and I will *never* be able to unsee.

"Oh, God," Mark says next to me in the car as the texts start to come through, one by one. He makes a face and turns away.

"Uh-uh, I will *not* shoulder this burden alone," I say, tugging on Mark's ear to force him to look. We take turns groaning and gagging as the pictures download to my phone. I finally can't take it anymore and text Kyle to tell him we have what we need.

The nearest FedEx Office is a ten-minute drive away in Whiting, the town on the other side of the fairgrounds. I don't know how we don't set off any red flags, but a kid with long hair and unusually bloodshot eyes prints everything we need without question, albeit at his own pace. Mark pays for the prints (because he insists this is still technically part of the date), and we head back to the Renaissance Faire.

We identify Roy's truck—he's one of those dudes who is posing with his truck in his profile picture on Facebook—and Mark parks his car a few rows away in the only free spot. The icing on this revenge cake will be how masterfully we now use Roy's beloved truck for our prank masterpiece. I get to work and Mark goes back to the front gate to keep an eye on Roy's movements.

An hour later, Mark emerges, jogging up to me as I put the finishing touches on Roy's truck. He's breathless, his eyes sparking with mischief. "His last show just ended. I could hear the crowd cheering on the way over," he says, his eyes trailing over my disgusting masterpiece. "Holy shit, Ellie."

I jump from the truck bed to admire my work. Mixed in with the eight-by-ten prints of College Roy, I've written on the windshield and windows and all over the body of the truck the names of people Roy tortured in high school.

Mr. Hugo. Jenny Sanders, who left in ninth grade after Roy spread a rumor that she had hairy nipples (and the entire school nicknamed her Sasquatch). David Duncan. Emma Lovett. Darla King. Devon Greenwood, who Roy outed junior year over the morning announcements. On and on.

Kids like Roy usually have a reason for lashing out at everyone around them, but not always. Eventually, the Roys of the world grow up to be adults, and maybe they grow out of it, but they always leave a row of casualties in their wake.

I add Roxy's name last. Mark doesn't say anything, but I can tell that he wants to. I know he probably will once this is all over. I'm thankful that he can tell that now is not the time.

Now, we wait.

We hide a few cars away, crouched in the gravel and dirt. Just before sunset, Roy, accompanied by a few castmates and Ren Faire employees, exits the park. Without his costume, he looks more like the Roy we used to know. He's filled out some, and his features are sharper and harder, but he's unmistakably Roy. He smacks one of the women beside him right on the ass, and she jumps. Her features tighten, but she doesn't say anything and just rolls her eyes instead.

I guess our bully never grew out of it.

One of the guys slaps Roy on the shoulder, pointing toward his truck. Mark lifts his phone, open to the camera, and begins recording. Roy's eyes trail over the row of cars to settle on his truck. His face screws up in confusion.

"What the fuck?" he says, but we can only see him form the words. He's still too far away to hear.

He runs for his truck. Behind him, his friends—if that's what they are—cackle. The girl Roy assaulted stays quiet, looking nervous, but even from here, I can see a tentative smile twitch across her lips.

Roy reaches his truck, taking in the sight. His face twists, rage and embarrassment warring for real estate. He grabs the picture taped to his dash. It's of him, no doubt drunk off his ass, wearing nothing but a stupid smile on his face and a pair of black socks, about to chug beer from a bong. He's fat and bloated, with a bulging Natty Light belly, and he's the only one laughing in the picture.

That's the thing about candid shots. The truth about how other people see you comes into sharp focus.

His eyes flick over the pictures, and he reads the names, as his friends come up behind him. Their phones are out. The flash on. Every shot is followed by a burst of light.

"Holy fuck, is that you?" one asks, and he points to a photo of Roy passed out, with someone whose face is just out of frame holding a used condom above his mouth.

"Oh my God, this is disgusting," another laughs and gags. They think this is all good fun. They don't know who they're dealing with.

Roy's face contorts. But not with rage, not angry, malicious, or cruel. For a brief, horrible moment, he looks sad. And scared. He doesn't look like the Bawdy Buccaneer or Roy Willard, Class Clown, who was really just a bully. He looks like a small, freaked-out kid.

Mark moves his finger to stop recording, and I know he saw it, too.

Too bad, right at that moment, Roy turns to his friend, and his eyes pass over the car Mark and I are hiding behind.

"Who the fuck?" He smacks the camera out of his friend's hand, pushing him out of the way. "Mark fucking Wright?" he asks, his voice deadly still.

"Oh, shit," Mark says.

Roy's eyes trail to me. He doesn't know me. I can tell he's trying to place me, call my face up from the recesses of his brain. I don't want to wait around to let him.

"Time to go!" I say, grabbing Mark by the wrist and launching into a run.

We don't look back to see if he follows. We can hear him running along the gravel, a string of expletives flying at us like arrows. My lungs burn as we round the row of cars where we parked. Mark releases a terrified, exhilarated laugh into the air. He fumbles with his key fob, pressing the button to unlock the car.

With a screech, we yank the doors open, slam into the seats.

I hit the locks. Mark turns the key in the ignition.

We peel out, but not before Roy runs up to my window and smacks it with his fist.

"Oh my God," I spit, struggling to catch my breath. My hands are shaking with adrenaline as I pull my seat belt over my chest and buckle it.

Mark blares his horn a few times and says, "Number eight: check."

My heart nearly explodes from the exertion.

Exhausted, I lean over and press my lips to his cheek, winding my arms around his neck.

I pull back to let my head fall against the headrest, watching him through the haze of my adrenaline as it drops back down. We're quiet for a second and then Mark says, "I don't think we should send that video to Kyle."

I know what he means. Kyle wouldn't be able to keep it to himself, and as fun as it might sound in theory, revenge is a dish that gives me indigestion.

"We gave him a taste of his own medicine," I say. "That's good enough for the list."

Mark nods his agreement and sighs. "It felt pretty fucking amazing to stick it to that prick."

I close my eyes, feeling the up-down of the car as it cruises away from the dirt paths around the Ren Faire and back into town. After a few minutes of easy quiet, my eyes drift open and fix on the line of his neck. I watch his Adam's apple bob as he swallows, and then his chest heaves with an extra-deep inhale.

"As far as first dates go," I start, letting my fingertips tuck into the hair at the nape of his neck, "this definitely tops the Cheesecake Factory." His whole body goes still.

"Ellie," he says, clutching my hand resting on his lap.

I smirk. "What, am I distracting you?"

He nods, and suddenly the only thing I can think about is running my hands over his chest. Winding my legs around him until I'm sitting on his lap. Kissing his lips until he begs me to stop.

"Fuck," Mark says.

I look up, following his eyes through the front windshield. We're on his street. In front of his townhouse. The one he shared with Liz.

"Autopilot," he says, his voice constricted.

There's a small U-Haul trailer attached to a Jeep out front. The front door hangs open. Before he has a chance to put the car in reverse, Liz, followed by a brawny redheaded guy wearing a Station 49 fireman's shirt, exits the townhouse.

Liz stops, her small hands faltering around the box she's carrying.

"Who's that with her?"

"Jamie," Mark says, just as Jamie's eyes trail to Mark's car. "Liz's big brother."

I recognize him easily now. Jamie played football in the grade above us. I vaguely remember hearing about him breaking someone's jaw in a championship game.

Jamie's eyes lock with mine through the windshield and then trace back over to Mark's.

I watch him go from zero to seeing red in less than three seconds. He flings the box he's carrying to one side.

Fuck is right.

CHAPTER 29

Hold me back, Liz, hold me back!" Jamie puffs up his chest like a WWE wrestler and walks toward the car like a gorilla, pounding his chest with alternating fists.

"What is he doing?" I sink down into my seat.

"Embarrassing himself and all of mankind." Mark locks the doors and puts the car in park. "He's a fucking Neanderthal."

Outside, Liz watches in horror as her brother Hulks up to the driver's side of Mark's car. "Jamie, please," she pleads in a vain attempt to break through the silverback gorilla haze. She rolls her eyes, and they find mine in the car, apologetic.

Jamie's massive hand comes down on the car door handle and yanks. A few times. He looks thwarted but not deterred. I assume his initial plan was to drag Mark out and pummel him. Thank God it's locked.

Mark is pale as a ghost.

"Is this real life?" I exhale as Jamie makes a loop around the car like a wild animal circling its prey. I've witnessed more crazy in the last four days in Stonybrook than I have in six years in Los Angeles.

Mark leans away from the window, tapping the button a few times to crack open the glass just enough so Jamie can hear him. "Can you please calm down?"

"You show up here with that slut and tell *me* to fucking calm down?" He smacks his pecs again.

"Jamie!" Liz looks pissed. "That word is degrading. To all women." Jamie stops at Mark's door and bends to put his eyes in line with the crack in the window.

"Why don't you come out here and face me like a man?"

"Why is that the barometer for manliness? Fistfighting and whatnot?" I ask, and it's a mistake because now Jamie's attention is on me.

"I'm sorry, did you say something?" Jamie cups his hand around his ear. "I can't hear you with Mark's dick in your mouth."

Mark steams. Like, were I to pour water on him, the car would fill with white haze.

"That's enough!" Mark unlocks the door and opens it as hard and as fast as he can. It slams into Jamie and he stumbles, falling back a few feet. Mark's out the door, his finger pointing toward Jamie in accusation. "Say what you want about me, but leave Ellie out of it."

No one's ever defended my honor before. How romantic!

Jamie regains his footing, rising up to full height. Okay, whoa. This fucker is *huge*.

Mark, get back in the car and drive away! He broke a guy's jaw once! Fuck my honor!

Somehow my telepathy doesn't work. Mark tries to make

himself bigger, and it's seriously cute and dorky, and it makes my stomach flip-flop all over the place.

Jamie's chest is a barrel, and he's got the kind of muscles that strain the skin. He gives Mark a shit-eating grin, eyes sliding up and down, before charging him like a bull to a matador.

All lovey-dovey feelings evaporate.

Jamie's shoulder lands square in Mark's side and they topple to the ground like players on a football field.

"Oh my God!" Liz yells, dropping the box in her hands and running toward the fray.

I jump up in my seat, and the belt grabs my shoulder. I reach down to unbuckle it. Jamie leans up, hovering over Mark, but is distracted momentarily by Liz screaming his name and running directly at him. Mark wisely takes the advantage. His knuckles make contact with Jamie's jaw in a loud *crack*.

Mark doubles over as Jamie rolls off. I think the crack was his knuckles.

Shit.

They both struggle to stand, heaving in air.

I think it's over. It has to be over. Mark shakes out his hand.

Liz's fingers are inches from her brother's shoulder when Jamie lunges again. His fist lands squarely on Mark's jaw. I scream and try to leap out of the car, only to get my boot stuck in the center console.

By the time I make it out of the car, screaming my brains out, Liz is thinking ten steps ahead of me and is holding the garden hose. She turns the setting all the way up to *powerwash*, and a powerful stream of spray hits her brother directly in the head. He's knocked away from Mark, and he spins around to wrestle the hose from his sister.

"What the fuck are you doing?" Jamie shouts.

"Making you stop." She sprays him again, right in his face.

Mark is on the ground—not bleeding, thank God—but he clutches his jaw and I can tell he's in a lot of pain. His knuckles are bruising, too, and starting to swell.

I kneel down beside him. All I want to do is get away from here. Far, far away. Maybe back to LA, where I can get us In-N-Out to take back to my apartment so I can snuggle Mark back to health in the king-sized bed I invested in with the secret hope I'd have someone to share it with.

Now, here he is, the boy, man, this person I've always dreamed about—curled up on the ground—jaw swelling because of me. Because no matter how broken up they were, her brother still thinks it's too fast, and somehow we besmirched her honor.

"I don't need you to defend me," Liz screams at Jamie, still gripping the nozzle on the water hose and pointing it directly at his face.

"He shows up here with that—"

"Ellie," Liz says. "Her name is Ellie. She lives in LA and writes for that TV show that Lucy watches. *Cooler Than You?*"

She looks at me for confirmation, and I nod, my eyes wide in stunned surprise. What is this plot twist?

Jamie looks from Liz to me and back to Liz. "Does she know that kid? The one with the swoop?" He gestures to his hair to indicate the hairstyle, and I know exactly who he's talking about.

"Eddie Harper," I say, feeling hopeful that I can defuse the situation. Hollywood to the rescue! "Yeah, I know him."

All at once, Jamie is sheepish, shifting from foot to foot, his upper body soaked and dripping. "Do you think I could get his autograph for my kid? I'll be dad of the year."

I roll my eyes on the inside, but all I want is for everyone else to disappear so I can get Mark inside. "Sure. Send me your address, and I'll get you a signed poster."

"That's great, that's really great." He smiles wide and taps Liz on the elbow. "I'm gonna go call Lame-y and rub it in her face." I'm assuming "Lame-y" is code for Amy, an ex-wife? Oh, the hypocrisy. He practically skips down the sidewalk toward his Jeep and shouts back at Mark. "Sorry not sorry about your face, Marcus! Put some peas on it."

Mark sighs heavily, and I touch the faint shadow forming under his cheekbone. He recoils in pain, sucking in a breath.

"Sorry," I whisper.

He smiles at me weakly.

Liz drops the hose and approaches us both.

"I'm sorry about my brother," Liz says to me while I help Mark to his feet. There's an edge of upbeat in her voice. She's not totally unhappy that her brother pounded Mark's face to a pulp. "He's going through a rough divorce. His ex got custody of their only daughter. It's a whole thing. Mark knows all about it."

Her eyes flick to Mark's. He tries to smile at her, but winces instead.

"I'm gonna go…ice my face." Mark walks toward the front door. Before he reaches it, Jamie sticks his head over the roof of the Jeep.

"Hey, Marcus—does your face hurt? Because it's killing me!" Jamie whoops.

Mark looks back at me, beckoning me to follow. I gesture that I'll be there in one minute. He shrugs and raises his eyebrows, indicating *suit yourself*.

He leaves the front door open behind him.

"I'm going to be okay, you know," Liz says, quiet enough for just me to hear. Her eyes find mine and hold contact with intensity. She's already different. Clearer, steadier, head held higher—less of a woodland sprite and more Queen of the Fairies.

"I know," I say with a faint smile.

"Probably better," Liz adds. She's in pain. It's written all over her face. "We were more *convenient* than *meant to be*, but we didn't actually fit together." She's looking at me, clear and open.

I can see it in her eyes. How amazing she's going to be. There's a fire, a spark, that wasn't there before. Something awakened that was lying dormant, maybe out of uncertainty and boredom. She's like an uncaged bird now, and even though I can also see that she's scared, she's ready for the open air.

She'll fly soon.

"Definitely better," I say. I tilt my head to one side and smile at her. She doesn't smile back. Instead, she leans down to pick up the box she was holding and walks toward the U-Haul. She sets the box inside and waits for her brother to set the one he tossed aside on top before closing the hatch. I watch as she opens the passenger door to Jamie's Jeep. She hesitates and looks back at me, then past me at the condo where she and Mark were supposed to start their life together. Liz ducks into the Jeep and slams the door shut behind her.

I watch them drive away until they round the corner and disappear from view.

*

When I get inside, Mark is sitting on the couch with a bag of frozen broccoli cradling his jaw.

"No peas?" I ask. He shakes his head. I glance around. "It's pretty empty." I motion to the barren apartment. Apparently, Liz was the one doing all the decorating. Now it's just that ugly couch and a table and chairs.

I take a turn around the room. She didn't dust (why would she), so on every surface where a picture frame sat, the evidence still remains. Gone, but not erased. Mark is watching me, but I don't stop. I walk into the kitchen. There's a Ninja blender on the counter. A Mr. Coffee. Two magnets hang on the fridge: a Michonne sword with *The Walking Dead* logo beneath, and one from the bakery where Mark works. The rest of the kitchen is bare. I bet if I opened the cabinets, they'd be mostly empty.

"She and her mom went shopping when we moved in together," Mark says, his voice making me jump. I whirl. He's standing in the doorway, bag of broccoli in hand.

My heart thumps hard against my ribs.

It's just me and him and the graveyard of his former life.

Me and him and a shitty IKEA couch he bought before he fell in love with a strawberry-haired woodland sprite. Before he gave up on his dream, or maybe exactly right when he did. Maybe buying that couch was the moment Mark Wright settled for normal.

Jesus, I can see it just past him through the door. A hideous gray omen.

My stomach drops as I realize maybe he's regretting ending things with Liz.

"Your eyes have tripled in size," Mark says. "What are you thinking?"

His face falls. It's already turning purple from where Jamie hit him.

"You have to get rid of that couch," I say.

His eyes snap to mine. His brow furrows.

"What?"

"It's like the carcass of your life with Liz," I say, my eyes trekking over the scene.

"It's the couch I bought when I moved home from New York."

"Even worse. It's the Couch of Failure."

His cheeks flush. He steps into the kitchen, closer to me, and I take a step back.

"So you want to redecorate?" he asks. "Right now?"

I nod, gulp. My heart thumps inside my chest so hard it hurts. He takes another step closer to me.

"What did you have in mind?" he asks. His brown eyes are smoldering. I break his gaze. It's too much, too intense. I'm afraid I'll go blind with the heat of it.

"We light that couch on fire," I say. "Burn it to the ground."

He laughs at my vicious couch-decimating fantasy. He reaches up to tuck some of my hair behind my ear. My eyes close, savoring the sensation. I love it when he touches my hair *so much*. "And?" he asks.

"We get you a new couch. Maybe one from Pottery Barn." I blink my eyes open and pin them on his.

"Pottery Barn. Fancy," he says, the corner of his mouth ticking up. He winces at the effort. His hand sweeps down my neck, across my collarbone, over my shoulder, trails down my arm until it comes to rest on my hip. It's a long, lingering touch that burns. "What then, Ellie?"

He squeezes my hip and I have no more words. They have all evaporated under the heat of his hand.

"How about I pull you down on that fancy Pottery Barn couch," he says, his voice low and soft, like a caress. "You bury your fingers in my hair and show me where you want me to touch you, and we'll discover all the ways we fit together."

My brain flashes back to Liz's words in the driveway. *We didn't actually* fit *together.*

Mark and I fit together just right.

I can feel the heat coming off his body, and all I want is for him to touch me. To pull me into him until every soft curve of my body fits with the hard lines of his.

I lift my face, and my nose brushes over his lips.

"I have some edits," I whisper. Our eyes lock. I don't shy away from the fire this time. Bring on the heat.

"Oh yeah?" he breathes.

"I take the edge of your shirt between my fingers," I say, reaching out and tugging. His hips bump mine. He doesn't resist. "I lean up, and my lips touch your skin right here."

I scoot closer, dipping my head to his swollen jaw. He tenses, and I plant a kiss beneath his ear.

"Ellie." My name sounds like a plea. He sucks in a breath and grips my shoulders as I press a little too hard against an extra tender spot in the center of his cheek. I pause for a few seconds before I continue my slow descent down his jawbone toward his chin. When I reach the tip of his chin, I pull back to look in his eyes.

Eyes so brown they're almost black. Charged up and alive with wanting.

"I really do hate that IKEA couch," I breathe against his lips.

He laughs, his thumb stroking the front of my hip, coming to rest in the tender spot where my thigh meets my hip bone. It warms my skin through my jeans, a subtle touch with the promise of so much more.

"How do you feel about an IKEA mattress?" he asks, leaning forward. I pull away, playfully denying contact before he can reach my lips. He understands the game and holds his hand out for me to take.

I slip my hand in his and follow Mark Wright up the stairs to his bed.

CHAPTER 30

Halfway up the stairs, Mark turns, stepping back to the one I'm balancing on. He leans in. His lips tug at a smile that he doesn't unleash as his finger hooks my chin, drawing my mouth to his. He presses his mouth to mine. My lips open. His tongue searches, tapping teeth, tickling, tasting. I inhale his breath. My body rises to his, chest to chest, hips to hips, but he backs away as soon as we touch.

He scales the next few stairs while I stand there staring at his ass in jeans.

It's been a long while since I had sex. The last time was with a guy who worked for another show on the network. He wore baseball caps and smelled good in the morning, like soap and aftershave. We'd pass in the office, share banter by the microwave in the break room. He was nice, and it felt good, but there were never any real fireworks.

It was easy to let it fizzle when it never really sparked.

My lips tingle with the leftover heat from Mark's kiss. Sixth

Grade Ellie, the one who fell in puppy love with Mark after he gave his oral report about whales to the class—and then spent years ignoring him from afar—would lose her shit if she knew she'd one day end up here. I went years thinking—fearing—that whatever it was that people felt in movies, or my friends felt with their significant others, was just not going to happen for me.

But the gravitational pull I feel right now in this beige townhouse in Stonybrook, Ohio, to the guy I was so into in high school, the one I was sure I'd blown my chances with in a spectacular way, who I wanted to pretend no longer existed for fear of being rejected—none of this is left over from Miscellaneous Ellie's daydreams.

This is not a dream.

This is real.

When I walk up those stairs, I'm going to have sex with Mark Wright.

Hot, sweaty, slippery, passionate sex with the real-life Mark Wright.

As I step onto the landing, my nerves get the best of me, and I'm winding my arms around Mark's waist from behind. His hand covers mine. His fingertips are soft, smooth. He turns to face me, making eye contact briefly before pulling me in for another long, deep, hot kiss that shoots flames right to my core. His hands grope at my waist, pulling me closer.

"Are you okay?" he asks, so soft, so gentle with me.

I nod and pull him back in for another kiss. He winces against me.

"I'm sorry," I say, pulling back from his mouth.

"It's worth it," he whispers.

I stare into his eyes, over his jaw. I press my lips lightly to where it's starting to bruise. "I like you a little roughed up."

This time, when I kiss him, he opens his mouth for me, and a moan that's not from pain rises in his throat. My hands search down the hard line of muscle on his back and tuck into his jeans. He tightens his grip on my waist, rumpling my shirt, sliding over my ass, winding back to the hem of my shirt and touching the skin beneath.

I back him into his bedroom before pulling away.

His lips are swollen from kissing, his jaw is dark from bruising, his eyes are shiny, dilated like he's drunk on me, and it's the hottest thing I've ever seen. Behind him, the bed sits, bare to the bone.

She took the sheets, bedding, and one of the lamps on the bedside table.

Jesus.

Mark follows my gaze, turning around to face the bed. For a second, I'm glad I can't see his face, because I want to give him the space to feel whatever it is this is going to make him feel. He reaches out his hand behind him for me to take.

I do, and he pulls me close. Our fingers lace together, locked.

"Hold on," he says after a beat, lifting my hand to press his lips lightly to the back of it.

He walks to the bathroom and opens a cabinet. I hear him rummaging around inside and then the door shuts with a puff. He walks back out holding a set of black plaid sheets.

"These were mine before Liz and I moved in together. We only used them for company because they didn't match her bedding. It's all I have left."

My heart cracks a little, and I want to take him in my arms.

"You take that side," I say, walking around to the other side of the bed.

Mark doesn't move right away. He stands in the doorway to his bathroom, holding sheets and staring at me. His eyes are soft. The hot fire from earlier has dimmed, but what's there now is better somehow. Sweet and vulnerable and all for me.

He walks back to the bed, unfurling the sheet and tossing it in the air. I grab my edge and we work together to put the bedding on. As we pass around, tucking in the edges, our bodies brush. My pulse quickens, the thud of my heart a drum against the walls of my ribs. He sets the pillows on the bed. I fold back the top sheet. Our eyes meet across the mattress.

I whirl, dropping to the edge of the bed to unzip my boots. I hear him move behind me, his shoes hitting the ground as he climbs over the bed. His fingers brush the hair off my neck, sending a shiver down my spine. He touches his lips to the curve where my neck meets my shoulder, and I close my eyes. A small breath escapes my mouth. He layers gentle kisses up my neck until his lips tuck behind my ear, light, soft, and full of longing.

He pulls back, and I turn, drawing my leg up to the bed so we are facing each other. His eyes have ignited. The dark mocha brown is now black with desire, sharp and hungry. He focuses on my lips, trailing down to my chest and the triangle of skin exposed where my shirt is unbuttoned. I undo the first button of my blouse, holding eye contact with him as I do.

"Do you mind if I take the rest?" he asks. He swallows hard, and I can tell his breathing is more shallow than usual. I'm making Mark Wright nervous, and I fucking love it.

I drop my hands.

"Go right ahead," I say. *Yes, please, and fast.*

His fingers are swift, deft with the slick pearl buttons. When he reaches the bottom, he stops to take in his handiwork. He's seen me without my top on before, in a rush, our passion tainted with shame and guilt. This time it's different.

He carefully uncovers my shoulders, and I let the fabric fall away.

Thank God I had the foresight to wear a cute bra.

He's looking at me like I have the most beautiful body he's ever seen, and it's sexy to see in his eyes how much he wants me, but I want to feel him all over me, to feel in every single part of my body how much he wants me. I pull on his shirt, tugging him closer, and after a single kiss to his lips, I break away to drag his shirt over his head.

Our lips crash together. Our tongues tangle. We slide over so we're lying on the bed, and I press against him with the full length of my body. His hands run over my back, over my bra clasp, undoing it. Skin to skin, we fold into each other, twining our legs. I feel around for the button of his jeans.

Undo it.

The zipper opens. I press into him.

He moans.

I smile against his mouth. He clutches my ass, pulls at the waistband of my jeans, and then his hands work the button free. We slip everything off.

I have to look. Mark Wright is naked next to me. I've definitely had some fantasies about that. The setting sun streams through the white linen curtains. His tanned body is slick with heat, and he's perfect.

Perfect for me.

We glide together under the sheets. He kisses my breasts, using his hand to stroke up the inside of my thigh, a slow ascension to where my body aches for him most. Everywhere he touches me is lit up, and everywhere he doesn't is begging for attention. I pull him on top of me, feeling his weight and his lust, my fingers gripping his skin, trying to get him closer.

He pushes up, securing his hand on the pillow beneath my head.

"Where are you going?" I ask, opening my eyes and shivering at the loss of his heat.

"I need to get something," he says, and he rolls away, walking to the bathroom and opening a single drawer. I shamelessly watch him come back to the bed, even though he's definitely blushing now beneath his bruise. He tears open a tiny silver wrapper.

He lifts the sheet, uncovering me completely before he lets it fall down over his back. He neatly applies the condom before pulling me carefully back into his arms. Our lips press together, light at first, then harder, and his hand clutches my breast in a firm but gentle squeeze. I grip him, working my legs around until he's back on top.

He leans up, looking me in the eyes. He doesn't say anything, but he doesn't have to. His lips touch mine, and then I can feel him, hot and hard between my legs.

One slow slide and he's inside me, stretching me wide, filling me up body and soul.

My breath puffs against the side of his face as he presses his mouth to my neck. Every thrust of his hips is a spark igniting a flame, a secret feeling that has long lain dormant inside of me. We're in sync, moving together.

I'm so close to the edge I can feel myself slipping, and then I'm falling, falling, and he's falling with me.

We fall together—weightless with desire and trembling with release.

When it's over, we disentangle our bodies from the sea of hideous black plaid and laugh about how high school we feel right now, all awkward bedding and nervous fumbling. Mark tells me that he's never felt this way about anyone, and I tell him that I've always felt this way about him.

He smiles against my lips before his head dips down, and we find new ways we fit together just right.

CHAPTER 31

It's super late when we finally come up for air. We doze lazily, me resting my head on his shoulder, him with his arm draped across my stomach. He traces slow circles on my skin, across my ribs and down to my belly button. It feels so good I could die. Happily. Right here in his arms.

My stomach decides to interrupt this perfect moment with a chorus of angry growls.

"Hungry?" Mark asks, kissing the top of my head.

My stomach answers him, loudly.

"I think that one shook the house," he says. I grimace as he drifts out of my embrace and into boxers, then sweatpants and a T-shirt. "I'll order a pizza."

I toga myself up in the plaid bedsheet and follow him down the stairs to the kitchen. I plop down on the horrible couch while he pours two glasses of water and orders a pepperoni pizza.

"With mushrooms?" he asks. I wrinkle my nose. "Scratch that. Olives?" Thumbs-up. "Extra olives."

He hangs up and sits next to me, admiring my makeshift outfit. He hands me a glass of water, and I chug the whole thing. Some of it drips down my chin. When I'm done, he's staring at me with a funny look on his face.

"What?"

"You're different."

"Gee, thanks."

"No, I mean it in a good way," he says. "There's nobody like you."

I consider that for a moment. "What do you mean?"

"You just are who you are," he says. "You don't make any apologies for being you. For being Ellie."

I lean back. "That's different from high school, I guess."

"You were always like that," he says, tilting his head. "Remember ninth grade English class when we all did a dramatic reading of *Romeo and Juliet*? And you played Romeo."

I drop my face into my hands. "Please, don't remind me."

He wraps a hand around the wrist closest to him, and I peek at him through the cage of my fingers. "You got so into your death scene that Ms. Kipler thought for sure you'd cracked your head open."

"I had a knot on the back of my head for weeks," I admit.

"You committed," he says. "You commit to everything." He looks away sadly, and I lower my hands to my lap. I chew on my bottom lip, unsure of what to say next, because his compliment is laced with his own uncertainty. He couldn't commit to the life laid out for him—and not just the one he was going to have with Liz.

Mark Wright's story is tainted with indecision.

"It's better not to commit," I say, "than to commit to the wrong thing."

"I'm not thinking about Liz," Mark says, his gaze flicking back to me. He holds my eyes intently, making sure he gets his point across. "I'm sure about you."

But how could he be? We've literally been dating for twenty-four hours. He was engaged to and allegedly in love with another woman...last week. He could have had sex with Liz like, last month or even a week ago or...jealousy winds itself up around my guts. My face screws up, and I manage to flatten it back out before he looks over.

I don't want to say all of that out loud, even if it's true. This moment is bigger than a big fat reality check from me. I just want to sit, wrapped up naked under our sexy-time bedsheets on his repulsive couch and pretend the rest of life isn't waiting on the other side of that front door.

"When do you have to go back?" Mark asks.

"I'm an adult. It's not like I have a curfew," I say, trying to stay on track.

Sexy sheets. Happy bubble. Don't pop.

"You know what I mean," he says with a sad smile.

"Friday."

The doorbell rings. Thank God. Mark stands, walking toward the door. He's wearing slightly more clothes than me. When he opens the door, the same pimply-faced pizza guy who delivered pizzas to Rachel's house last night and got his lights punched out stands on the other side.

I bite back a laugh. His nose is bruised, but doesn't seem broken, and Mark points to the purple bruise still darkening over his own jaw. "We match," he says with a grin.

The pizza guy looks a little freaked when he recognizes Mark from yesterday. His eyes shift to me, toga-ing it up on the couch. I see his Adam's apple bob as he swallows.

"That'll be fourteen-fifty." There's a definite whimper in his voice.

Mark fishes out a twenty and a few extra dollars for the tip this poor kid didn't get yesterday. The pizza guy takes the money, shoves the box into Mark's hands, and runs as fast as he can to his car. Mark shuts the door and turns back to face the sofa, just as we hear the sound of tires squealing as the pizza guy makes a speedy escape.

My laugh comes in a burst, and Mark's shoulders shake with his.

Thankfully, when he sets the pizza box on the couch between us, he doesn't return to our previous conversation. I greedily grab a slice and stuff my face with it. He watches me eat pizza with the same voracious appetite I used to tear into the turkey leg at the Ren Faire.

"Sex makes me hungry," I say over a mouthful of cheesy goodness.

"Then we should have a lot more of it," Mark says. "Where do you put all of that food?"

"My butt," I say quickly, and he nods his head in enthusiastic agreement.

After we've polished off the pizza, we flip on the TV. Since I got back to Stonybrook, it's been an almost nonstop roller coaster of insane, and all I want is to chill. Even if the whole sad Mark face and Ellie reality check thing still linger in the back of my mind. We agree that Bob Ross is a national treasure and a master of public television. We turn it into a game—every time Bob draws a tree or talks about a squirrel, we take off an article of clothing. Of course, I am only wearing a bedsheet, so that slips off fairly quickly and then we are back at it on top of my discarded "clothing" item.

"I have succumbed to the IKEA couch." I heave a loaded sigh, scooting up to rest my head on the throw pillow. Mark leans back against the cushions, adjusting my legs so they are draped over his lap comfortably.

"How does it feel to stoop this low?" Mark asks.

"I don't know. I kind of like it," I admit.

He gasps. "Shocking."

"It's so crappy, I'm not afraid to fuck it up."

It's a choice of words that leads to more sexy petting, and when we're done, I can barely keep my eyes open. It's that time of the night when it stops getting darker and starts to get lighter instead. My eyes laze until my lids become a weight I can't carry. I fall asleep naked in Mark's arms on a couch that has somehow become one of my favorite places in the whole world.

The sound of my purse buzzing incessantly wakes me. Rudely. I fumble up, my mouth dry as a bone and tasting like feet, and yank my phone out, expecting to see MOM flashing on the screen, worried that I never came home.

Instead, it's an Ohio number I don't recognize. Usually I let these calls go to voicemail, but the last time I did that, it was Roxy. After the way we ended things at the Ren Faire, a small part of me wants to answer. Just in case it's her.

"Hello?"

"Ellie, it's Brock."

My voice turns to ice. "How the hell did you get this number?"

Mark shoots up beside me, half asleep and alarmed by the sudden shift in my voice.

"Listen, fuck—"

"Don't ever call me," I interrupt, ready to hang up.

"Roxy's in the hospital."

Blood roars through my ears, then I feel it drain from my face. Mark's brow furrows, his face screwed up in question. I pinch my lips and give him a single shake of my head.

"What? Why? How?" I spit the questions.

"She's at All Saints—can you just come? Please?" His voice catches, and it's surprising to hear him in so much distress over anyone but himself. "I can't stay."

The line beeps to signal the call has ended. I hold the phone to my ear for a few more seconds before my hand drops to my lap, and I turn to Mark.

Mark looks all hot and rugged from our all-night sex-capades. Add his sleepy worried face to the mix, and he's even more delectable, although gradually growing more alert in his confusion. He waits for me to say something. To fill him in. All I want to do is stay here, covered in this haze of romance with Mark, but I can't. I know I shouldn't. I groan.

"I have to go."

CHAPTER 32

We pull up to the emergency room entrance of the hospital.

There's an ambulance parked at the doors, the lights still spinning even though they've turned off the siren.

Mark puts his car in park.

The lights whirl, sending beams of red around and around.

My head is full and heavy.

I threw on the same clothes I wore to the Renaissance Faire, twisted my hair in a bun, and washed off all my makeup.

I feel bare and weird and scared. I want to go back to Mark's, but I can't. I want to be pissed at Roxy, and I am, but I'm also afraid that the last thing I ever said to her—after ten years of nothing and two days of something almost like redemption—will be *fuck you*.

"I'll go find a space," Mark says. His hand squeezes mine in my lap.

"I think I need to go in," I say, already unbuckling. "Alone."

"Ellie," he tries, but I've got the door open. He reaches for me, hand on the sleeve of my coat. I pull forward, stepping one foot out of the car.

"I don't know what to expect in there," I say. "But I know that her seeing you with me won't help. It has to be just me. You can go home, and I'll text you later." I grab my purse before shoving out of the car.

I don't look back, because I know he'll be watching. He doesn't drive off right away. He's probably warring with himself, trying to decide whether letting me go in by myself is the right thing to do. Maybe he's right, and I'm wrong.

All I know is that whatever's happening in there, Roxy needs *me*. Not diabolical Brock Crawley.

My brain flashes with an image of Brock slithering out of the ER like the yellow-bellied snake that he is before Mark runs him over with his car and leaves him to bleed out on the pavement.

Move over, Dexter. Maybe I'm the real vigilante serial killer.

The automatic doors *whoosh* open.

The emergency room at All Saints Hospital is about twenty minutes from Stonybrook and isn't exactly Seattle Grace of *Grey's Anatomy*. It's dingy and mostly empty, and the heavy-set nurse behind the counter wears multicolored, cat-patterned scrubs.

Roxy isn't in the waiting room. I imagine Brock driving up in his douchebag car, opening the passenger door, and kicking her out before speeding off in a blur of shiny black and chrome. He didn't tell me what happened or why she's here, and I don't know if she had an ID or anything. I don't know if they'll let me in to see her.

I don't even know if she's still alive for me to see.

I shake off the thought and speed-walk up to the intake counter. The nurse, *Rhonda* by her nametag, doesn't immediately look up.

"Hi," I say, setting my purse on the counter.

"There's a wait," she says, eyes on her computer screen. I look around at the one person sitting in a chair by the double doors, passed out.

"You're clearly swamped," I say, my voice syrupy. I'm not great at the catching-flies-with-honey thing. "I'm looking for my . . . fr—sister."

The word feels strange in my mouth. Not the truth, but not a lie, either.

After an overlong beat, Rhonda turns her murky-green eyes in my direction. She's got jowls that make her look a little like a bulldog. She takes me in with a disapproving gaze, her full lips pouting into a Droopy Dog frown. "She got a name, this *fr-sister*?"

I show her all my teeth in the imitation of a smile. "Roxy Draper. But she may not have given a name—she may not have been able to." I fiddle nervously with the strap of my purse.

"Dark hair, medieval wench costume?" Rhonda asks, fully deadpan.

"That's her," I say, exhaling.

"She's inside. You'll have to wait," Rhonda says in the least concerned voice she can possibly muster. She goes back to typing at her computer, pretending to be doing something important. I watch her through narrowed eyes. I bet she's on Facebook.

"Is she okay?" I ask, feeling desperate. Rhonda doesn't stop typing or even look up. Who hires these people? To guard the gates of ER hell, no less.

"Somebody dropped her off at the doors, unconscious and covered in her own vomit. Probably alcohol poisoning."

"Is she awake—did she wake up?" I ask, my pulse ratcheting.

"They pumped her stomach and gave her fluids and now they're running some tests. Last I heard, she's not awake yet."

"Can I go back there? I don't want her to wake up alone." And I realize, as I say it, that it's true. Rhonda looks skeptical, like me going back there is not allowed or a good idea.

"Befri stends," I say to her finally, in a last-ditch effort.

"Excuse me?" she says, squinting her eyes at me, like she's worried I might be having a stroke.

"Befri stends," I say again. I take a deep breath. I think I've earned a speech. "Rhonda, have you ever had a friend—I mean, sister—who made you feel on edge and a little terrified, but also when you were together, you felt completely understood? For me, in my life, since I was a kid, Roxy has always been that . . . sister."

Rhonda's brows cinch together. I'm not sure Rhonda has friends. Or sisters. Or a pulse.

"When everyone else made us feel two inches tall because we didn't wear the most expensive clothes, or get invited to the best parties or give blow jobs in the back of the bus—well, Roxy may have done that one, but—Roxy and I believed in each other. Even when it got complicated, even when one of us betrayed the other, even when we did stupid, fucked-up shit. Deep down, beneath the insecurity and the bullshit, we have always mattered . . . to *each other*."

Rhonda tilts her head back. I'm pretty sure I see a glimmer of understanding in her eyes. *Come on, Ellie. We can do this.*

"Befri stends," I say again, in the most dramatic voice I

can muster. "Best friends who love each other in spite of each other."

Rhonda nods her head a little, like she's finally starting to get it. *One more push, Ellie.*

"Roxy is in there right now, scared and alone," I say. "She needs someone to be there with her when she wakes up. She needs her befri stend. She needs to know that if something happens to her, it matters. She matters. She matters to me."

With a heavy intake of breath, Rhonda leans forward, moving her hand under the desk. The double doors that lead back to triage open. My smile this time is one hundred percent genuine.

"I could kiss you, Rhonda!" I blow her a kiss, already running toward the doors.

"Room one-forty-seven," she calls after me.

On the other side of the doors, there are more nurses, carts with hospital food, and a few gurneys. I follow the signs to patient rooms, eyes peeled for Roxy's. When I reach it, the door hangs open, a dim blue light emanating from the other side. All the adrenaline coursing through me falls away, and I stop, frozen, outside the door.

My mind spins backward.

Back to when Roxy and I officially became friends.

Second grade. First day of school. Recess. The swing set by the gymnasium.

I sat on the stiff, warm rubber of a single swing, alone and lonely, watching the rest of my class play on the big jungle gym at the center of the playground.

"Sheep," a voice came from nearby. I blinked, looking over to see a small dark shape leaning against the metal post of the swing set. Her hair was short and wildly curly. She wore a black Scary Spice T-shirt and leopard-print purple jeans. I knew her from ballet class. Our moms were friends first. They talked while we learned how to plié. Roxy smiled with all of her teeth. She mostly scared me.

She was scaring me now.

"Sheep?" I asked, not sure what this tiny ominous human was talking about. Why was she talking to me? People talked to me because they wanted me to help with a math problem or tell them the definition of a word, or because I was sitting in their spot at the lunch table and they wanted me to move.

She walked over, folding into the swing beside me. "They're sheep; we're wolves."

"Okay," I said. "What do we do?"

"We sit here," she said, "and howl."

Then she howled. *Awoooo!* A few kids playing nearby looked over. She snarled at them like a wild animal. They ran away, and she kicked her feet up and laughed.

"You try," she said to me.

I said nothing at first, just watched these so-called sheep chase each other, wearing the same clothes and the same braids in their hair. Playing the same games at recess day after day. Buying the same toys. Liking the same boys and the same TV shows and the same music. I knew in that moment that friendship with Roxy was inevitable, because try as I might to fit in, I could never be a sheep. I needed more.

I took a deep breath.

Awoooo!

Roxy laughed and clapped her hands. It was actually kind of exhilarating.

"Wolf pact," she said, spitting in her hand before extending it to me. My eyes widened. I reluctantly reached out to shake, and she pulled her hand away. My cheeks warmed. Was this a prank? "You didn't spit."

It was the most disgusting thing anyone had ever asked me to do, but no one had ever wanted to ally with me before. It felt important. Sacred. I spit in my hand.

"I'm Roxy," she said, pumping her legs as she started to swing.

"Ellie."

"Ellie." She tested the name on her tongue. "Race you to the top."

We both pumped our legs as hard as we could, back and forth, as high as we could go. The iron chains squealed, and the swing set shook with the force of our new friendship.

And when we got to the top, we howled together.

"*Ma'am.*"

The word snaps me back to the hospital. "Ma'am?" the nurse asks again. "Are you family?" She motions to the door I know Roxy is behind.

I blink. Focus on her face. The nurse's big brown eyes are round, the edges crinkled up in concern.

"Yes—I'm Ellie." Like that means anything to her. I clear my throat. "Draper. Her sister."

"Ellie." She smiles, kind. "She's still asleep."

"Is she okay? Going to be okay, I mean—do you know?" I ask.

"She's stable," the nurse replies, which feels like the wrong word. Stable people don't almost kill themselves with alcohol. "You can go in, if you want." I take a long pause to reply, and she places a hand on my shoulder. "It might help her to know you're here."

I should call her mom. But Maureen will likely hurt more than she helps in this delicate situation. She's been known to bust into rooms screaming, especially where Roxy's transgressions are concerned. I should call *someone*. But Roxy's dad hasn't been in the picture in any way other than child support since he left her mom. And Brock is the coward who dropped her off at this place like dropping a dog off at the pound. He left her here all by herself. Fucking psychopath.

I suck in a breath. I'm here now. It's all up to me. Roxy's befri stend. I can do this.

I push the door open and step inside.

CHAPTER 33

Roxy wears a blue and white hospital gown.

She looks small, even though she's not. She's tall, and her bold personality makes her seem big and always powerful, even when she feels weak.

Her arms are stretched out beside her on top of the sheet that covers her up to her stomach. The nail polish on her fingers is chipped to hell. That metallic black manicure she must've gotten for the reunion is falling apart right along with her. Her eyelids look dark, probably from smudged mascara and years of not-enough sleep. The monitors beep with her pulse, and they've hooked her up to an IV drip.

I pull up the chair from beside the window and sit. Leaning back, I tuck my purse in beside me, and watch the slow, steady up-and-down of her breathing. They put an oxygen cannula in her nose, and I hear a squeak as it releases some air directly into her nostrils.

My phone is lit up with texts from Mom, from Vic and

Tina, and, most recently, from Mark. I open the thread from my mom. She's sent me about twenty messages wondering where I am, pointedly not asking me about Mark, even though she's definitely curious and disapproving in her silence. I tell her about Roxy and insist she *not* call Maureen. She doesn't argue, but she does ask:

Does this mean you two are friends again?

I ignore it and shove my phone in my pocket. Ain't nobody got time for that.

"Ellie Jenkins to the rescue," Roxy rasps, yanking my attention from my phone.

"You look like shit," I say.

It takes some effort for her lip to kick up at the corner. "Hospital chic. You're just jealous." Her eyes are dilated. They shift around, like she's trying to get them to focus.

Something that feels dangerously close to pity catches in my throat, in my heart, and I strike it down fast. I don't want to feel sorry for Roxy. She's too cool for that.

Even now, hooked up to machines, clearly at her rock bottom—she's the baddest bitch I know. She can get through this. She's going to be fine. Or she's not. Either way, I'm here.

"Brock called," I say, showing her his number, which I can't believe is in my phone. I wrinkle my nose in disgust. "He's a real catch."

"Guess I should throw him back." Her laugh is weak and forced. She looks down at herself and takes in all the wreckage.

"What the hell happened, Rox?" I hear the plunk of her

sobriety medallion from the night before the reunion in the bathroom of the Local. "This is the kind of shit people do in high school—college, maybe. You're twenty-eight."

"If you came here to preach, then you can find the fucking door on your own," she says, glaring daggers at me. The effect is dampened by the cannula in her nose and the way her eyes can't focus on mine for very long. "Nothing ever changes."

Her eyes prick with tears that she blinks back. She never cries. She probably needs to cry.

I pinch my lips together, watching her. Not walking away. I won't walk away. Not ever again. "A lot has changed."

And it's true. A lot *has* changed. For me. I left this place. I started a new life, all on my own. I have a job, a good job, even if it isn't exactly the dream job yet. I have good friends and a decent apartment in the city I've always dreamed about living in. I'm on my way. After this weekend, I will be one step closer to having everything I want.

Maybe.

Mark's face pushes into my mind's eye, and I shove it to the back of my brain.

But for Roxy—her life is the same. The same town, the same people, the same parties, the same bad habits she had back in high school. Her mom is still sick. Her dad is still not in her life. She's still a lone wolf. Her life hasn't budged from where I last left her.

And maybe that's okay.

"Do you know the first thing Christine said to me when I showed up at the Local that night?" she asks me.

I shake my head.

Roxy imitates Christine with her whiniest bitch voice: "*Well, well, there she is. Still brightening up everyone's day with your tits?*"

"Damn," I say. Even the jokes about Roxy haven't changed. "Someone needs to get *her* the memo that slut-shaming is no longer in vogue."

"Was it ever? Bitch needs to die," Roxy says. I know she justifies her affair with Brock because of how much she abhors his wife. Brock and Christine are both reprehensible human beings who deserve each other.

Roxy tries to push herself up against her pillow, but her eyes roll, and she swoons a little.

"You have a button thing, to make it sit up more," I say, motioning to the control for her bed. I reach out to help, and she smacks my hand away. Her finger presses the arrow up, and it inches higher at an almost comical rate. The whole time she holds my eyes, her lips curling up into a shit-eating grin. I bite back a laugh, covering my mouth with my hand.

She stops the bed before she's fully upright and shoves the controller behind her pillow.

After a second, she lets out a huff of air, her shoulders rising. My giggle is edged with nerves. I hate hospitals, and being here with Roxy feels so foreign. Almost like I'm having an out-of-body experience.

"I need one of these for my house," she says.

"My parents have one for their bed," I say with a shrug.

"No shit. Can they hook me up?"

"Sure—Tempur-Pedic?"

"Oh, hell yeah. Get that invalid life on lock."

We laugh together until it fades away and is replaced by

something else. Something passes over Roxy's face. She frowns and bites her lip, her eyebrows scrunching together and up. Is it anxiety? Fear?

"What's wrong?" I ask. I reach for her hand on the bed. Her fingers look so pale and ragged in mine.

"Does Maureen know I'm here?" Roxy holds her breath waiting for my answer. She stares at the blank wall opposite me like she's staring out a window.

"Hell no," I say. "I don't have earplugs with me."

"Thank God." Roxy lets out a long, steady stream of air.

"What happened with your mom?" I ask. I can tell it's the million-dollar question from the way Roxy's face screws up in pain. I squeeze her hand.

"Still sick," Roxy says. "Worse."

My face falls. Not what I was hoping to hear.

"She was having these episodes, and it kept getting worse. And then one day she called me because she couldn't see anything. She actually called the neighbor, and then the neighbor called me."

I squeeze her hand.

"Multiple sclerosis," she pronounces every syllable deliberately. "The official diagnosis."

My heart sinks.

"I'm so sorry" is all I can squeak out.

"Nah, don't be." Roxy heaves a heavy sigh. "Maybe a circuit will trip somewhere in her brain, and she'll actually like me."

I don't laugh. I can't. My heart is breaking for my once best friend, who has, despite all my best efforts, started to weasel her way back into my heart.

"She loves you, Rox," I say softly, still gripping her hand.

"She's shit at showing it, but I know she wouldn't want to see you like this."

"That's for fucking sure." Roxy's sardonic laugh turns into a cough. I go to buzz the nurse, but Roxy shakes her head and lets out one final hack. "I need to quit smoking."

"You need to quit everything," I say.

I'm right. We laugh. It's nice.

"Seriously, though, Brock Crawley is gutter sludge." I can't help it. I hate him. Especially after that after-party—I'd like to put him in my trunk.

"I don't want to talk about this," she says. She looks at the ceiling like there's something more interesting up there than fluorescent lighting.

"Oh, we're talking about it."

Roxy pretends to sleep. I say her name like her mom used to when she was mad, and her eyes fly open.

"Oh my God," she says, holding a hand to her chest. "I thought for a second it was actually her and almost had a panic attack."

"Brock. Crawley."

"I'm having chest pains."

"Roxy!"

"Okay, okay," she concedes. "I don't know. We've been off and on for a few years."

"And?"

"And...I keep thinking at some point he'll actually admit that he cares about me."

"It's Brock Crawley, Rox. The only thing Brock cares about is making Daddy proud by following in his mediocre political footsteps."

"And his car," Roxy adds.

"That vanity plate though," I say, covering my mouth with my hand to stifle a laugh.

"I know, it's awful," Roxy says. She winces almost as if she's in pain from the embarrassment.

She shakes her head and chews on her lip, almost as if she's mustering up the courage to tell me something.

"What is it?" I ask.

She sighs.

"After we saw you and Mark at the Ren Faire, Brock and I left, and he tried to convince me to go back to the motel and wait until he was done with Christine. She kept calling. I could hear them on the phone, planning what they were going to wear for their Halloween party. They landed on Barbie and Ken, by the way—real fucking original. And he kept calling her baby," she says, and my face screws up in disgust. "And she was worried. She kept asking where he was, when he was going to be home. What does he want for dinner. Blah, blah, blah."

We both gag.

"But I had some shit in my bag," she continues. "And Brock has never been able to turn down fucked-up sex."

Gross.

"What kind of *shit*?"

"Pills, I don't know. It's not like I have a script for them. And I had too much to drink. I blacked out." She twists her lips into a scowl. "I never black out. I'm a stand-up drunk. Tolerance of a Scottish clansman."

"Roxy—"

"He doesn't love me, Ellie." Her face breaks down, but she doesn't cry. "He's been sleeping with me for years. And sleeping with her. He just can't be alone. He can't be on his own for even a few hours because then he might actually realize he's the fucked-up kid everyone thought he would be, and that scares the shit out of him."

"He *is* fucked up," I point out. "He's vile."

Roxy doesn't say anything to that. Just looks around the room. "I need a drink."

I cross my arms over my chest. "Like hell you do."

She sighs and shifts her weight around the bed, trying to get comfortable. Her discomfort turns to frustration, and she tries to pull the various tubes out of her body.

"Hey, hey, hey—stop it!" I grab at her hands and pin them to the bed. Tears well up in her eyes.

"I think I love him." It squeaks out on a sob. I'm frozen in place. She's crying, she never cries. What do I do? This is uncharted Roxy territory.

I decide to slide my arms behind her to hug her upper body. She doesn't hug me back, but instead balls her hands up into shaking white-knuckled fists. She's in so much pain, and I wish I could show her that it has nothing to do with scumbag Brock.

"You don't love him," I say. My thoughts drift back to her mom. Roxy has never handled complicated emotions well. A lifetime of stuffing down feelings will ravage your soul. Ask me how I know.

She shakes her head. "I don't want to love him," she says, trying to breathe through the feelings. "I want to hate his guts just like you, just like everyone else."

"What do you see in him?" I ask her, trying to figure it out.

"Someone broken," she croaks. "Like me."

I pull away and sit next to her on the bed. I push a stray hair away that is stuck to her wet face. "You're not broken. Fragile right now, maybe. But not broken."

"Ellie." She swoops her finger in a circle around the room. *Look where I am.*

"A minor hiccup," I say, trying to sound optimistic.

Roxy rolls her eyes. "How's your happily ever forty-eight hours after going?" Roxy sees my answering dagger eyes and reneges. "Sorry, sorry—not trying to be a dick. Just genuinely curious."

"He's better than fiction," I say with a dreamy sigh.

"Oh, God." She makes a gagging sound. She is always herself, even in her current weakened state.

"It's weird," I say, ignoring her. "It's like a second chance at a first chance. I had this fantasy about him playing in my head since middle school. I was so afraid to actually be with him because...what if he didn't live up to the fantasy? But the fantasy doesn't live up to reality. Surprise, surprise—reality is so much better."

"Shocking," Roxy says, trying not to roll her eyes at my lovesick speech. "You're saying his dick is bigger than you thought it was?"

I blush bright red.

"Aha!" Roxy says with a knowing smile. "You two bumped uglies."

"*Please* don't say it like that."

"You always were such a prude," Roxy says. "*So* Ellie Jenkins finally got into Mark Wright's pants—now what?"

I frown. "What do you mean?"

"What do you mean, what do I mean? Does he sell his place

and move to LA? Rent an apartment and find a job out there? Now what?"

Cold settles over me at her words. It's not something we've talked about. It's not something I even *want* to talk to him about—at least, not yet. Moving to LA is a huge, complicated, *expensive* commitment. It may have been a dream of Mark's at one time, but from the looks of it, it was still a long way off. Until I showed up. Mark and I have been in the Stonybrook love bubble, where we make all kinds of semi-sense.

But what happens when I have to go back to LA?

What does Mark really want—on his own, without me as a factor? I know what I want. I always have.

"You'll figure it out," she says, patting my hand, probably realizing that shit just got mad complicated inside my head.

"One day at a time, right?" I say with a nervous laugh. One side of her lips twitches, but she doesn't smile. "Speaking of one day at a time, you're done now, right? You're sober? And tomorrow is a new day."

"The first day of forever," she says, her voice straining. "That's the worst part. One day at a time for the rest of your life. And every time you go to dinner, on a date, to the grocery store or gas station, birthday parties, weddings, anywhere, you're the only one ordering club soda."

"You're forgetting pregnant women and Mormons," I say.

"One day at a time forever is a really fucking tall order."

"You can do it," I say. "Don't you know what you are?"

"What?" Roxy asks. Her head tilts to the side, like she has no idea what I'm about to say.

"You're a wolf," I remind her.

She smiles, baring all of her teeth. We both howl.

Awoooooooo!

Until a nurse comes in to shush us. When she shuts the door behind her, Roxy snarls after her. I laugh and pat her hand.

"You're gonna be fine, Rox," I tell her. I don't know how I know it, but I do know it.

"Fine would be a nice change of pace," she replies.

We talk and giggle and occasionally howl until the annoyed nurse comes back in to tell me I need to leave, because Roxy needs her rest. When I open my phone to call someone to pick me up, Mom's text is still there, staring back at me from the screen.

Does this mean you two are friends again?

There are some people you never stop being friends with, no matter how much time passes between talking, or what you do to each other, what goes unsaid, is misunderstood, or feels broken.

I text her back.

BEFRI STENDS Forever

CHAPTER 34

My childhood desk is white painted wood with a pink upholstered chair. There's a slim drawer in the front, with pens and Post-its still stashed inside. I pull one out, a red one, and take it with me to the bed. Mark's script sits there, crisp, bound by brads, his name printed in ink on the front beneath the title.

Dad came to get me from the hospital. I couldn't call Mark.

I can't stop thinking about what Roxy asked, about what comes next. Am I really going to ask Mark to move to LA after we've only been on one date? After one night of (okay, delicious) screwing around? Mark is still a man who just broke up with his fiancée, a woman he allegedly loved and was in a long-term relationship with for three years. He's still a man who is only just starting to figure out the life he wants outside my favorite Stonybrook bakery.

He's still a man who has a lot of shit to untangle.

I'm still a woman who has a job and a life far away from everything he knows, from everything that's familiar and easy for him. In the short time we've been together, he's never once said he was ready to drop it all and move to LA. He never said he wanted to do what it takes to make his dreams come true. He didn't even say what his dreams actually were.

As sure as I am that I want more than these few days with Mark, I am not sure if I can give up the opportunities waiting for me back in LA to stay here and sort out what we mean to each other. Mark is a teenage dream come true, but co-EP is part of a lifelong goal that's about to crack open my career after five years of being stuck. They can't really compete—both are desires of my heart. And one of them, I've worked too hard to reach just to let it slip away now.

I can't call Mark. If I ask him all my questions and he doesn't have an answer, what happens? What if he does, but his answer isn't what I hope it will be? Because anything less than "I'm packing my bags and hawking the couch on Craigslist" will mean he isn't sure. And I want him to be sure. About me, about his choices, about what comes next. Mark needs space to figure all of this out, and I need to get back to LA.

I press play on "11 Hours Straight of High Quality Stereo Ocean Sounds for Sleep, Study & Play" on YouTube and settle in to read.

We had a deal, and he held up his end of the bargain.

Now, it's time for me to hold up mine.

It never takes long to read a good script. Especially one that makes you laugh.

I leave a slew of notes in the margins, mostly addressing

pacing problems and second act wobbles, but it's good. Better than I expected, despite the facts that I've always thought he was smart and that in the last few days I've discovered that he knows how to make me laugh. It gives me a little inkling of hope that he's got the spark, and he'll be able to do the work if he wants to. If he decides to see it through.

But that's his decision, not mine.

I slide the script and a small handwritten note into a large manila envelope and seal it. I'm the asshole who nails the coffin shut on a dying relationship and buries it deep, leaving the guy in the dust.

I tell myself that whatever happens with Mark in the future, what we had this week was still worth it. It will still feel right to him, even if I'm not here in the morning to wake up to. He's sent me more than a few texts and called three times. I haven't replied at all. When he gets this, he'll know.

He'll understand everything. Or maybe he won't.

I just hope he doesn't hate me forever.

What are you doing, Ellie? What the hell *are you doing?*

My heart palpitates its dissent, and I chalk it up to acid reflux, popping a few Tums for good measure just as my phone starts to ring with a FaceTime call from Vic and Tina. I answer, propping the phone on my vanity so I can talk while I pack.

"You didn't finish the list! Why the hell are you coming home?" Vic asks, his slightly shrill but totally endearing voice like music to my ears.

"The rest of the superlatives on the list aren't in Stonybrook," I say. "The *Ellie Is Cool Now* list will have to wrap up back in LA—probably over Zoom."

I only hope they don't dig any deeper into it. I could stay and squeeze out a couple more days with Mark, but then what? I'd still have the same questions, still have to return to LA no matter what. More time in Stonybrook will simply give me more chances to get closer to feeling the big L word.

This is the right move.

Tina yanks the phone so the camera is fully facing her beautiful and slightly surgically enhanced face. "You and Mark did the dirty, didn't you?"

Vic yanks it back. "They better have."

"We had sex. Can we call it that, please?"

They *oooh* in the most annoying way possible and immediately want to know all the juicy details.

I feel my lower lip quiver and suck it under my front teeth to quell the sensation. I do not want to cry. I don't feel ready to talk about that part with anyone, not even Vic and Tina, no matter how much I love them, no matter how much they want to know. The resolution of Mark and Ellie's romantic arc isn't fodder for TV. Or for my friends to dissect. I grab the phone with one hand, holding a pair of underwear in the other.

"I don't want to talk about it. I love you guys, and at some point, after enough rum—and time—I'll tell you the whole sexy tale," I say, staring at their eyes through the camera lens. "But not yet."

My stupid lip wobbles again.

"Oh, sweetie," Vic says, frowning.

"We're here when you're ready—*if* you're ever ready," Tina adds.

"I hope she's ready at some point."

"But if she isn't, that's fine, too."

"Talking about painful things can help bring closure."

They bicker back and forth playfully while I pack, and I'm grateful for the noise, and the space, and when they finally move on from their faux-squabbling, I *do* tell them about Rachel Bumpass and Roy Willard, about how much I love David, and how I'm completely rooting for Roxy.

"Fuck, that's good TV," Vic says through tears.

Tina hands him a roll of toilet paper from her bathroom, mouthing the words *drama king* while he dabs his eyes. I grin.

I'm so ready to get back to LA.

The next morning, Mom makes me waffles for breakfast before my flight. She whips cream for the top and cuts fresh strawberries. When I come downstairs, she's frying bacon, and fresh coffee is brewing in the pot.

"You tried to sneak out without getting your Mom-style breakfast," she says, smiling at me over her shoulder.

When I was growing up, my mother worked full-time. Mornings before school were hectic, with her checking homework and packing herself, Dad, and me all healthy lunches. She'd usually direct me to a bowl of cereal or a box of Pop-Tarts. But Saturday mornings were for homemade breakfast. Pancakes and eggs and bacon and waffles, all the things she loved, lovingly prepared with ease. We'd sit down together as a family, the three of us. This went on as long as I lived at home, and every time I came back during college, she always made a point to cook me at least one full Mom-style breakfast. She still does when I come home to visit from LA.

I set my purse and computer bag by the kitchen table and walk over to where she stands at the stove. I wrap my arms around her shoulders, tugging her close and planting a kiss on her cheek. She smiles. I love her smile.

"What's that for?" she asks. "Surely you can get better food in LA than my cooking."

"There's nothing better than your cooking, Momma." Because it's true, and I know it means a lot to her to hear me say that.

I pour a cup of coffee and take my seat at the table. "Where's Dad?"

"Oh, you know him. Up at the crack of dawn raking up the leaves on the front lawn. It's October. The grass is barely even growing." She rolls her eyes as she turns, bringing the bacon over to the table on a plate. She sets it down with the rest of the food and settles into her seat.

We eat in comfortable silence for longer than I expect.

"Maureen called," Mom says finally, taking a sip of her coffee. There it is.

I crash my fork onto my plate. Syrup splatters. "You didn't tell her about Roxy, did you?"

"Ellie, she's her mother. The hospital called. Apparently, Roxy's insurance lapsed."

"Damn it, Roxy's going to lose her shit." I pull out my phone to text Roxy.

"Maureen told me to thank you for stopping by."

"She doesn't need to thank me," I say, clipped. *Let's be wolves.*

I hear Roxy's voice in my head. Most of the time being a wolf with Roxy meant being Maureen's nemesis.

"Maureen told me about her diagnosis," Mom says. "That's just awful. Is that why Roxy relapsed?"

I shrug. "I'm sure the twenty-eight years Maureen was a dick to her didn't help."

"Ellie!"

"Well!"

Mom shakes her head with defeat and moves her eggs over on her plate, making room for another waffle. She's pouring the maple syrup when she asks, "How's Mark?"

"Mom," I groan. "I leave for the airport in fifteen minutes. We're so close to ending this visit on a high note."

"Fine, but I'm just going to say one more thing."

"I wish you wouldn't."

"Are you sure you want to leave him behind without saying anything? Even goodbye?" She gives me one of her signature steely-eyed stare-downs.

I don't hesitate. I've made my decision, and there's no room for uncertainty. Even if my guts are screaming at me that something *isn't right.*

"I'm sure," I say, turning to reach inside my computer bag.

I set a manila envelope addressed to Mark on the table beside the plate of bacon. She reads the address. Her eyes flick up to mine, a visible question in them. I clear my throat, laying my fork down beside my plate.

"Make sure he gets this. It's important."

She reaches under the table and squeezes my knee. "Finish your eggs. You need the protein."

We don't say another word about the envelope. Or Mark.

When she drops me off at the airport, she gives me a hug before I walk into the terminal to check in for my flight, and I don't want to let go.

I don't want to say goodbye, no matter how ready I am to leave.

CHAPTER 35

I get off the airplane and go right to the studio. LA is three hours behind Ohio time, so the writers' room is taking a late working lunch when I walk in. Everyone except for Vic and Tina is surprised to see me, and even Andy's face flashes with confusion before it returns to its usual state of generally bored and slightly amused.

Everyone in the room starts clapping and cheering.

Oh. Oh no. I was not expecting this. I forgot about the whole promotion thing. I am not in the mood to be clapped for.

A few writers pat me on the back and sing my praises, telling me I deserve this. Blah, blah, blah. I suddenly feel like I'm standing in a wind tunnel, and I need to get out of there. I back the hell out of the room with profuse *thank-yous* directed to no one in particular, and definitely not to Andy, who doesn't say a word.

My little cubicle feels like a safe haven. I sit down and pull out my laptop.

322   VICTORIA FULTON & FAITH McCLAREN

Home sweet home.

Vic and Tina stop by with a bottle of Veuve and hugs, even if I can still feel all their questions underneath every line of banter they throw my way. We clink glasses, and I take a single pathetic sip before I sit back down to my laptop, searching for a distraction. Vic and Tina take the hint, and with another gentle group hug, they leave me in solitude.

I glance at my phone.

Mark hasn't called or texted again. I think Mom must have given him my notes on his script. That means he got my other note. He might even be reading it as I sit here, watching celebratory champagne bubbles dance in my glass.

My hair prickles up on the back of my neck as I feel a presence looming behind me. "Hi, Andy," I say without turning around.

"How's your follow-through, Jenkins?" he asks. I suck in a deep breath and turn around. He leans against the cubicle with a cup of coffee in one hand and a script tucked under the other arm.

I know that part of this challenge was to see if I cared enough about this job to see it through to the end. Every showrunner worries that their best writers will get poached by better, more critically acclaimed shows, shows that pay more or are more satisfying creatively. And honestly, before *Ellie Is Cool Now*, I would have taken any job that so much as batted its eyes in my general direction. Post–*Ellie Is Cool Now*? I like my job. I like my boss and my work friends. My work, this show, this job— it all has the meaning I give it. Just like high school—how I feel about high school and the people I went to school with— it's all up to me. I decide.

I choose to believe it's all leading toward my destiny. No matter what.

"Most Artistic is in Berlin," I say and hand him a crappy sketch of my parents' cat. "We Skyped this morning at two a.m. Eastern." I smile. "I'll send you my bill for art supplies."

He examines my "art." A single brow shoots up.

"I said I could write, not draw, okay?" I snap. He tucks the sheet of paper under his arm next to his script, eyeing me for a second as he sips his coffee.

"What about number nine?" is his next question. All business. If he notices my mood, he doesn't let on. Thank God. I can't handle anything that even smells like sympathy from Andy Biermann.

"Glad you asked," I say with a triumphant crack of my knuckles. I spin my laptop screen around to face him. A You Win pop-up flashes across my screen over a game of online chess against—you guessed it—Most Athletic.

Win a game against Most Athletic.

"Turns out Most Athletic sucks at chess," I say with a smug grin on my face.

Andy raises the opposite eyebrow.

"Hey, it's a game, and I have won it." I defend myself with a *what-more-do-you-want-from-me* shrug.

Andy's lips twitch. Despite the skeptical act, I can tell he's impressed. "And number ten?" he asks, and it's so obvious that he's fighting a smirk, I could almost scream.

I frown, turning away from him to start sorting through the pile of papers on my desk.

"I completed the list," I say. "I have a whole new lease on life. The freshest of perspectives."

I pick up a stack of papers and jog them against my desk, just because it feels productive and also because it hides the mixed emotions warring on my face.

"Now it's back to business as usual."

"Hmmm" is all he says before he takes a slurpy sip of his coffee and slowly drifts away.

I sigh and slouch down in my chair.

I did it. I attended my class reunion. I proved to everyone— or at least a few people—that I'm actually somebody and not the nobody I was in high school. I rekindled a friendship with my childhood best friend. I ruffled a few feathers and learned some valuable lessons (like always use your Hollywood status to defuse a violent altercation).

I finally kissed my high school crush.

And—okay, I kinda sorta maybe left him with his life in shambles.

Oops.

My skin warms. My eyes sting.

I run my finger over the trackpad on my laptop, clearing my throat, blinking back tears. The words of my note flashing in my mind.

Catch you on the flip side.
E

I hope that I do.

*

THREE MONTHS LATER

It's my first day back after winter hiatus, my first day on the new, improved job. Same office, same show, same people—new title, new responsibilities, new parking spot. I'm a bundle of nerves, and chock-full of Tums, but I'm more twisted up with excitement than fear. It's like that feeling you get right before the plane takes off. Right before you're flying thousands of feet in the air, leaving the earth behind.

I met Mom and Dad at a cute vacation cabin in Big Bear for Christmas. We hunkered down away from the world, drinking vats of hot cocoa and taking long walks in the snow-capped mountains. A perfect, socially distanced Christmas, and just the quiet distraction I needed since I couldn't bring myself to make another trek back to Ohio.

Roxy has been sober for almost three months. She texts me frequently. She has a sponsor at AA she finally really likes. Well, as much as Roxy likes anyone. Her new sponsor gave her a scarf and a card that said "Merry Fucking Christmas, bitch." Apparently, it went over well. She says she hasn't seen Brock since that fateful night at the hospital. I hope she's done with him for good.

I haven't heard a peep from Mark Wright since Mom dropped off my notes to him the morning I left for Los Angeles after the reunion. No calls. Not a single text. I sent and then deleted a Facebook friend request about ten times before it stuck.

He hasn't accepted.

I check his profile every once in a while to see if anything's different. It isn't. He has that same picture from New York, the same profile, no indication of his relationship status, no clue to where he's working, if he's still in Ohio, or whether he kept the

Couch of Failure. My brain spins with ideas about his life now. I try not to freak out when I think about what he's up to and who he's up to it with.

I wonder if he decided to get back together with Liz. I might have truly been a rebound, and when I was out of sight, his eyes cleared enough to see Liz standing there waiting. Not that she was waiting. I've stalked her Facebook profile a few times, too. Even though she changed her profile picture to a photo of just her instead of the dorky one she had before of them smiling with their heads tilted together, my brain can't help but go hog wild at all the possibilities.

I never let myself daydream about a happy ending for us. It hurts too much to think about how that might be the one dream that will never come true.

I walk into the writers' room and throw my empty Starbucks cup in the trash.

Andy always sits at the head of the table, and I usually sit somewhere in the middle, safely tucked between Tina and Vic, my favorite human shields. I set my bag on the seat at Andy's right-hand side. It's symbolic, and I know he'll probably read into it, but I'm okay with that. I want him and everyone else in the room to know how ready I am for what's next.

Because even though a lot of hurt came out of the *Ellie Is Cool Now* list, some truly incredible things did, too. Not the least of which is this: I'm going to co-executive produce a damn good season of TV.

My phone buzzes with a text. Roxy's name blinks back from the screen.

Andy's not here yet—he's always the last one in.

I swipe to reveal the text.

Today's the big day?

I reply:

I'm gonna blow chunks.

She says:

Talk about a power play on your first day as boss.

I snort.
She continues:

Welcome to the table read, y'all did good work 😭
now open your script to page two...

You sure you don't need a job? You have a knack for
making shit up

Speaking of writers in need of work, have you texted
Marky Mark?????

You know the answer

Coward.

Blunt as ever.
Writers start to file into the room, one by one.
It was a fling. But I don't believe it, and I know she
doesn't either.
I look up. Some of the other writers are whispering and
stealing quick glances at me. I shift uncomfortably in my

ergonomic office chair, starting to feel like maybe I made the wrong seat choice. Feeling self-conscious about the shirt I chose—a light-blue button-down with French cuffs. It felt powerful at the time. Now it feels snooty.

I reply to Roxy.

Gotta go. Wish me luck.

Luck.

She adds:

You fucking coward.

I click out of the text app, darkening the screen.

Even Vic and Tina don't look at me when they enter. They're unusually quiet, not even speaking to each other as they take their seats in the middle of the table, far away from me. Vic gets straight to work pulling out his notebook and laying out his pens. Anything not to make eye contact. Vic usually needs to be reprimanded at least twice before he stops fucking around.

What the hell is going on?

My pulse quickens as I start to panic. All the shifty eyes and the whispering and the not talking to me—I know we all work for a high school show, but come on!

I push back my chair, about to run to the bathroom to maybe throw up, when Andy appears in the doorway with a fresh cup of steaming hot coffee. The room goes silent. A few eyes dart to me before they settle on him. I swallow hard, frozen.

I expect Andy to sit down, but he doesn't. He hovers in

the doorway, same bored face as always. But something is different. There's a mischievous twinkle in his eye that I've never seen before.

"Welcome back, everyone," he says. "Hope you all had a memorable holiday."

He makes lazy eye contact with everyone, and I notice that his eyes linger on me for a second or two longer than the rest before he takes a sip of coffee from his mug.

"You've probably noticed that we've made a few changes around here. You all know that Ellie is now co-EP." He pauses, eyeing me again. "Which I guess is why she chose the best seat in the house, next to mine." A few of them actually snicker. "And we have some breaking news—our writers' assistant Susie is now writing on staff."

Light clapping titters around the table as everyone congratulates Susie. She turns beet red and waves an awkward *thanks* to the room. I harken back to the days of Susie fishing my reunion invitation out of the trash for Andy. She definitely deserves this.

"That leaves us without a writers' assistant," he says cryptically. "Fortunately for us, there's always some young Hollywood hopeful, fresh off the Mother Road."

He's referring to Route 66, of course. He hired an LA transplant? That's rare for Andy. He usually likes his hires a little bit seasoned within the industry, maybe even with a few battle scars. I was, of course, the rare exception.

"I hope you'll say *please* when you ask him to fetch your coffee," Andy says. The room laughs a little too loud. Andy motions with his head to someone outside the door.

All eyes are on me when Mark Wright steps into the room.

CHAPTER 36

I'm going to throw up.

I'm going to throttle Andy.

I'm going to hyperventilate.

I'm going to jump out the window and become morbid urban street art.

I'm going to—my eyes meet Mark's.

He looks so good. His hair is clean cut, styled loosely. His shirt is dark green, warm and soft against his creamy skin.

"I'm feeling a change of scenery today." Andy interrupts my panic-laced revelry.

"*Push Comes to Shove* isn't back from hiatus until next week," Tina chimes in.

"Perfect. Let's head over." Andy winks at me. "Ellie, maybe you can show Mark around the studio."

Everyone files out of the room. Vic and Tina finally look at me, and I mouth *You knew about this?* to both of them. They grit their teeth and shrug their apologies.

I'm going to throw them out the window—after I throw Andy first.

I don't forgive them. Or maybe I do. All of this is yet to be decided.

Vic wiggles his fingers in a wave at Mark as he passes. Mark doesn't turn his attention from me. Vic leans over and whispers something to Tina, who nods before shutting the door, leaving Mark and me alone inside the writers' room.

The room feels cavernous and claustrophobic all at once.

Mark doesn't move, just looks at me. I have to remind myself to breathe. I haven't heard from, seen, or spoken to this man in three months, and now he's standing right in front of me. In LA. With a job that is hierarchically beneath me, at the very bottom of the food chain. I am his motherfucking *boss*. What is happening?

He breaks the heavy silence.

"You did the thing" is all he says.

"The thing?" I ask, not sure what the fuck he's talking about.

"The thing where you pretend I don't exist," he explains. "Because you're scared."

"Oh," I say. "That thing."

He shifts his weight from foot to foot. I can tell he's nervous. I feel like I'm losing my mind. A pressure starts to build inside my chest. *Don't cry, Ellie. Whatever you do, do not cry.*

"I figured I'd just have to tell you in person," Mark says, shrugging.

"Tell me what?" I ask, genuinely confused. Still trying to hold back feelings.

He starts to circle around the table, stepping toward me cautiously, like I'm a wild animal that might bolt at any second, at any sudden movement.

"That I have a massive crush on you," Mark says.

Oh no, oh no.

"That I think you made a big mistake by running away from me," he continues.

His words catch inside my gut in just the right way, and I can't hold it back anymore. The tears start to flow freely.

"That I was always going to *catch you on the flip side*, so that I could do this." He takes my wrist and gently pulls me to my feet. Then he wraps his arms around my waist and pulls me close, kissing my tear-stained face like he hasn't seen me, heard from me, or talked to me in the last three months.

Because he hasn't. Because I ran away.

When Mark pulls away, he rests his forehead on mine. My heart is a hummingbird inside my chest.

"How did all of this happen?" I ask him. He pulls back to trace a tear streak down my cheek with his thumb.

"I got your notes on my script and your cryptic little card," he says. "I put my condo up for sale that same day and started looking for apartments in LA. And then out of nowhere, Andy fucking Biermann called me."

I make a mental note to strangle Andy to death and then bring him back to life so I can thank him.

"He said he heard I had a script, and he wanted to read it," he continues. "I was lucky you left me with such baller notes. Jesus, you're a genius."

I flush. He does the thing I love where he tucks one side of my hair behind my ear, his fingers tracing a line of fire down my neck to my collarbone. Maybe it was only forty-eight official hours that we spent together, but God, I missed this.

I missed him.

"Anyway, I revised the hell out of it for a week and a half and then sent it over. He called me up and offered me this job two hours later. But on one condition."

"What was that?" I ask, my brow furrowing.

"I wasn't allowed to tell you. About any of it."

"Oh, now he's really going to get it."

Mark laughs, shrugs. "He said he wanted an 'idealistic happily-ever-after for my favorite little cynic.' Direct quote."

"He certainly has a flair for the dramatic," I say, realizing that Andy Biermann is probably one of my favorite humans on the planet. And also one of my greatest teachers. And also I hate him.

"I know it's soon," Mark says. "And I know we've only been on one official date, and we haven't talked for three months— but I think I'm falling in love with you, Ellie."

I feel my Grinchy heart swell up three sizes. "I think I've always loved you, Mark Wright."

He pulls me into his arms, swooping me back in true climactic rom-com fashion to plant a deep kiss on my lips. My leg shoots out, and we laugh because we are one giant fucking romantic trope, and we love it.

We hear cheering in the hallway. The entire writers' room peeks in through the slit window in the door. Vic and Tina are at the front of the line, screaming and making kissy faces. Vic gives me a thumbs-up. Tina waggles her eyebrows. And at the back of the crowd, Andy watches with a pleased-as-punch grin on his face that he quickly tries to hide.

I roll my eyes at all of them.

Then I go back to kissing my high school crush.

ACKNOWLEDGMENTS

This book wouldn't exist if either of us had been "cool" in high school, or felt like we fit in, in our small suburban towns. After high school ended, we eventually found each other in an online writing class and challenged each other *so good* we had to be friends. We both wound up in the same big city (Go, Lakers?) and almost five years ago, we started writing a book together one chapter at a time on Wattpad. She had a janky Canva cover and a deep hatred for high school that ironically appealed to a lot of current high school students. The rest is history, as they say.

To *Ellie* finding her way into the world—and to the big dreams of two small town girls coming true—no high school reunion required. (Phew!)

We want to thank our Wattpad readers for falling in love (and occasionally being annoyed) with Ellie right from the very start. We loved watching the comments and votes roll in and seeing you engage with the story as we wrote it is an experience we'll not soon forget. There's nothing authors want more than to see their characters find their way into the hearts and lives (and funny bones!) of readers. You were the first to notice her spark, and we're so grateful you've joined us on this wild ride.

To Jenny Beres, without whom this book very well could have been a rando clump of words on the internet. You lent your brilliant mind to helping us promote this book in creative ways when it was just a few chapters old, and without you, *Ellie Is Cool Now* might not exist in its current clump-of-glued-paper state. We love you, fellow "cool now" friend.

To Sara Biren, who copyedited each new chapter of *Ellie* before we posted to Wattpad: you were our first line of defense against bad grammar, helping us make each chapter better than the last, and we owe you a margarita next time you're in LA.

To Ashleigh, Deanna, and the whole team at Wattpad: thank you for believing in *Ellie*, for championing her story to the publishing world, and for helping us get this book into the skillful hands of our Forever team. This dream come true wouldn't have happened without you and the community of readers and writers you've built through your platform.

To our incredibly clever editor, Madeleine Colavita: thank you for seeing the diamond in the rough draft. When *Ellie* came to you, she was a messy perfectionist who hated people. She's still that, but with your guidance, she's grown into a (hopefully) relatable heroine and a (hopefully) lovable curmudgeon, and now a co-executive producer we'd be happy to do a coffee run for.

To our whole Forever team, Lori Paximadis, Stacey Reid, Daniela Medina, Estelle Hallick, Grace Fischetti, and Ambriah Underwood: thank you for passionately helping us polish and shine *Ellie* into her coolest form yet. You took her from Charmander to Charizard, and we apologize for the uncool Pokémon reference.

Katie!! Our agent and the third unicorn in this mystical trifecta. Thank you for taking a chance on us and *Ellie*. Your patience and persistence paid off—she's a book now! In no small way because of you. You are pure magic, and the very best partner we could ever hope to have.

FAITH:

No one in the whole universe has believed in my big dreams more than my husband. Nathan, you are the person I love to fight with, adventure with, and spend my life beside. Thank you for fresh baked bread, martinis on the porch, and staring at the sunset over Los Angeles talking until it gets dark. I will never stop falling in love with you.

Sam, my son, you are the light in every dark day, and the first ever dream of mine to come true. Thank you for always knowing *Ellie* would be in bookstores and not being surprised now that you're proven correct.

There are a handful of humans who have been supporters of *Ellie* from the very first day she debuted on Wattpad. To my Beez, Liz Parker, Tracey Neithercott, and Sara Biren, you are the best CPs in the world, and my soulmate sisters, thank you for supporting this journey with memes, and commiseration, a lot of laughter, and even more love. Devin Ross, your guidance was invaluable. Sarah Fox, Hannah West, Rachel Fikes, and Samantha Pierce, you were all fans and friends—of me and of the incomparable Ellie Jenkins. Austin Siegemund-Broka and Emily Wibberly, for sending that email to Katie, and letting me read your romance novels for inspiration and aspiration.

My BTS crew, and especially my ARMY leaders, Alice and Cat: Loving BTS changed my life. I am grateful to have them and y'all in my corner.

To my parents, who never needed me to be cool to love me, and always knew I would wind up in Hollywood making my wild dreams come true.

Jenny Beres: you are Victoria's BFF but you're one of my all-time favorite humans, and none of this would have happened without you.

And last, but never, ever least, my tiger friend and coauthor, Victoria: We are the wolves. To running together into the wild unknown of publishing and beyond.

VICTORIA:

Mom and Dad. So grateful that all my childhood trauma came from school and not you (mostly—JK MOM). I love you both forever. Thank you for all your no-matter-what support.

Nick. You rat. I love you.

Jenny. EXCUSE ME. You're my bestest friend.

Jess. COO Extraordinaire. Tossing the author bouquet to you next, my friend.

Aunt Paige and Dan (Uncle Bob too!). Love you, fam. Thanks for buying/reading all of my crap :)

To people from high school—um, sorry. It wasn't you, it was me the whole time. I had to co-write an entire book to figure that out, but I get it now.

More people who deserve acknowledgment for their love and support: Beth and Mike, Theresa and fam, Leslie, Sofia, Dara,

Tim and Mary Jane, Timmy and Olivia, Cody and Shelby, Amy, Alyssa, Jake and Courtney, Jenn, Mandy, Senia, Karine, Kai, Demetra, Liz, Sara, Terra, Linda and Dave, Tina, Katie, Rachel, Cat, Alice, Janet, Tawnya, Hollie, Pilar, and Rocky.

If I forgot you—better luck next time, I guess.

And Faith! My cutie lil' writing partner. We did it, we're doing it, it's done—

I can't wait to see what's next!

ABOUT THE AUTHORS

VICTORIA FULTON and FAITH McCLAREN are best pals and coauthors of the international Wattpad phenomenon and 2018 Watty award–winning rom-com *Ellie Is Cool Now*, as well as the young adult psychological thriller *Horror Hotel*. Originally from Ohio and Texas, Victoria and Faith now live and write in too-sunny Los Angeles, California.

Victoria lives with her fiancé and their two cat children. She has a chemical engineering degree from the University of Dayton, so, naturally, she now co-runs a PR agency with her other bestie when she's not writing about smooching and serial killers.

Faith lives with her guitar-making husband, Pokémon-loving son, and two scruffy dogs. When she isn't listening to BTS or watching K-dramas, Faith writes contemporary romance novels and volunteers with wolves in a sanctuary outside of Los Angeles.

You can learn more at:
victoriaxfaith.com
Twitter @VictoriaxFaith
Instagram @VictoriaxFaith